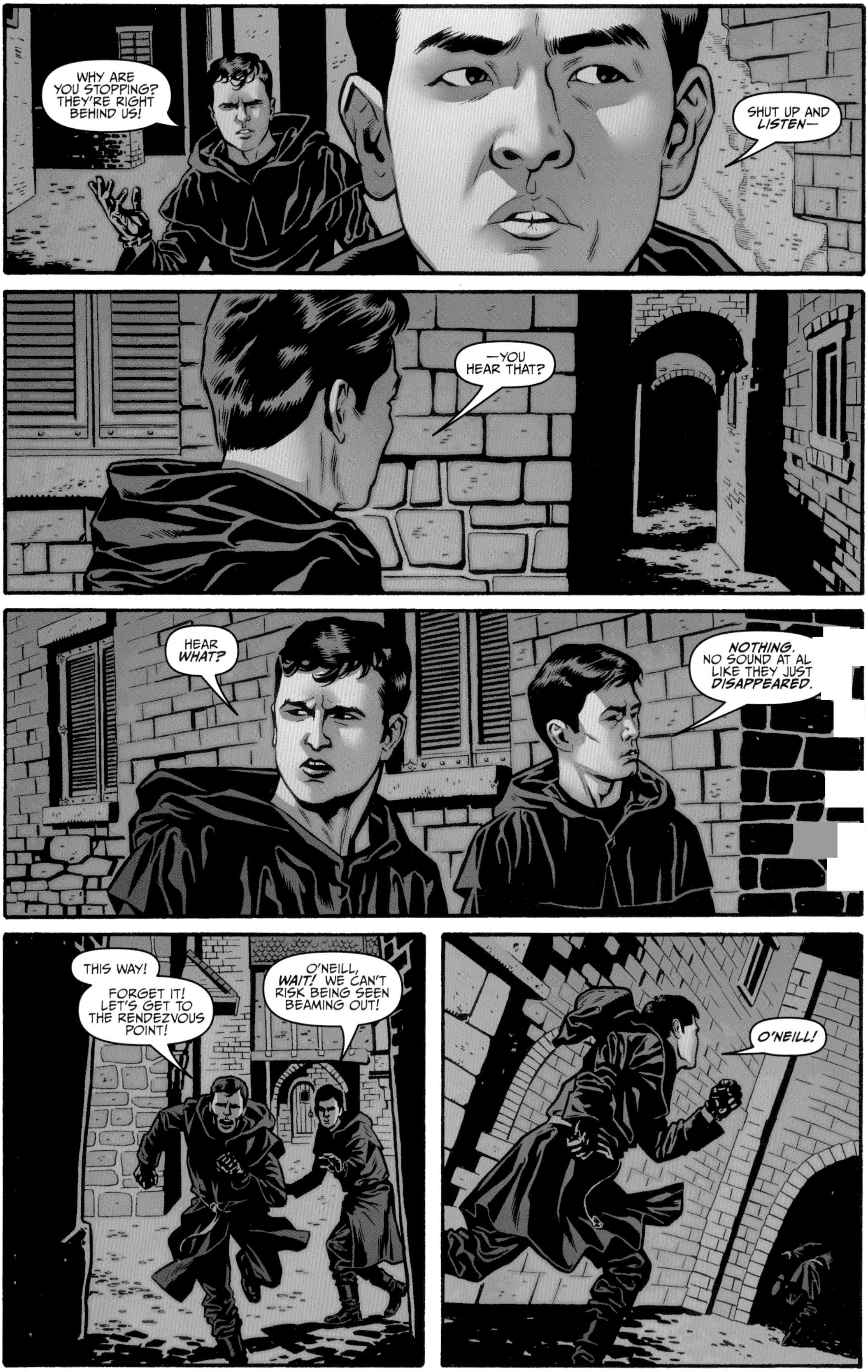
WHY ARE YOU STOPPING? THEY'RE RIGHT BEHIND US!
SHUT UP AND *LISTEN*—
—YOU HEAR THAT?
HEAR *WHAT?*
NOTHING. NO SOUND AT AL LIKE THEY JUST *DISAPPEARED.*
THIS WAY!
FORGET IT! LET'S GET TO THE RENDEZVOUS POINT!
O'NEILL, *WAIT!* WE CAN'T RISK BEING SEEN BEAMING OUT!
O'NEILL!

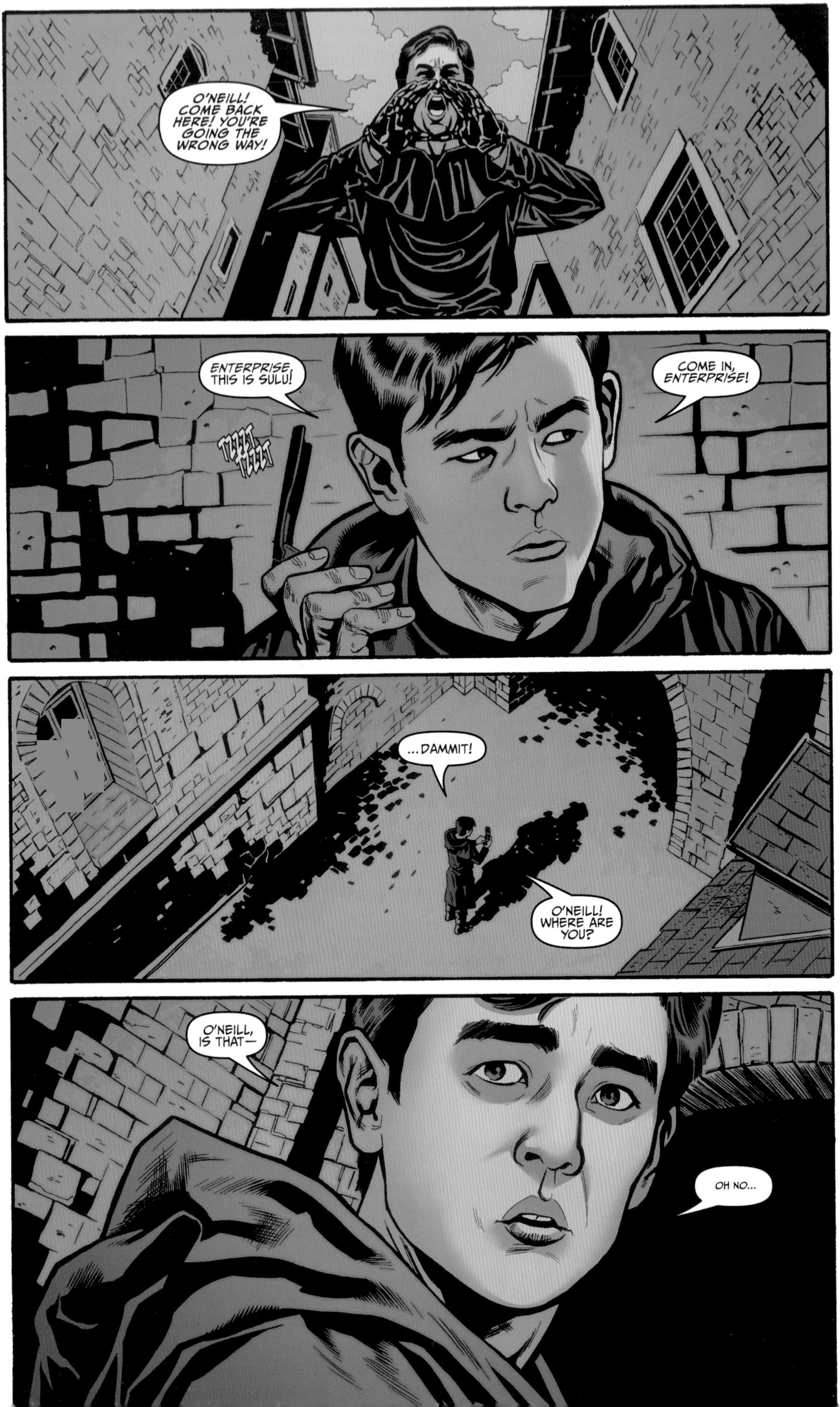
O'NEILL! COME BACK HERE! YOU'RE GOING THE WRONG WAY!
ENTERPRISE, THIS IS SULU!
COME IN, ENTERPRISE!
...DAMMIT!
O'NEILL! WHERE ARE YOU?
O'NEILL, IS THAT—
OH NO...

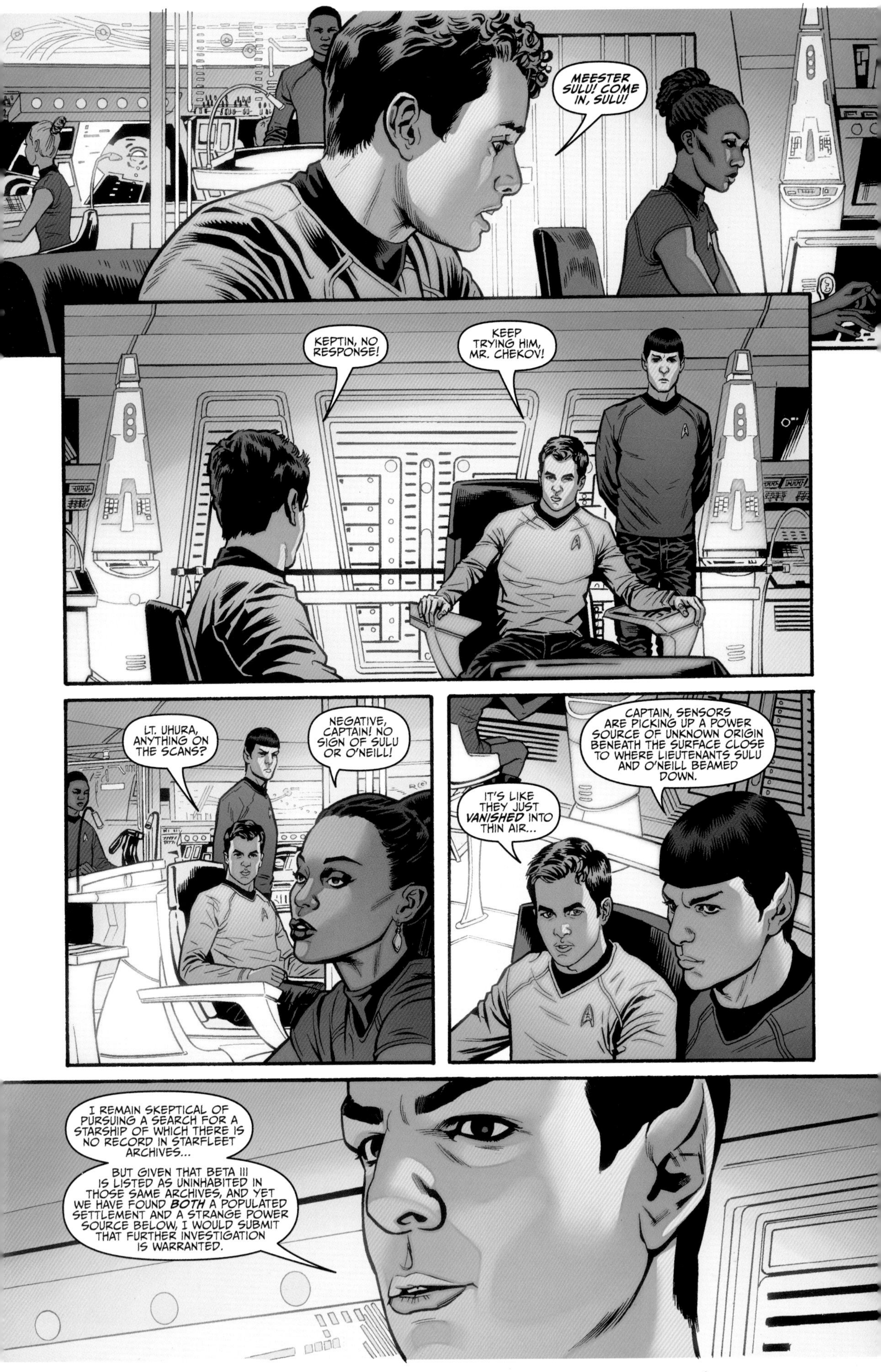
MEESTER SULU! COME IN, SULU!
KEPTIN, NO RESPONSE!
KEEP TRYING HIM, MR. CHEKOV!
LT. UHURA, ANYTHING ON THE SCANS?
NEGATIVE, CAPTAIN! NO SIGN OF SULU OR O'NEILL!
CAPTAIN, SENSORS ARE PICKING UP A POWER SOURCE OF UNKNOWN ORIGIN BENEATH THE SURFACE CLOSE TO WHERE LIEUTENANTS SULU AND O'NEILL BEAMED DOWN.
IT'S LIKE THEY JUST VANISHED INTO THIN AIR...
I REMAIN SKEPTICAL OF PURSUING A SEARCH FOR A STARSHIP OF WHICH THERE IS NO RECORD IN STARFLEET ARCHIVES...
BUT GIVEN THAT BETA III IS LISTED AS UNINHABITED IN THOSE SAME ARCHIVES, AND YET WE HAVE FOUND BOTH A POPULATED SETTLEMENT AND A STRANGE POWER SOURCE BELOW, I WOULD SUBMIT THAT FURTHER INVESTIGATION IS WARRANTED.

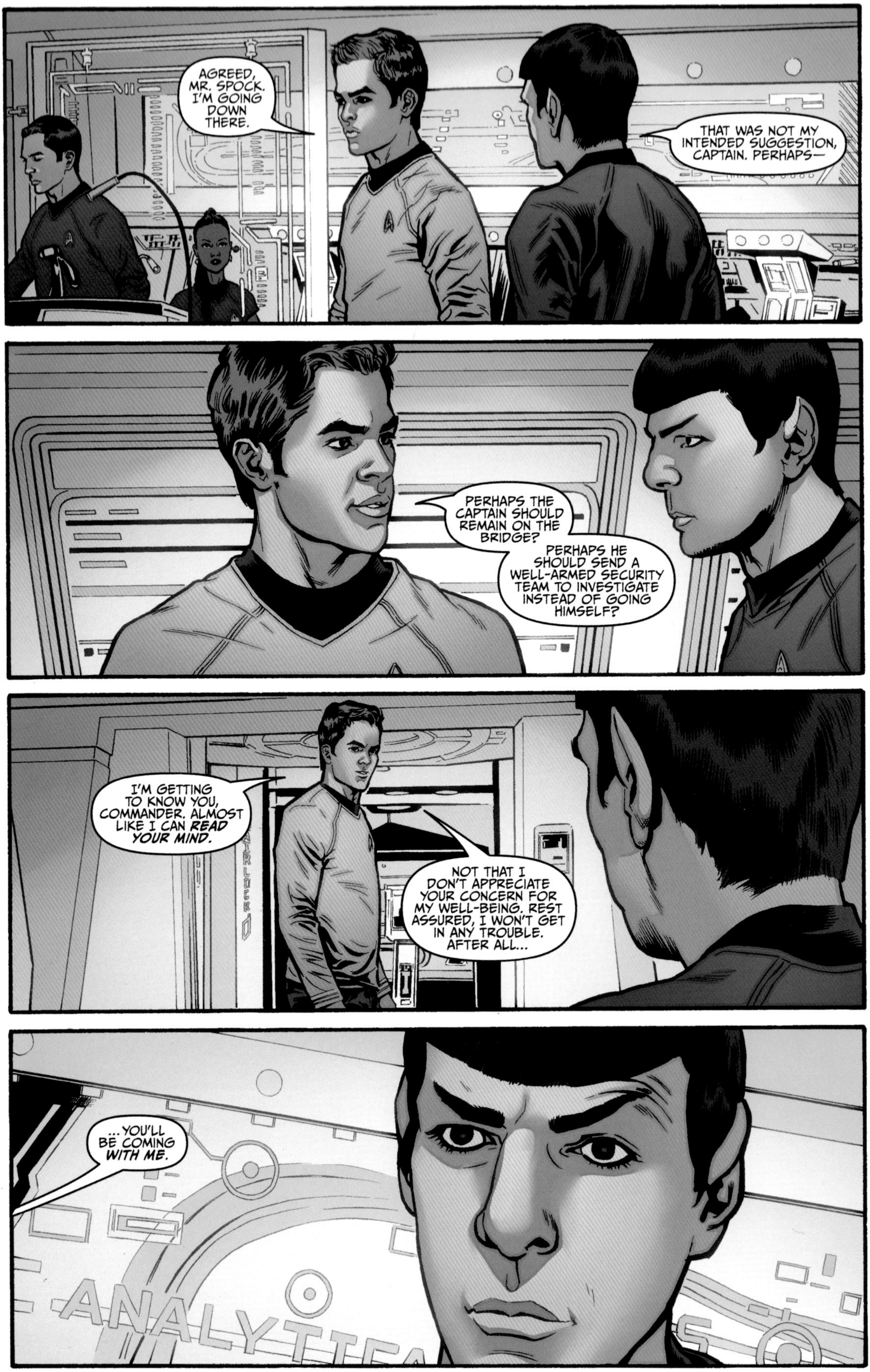
AGREED, MR. SPOCK. I'M GOING DOWN THERE.
THAT WAS NOT MY INTENDED SUGGESTION, CAPTAIN. PERHAPS—
PERHAPS THE CAPTAIN SHOULD REMAIN ON THE BRIDGE?
PERHAPS HE SHOULD SEND A WELL-ARMED SECURITY TEAM TO INVESTIGATE INSTEAD OF GOING HIMSELF?
I'M GETTING TO KNOW YOU, COMMANDER. ALMOST LIKE I CAN *READ YOUR MIND.*
NOT THAT I DON'T APPRECIATE YOUR CONCERN FOR MY WELL-BEING. REST ASSURED, I WON'T GET IN ANY TROUBLE. AFTER ALL...
...YOU'LL BE COMING *WITH ME.*

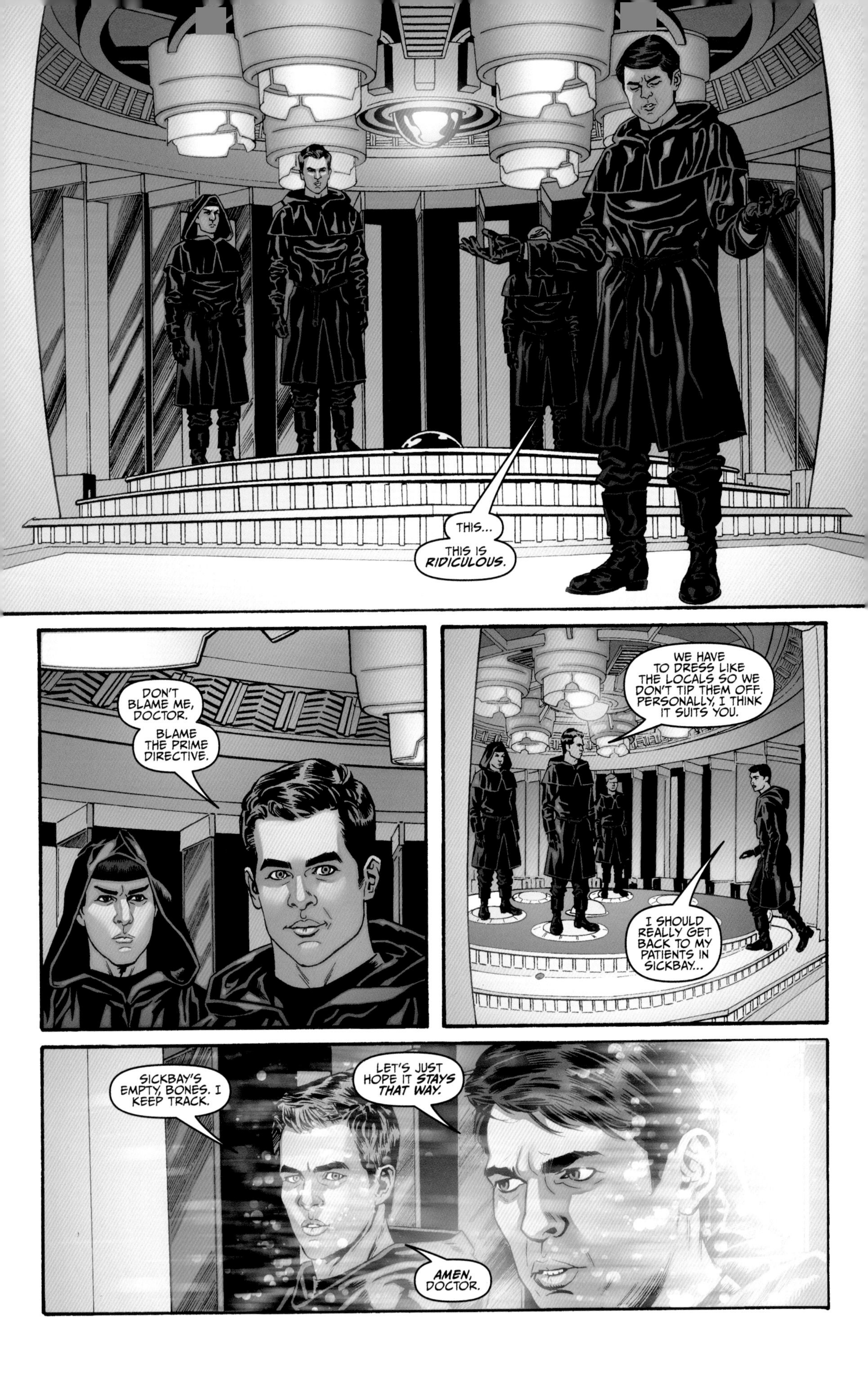
THIS...
THIS IS *RIDICULOUS*.
DON'T BLAME ME, DOCTOR.
BLAME THE PRIME DIRECTIVE.
WE HAVE TO DRESS LIKE THE LOCALS SO WE DON'T TIP THEM OFF. PERSONALLY, I THINK IT SUITS YOU.
I SHOULD REALLY GET BACK TO MY PATIENTS IN SICKBAY...
SICKBAY'S EMPTY, BONES. I KEEP TRACK.
LET'S JUST HOPE IT *STAYS THAT WAY.*
AMEN, DOCTOR.

OKAY, THIS IS OFFICIALLY *WEIRD*...

WE JUST WANDERED INTO THE *MIDDLE AGES!*

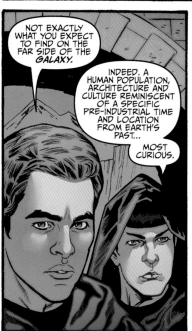

NOT EXACTLY WHAT YOU EXPECT TO FIND ON THE FAR SIDE OF THE *GALAXY.*

INDEED. A HUMAN POPULATION, ARCHITECTURE AND CULTURE REMINISCENT OF A SPECIFIC PRE-INDUSTRIAL TIME AND LOCATION FROM EARTH'S PAST...

MOST CURIOUS.

THEY DON'T APPEAR FAZED BY OUR PRESENCE. LOOK AT THEM. IT'S LIKE THEY'RE JUST... *DRIFTING* IN A DAZE...

KEEP YOUR EYES OPEN FOR SULU AND O'NEILL.

GREETINGS, TRAVELERS! *LANDRU* BE WITH YOU!

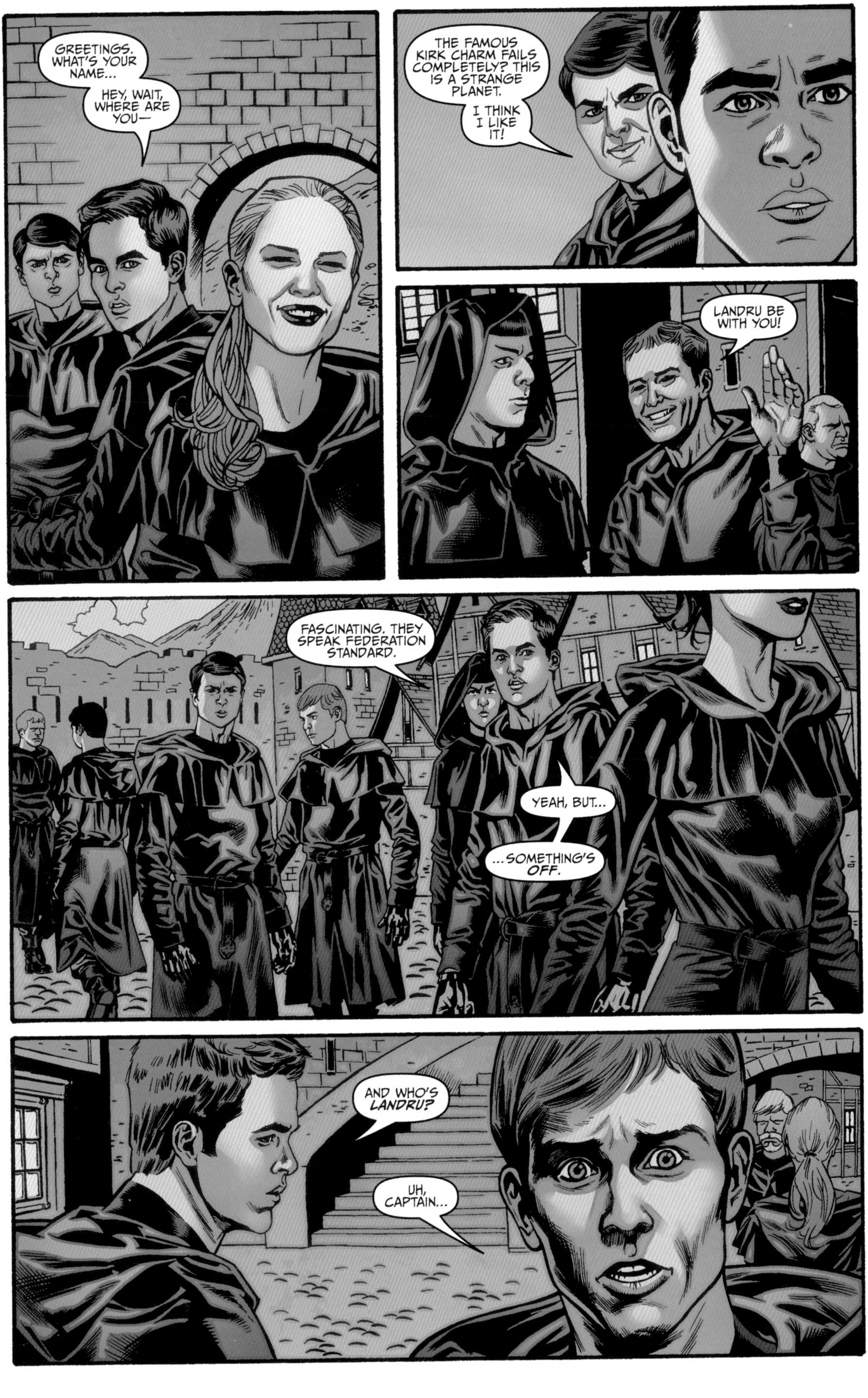
GREETINGS. WHAT'S YOUR NAME...
HEY, WAIT, WHERE ARE YOU—
THE FAMOUS KIRK CHARM FAILS COMPLETELY? THIS IS A STRANGE PLANET.
I THINK I LIKE IT!
LANDRU BE WITH YOU!
FASCINATING. THEY SPEAK FEDERATION STANDARD.
YEAH, BUT...
...SOMETHING'S *OFF.*
AND WHO'S *LANDRU?*
UH, CAPTAIN...

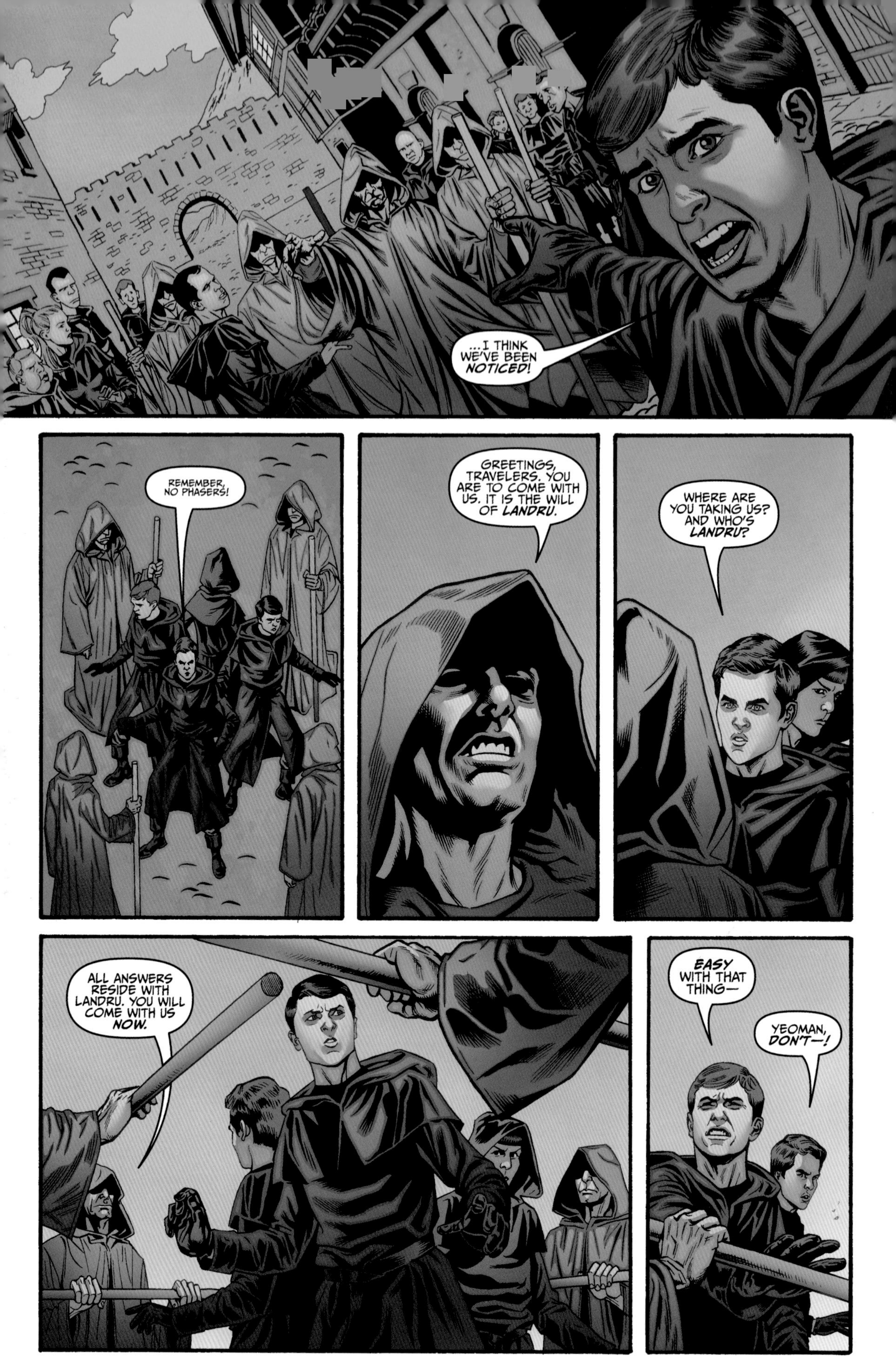
...I THINK WE'VE BEEN NOTICED!
REMEMBER, NO PHASERS!
GREETINGS, TRAVELERS. YOU ARE TO COME WITH US. IT IS THE WILL OF LANDRU.
WHERE ARE YOU TAKING US? AND WHO'S LANDRU?
ALL ANSWERS RESIDE WITH LANDRU. YOU WILL COME WITH US NOW.
EASY WITH THAT THING—
YEOMAN, DON'T—!

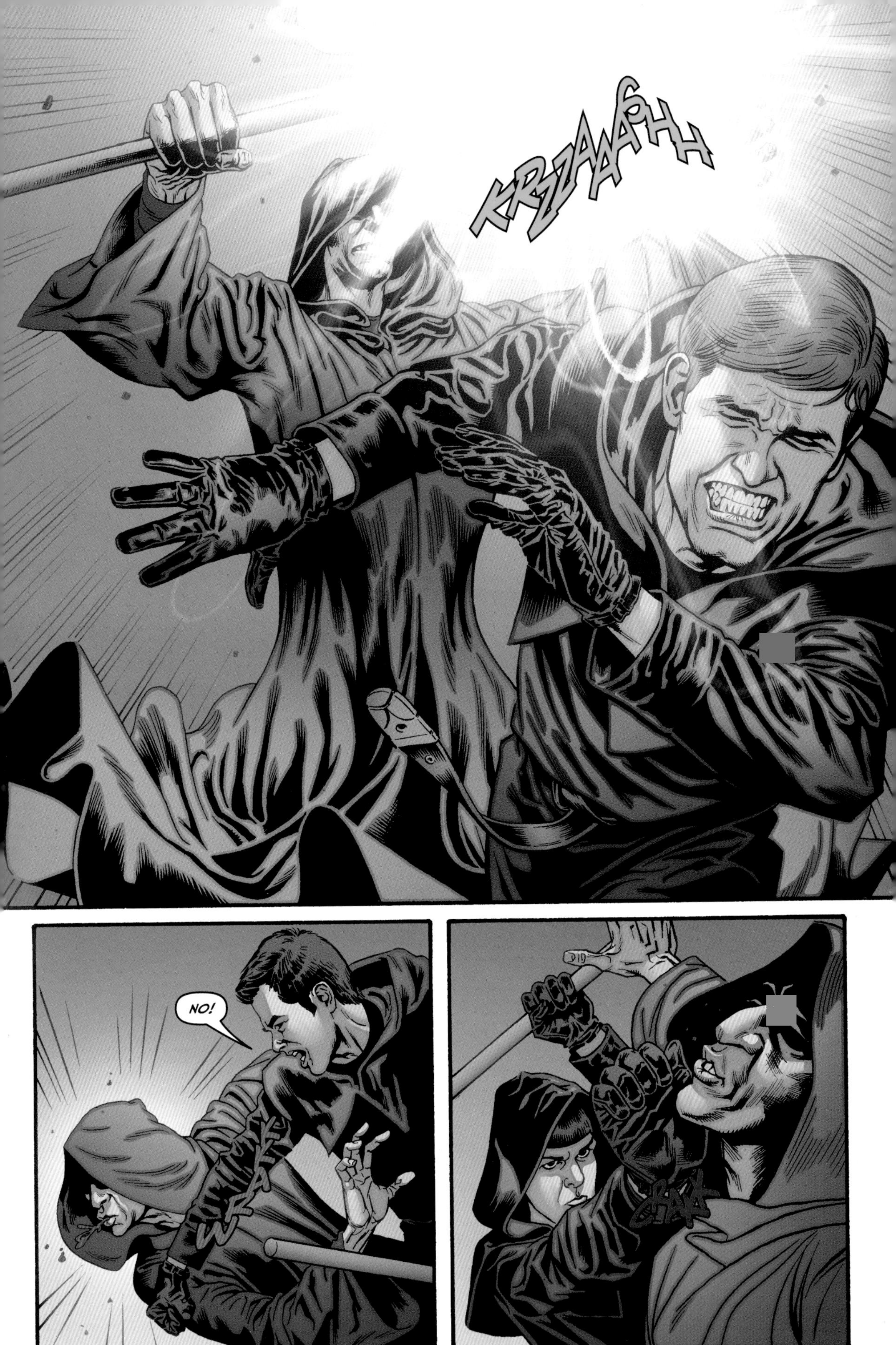
KRZZAAASHH
NO!

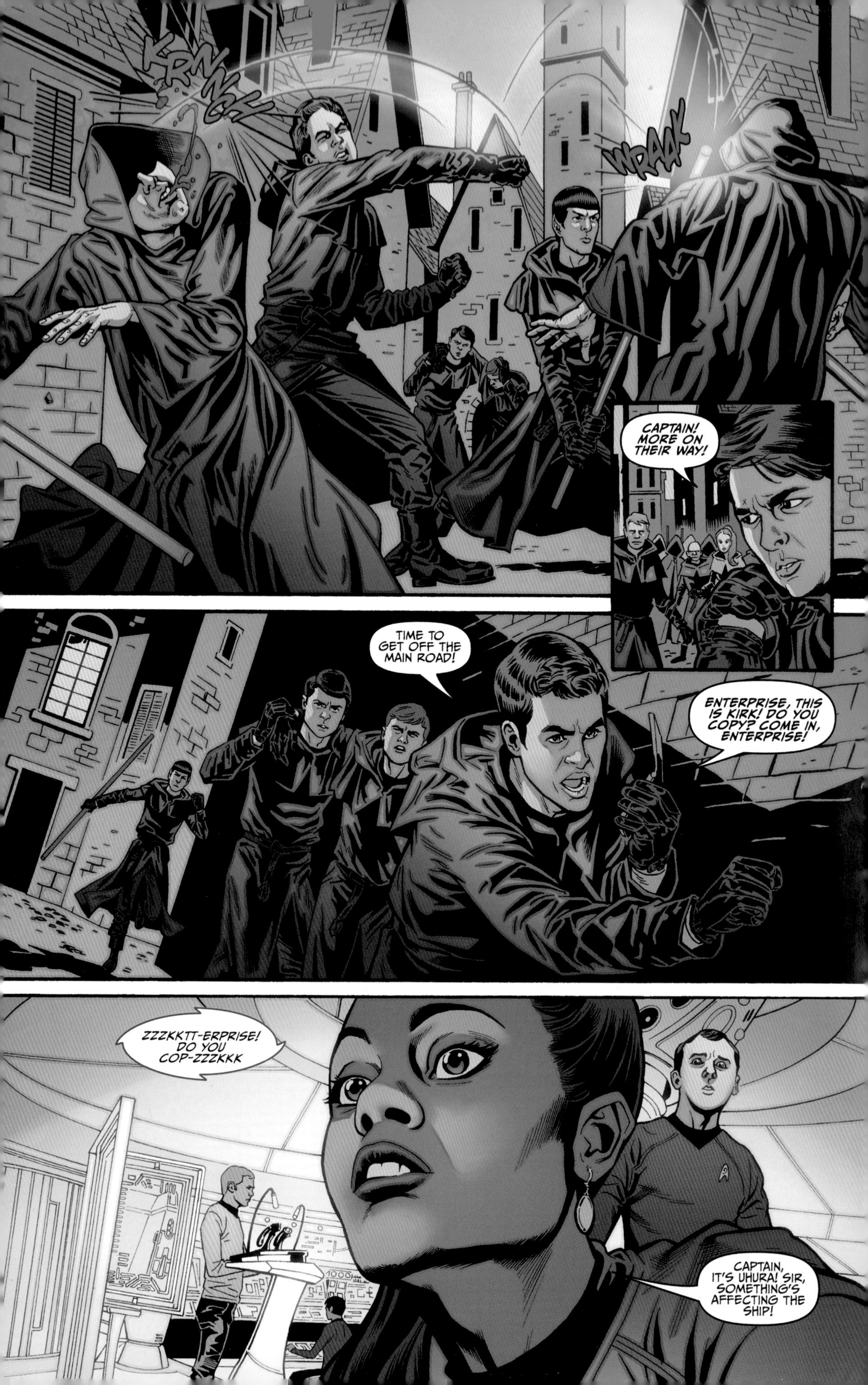
KRNNCH
WRAAK
CAPTAIN! MORE ON THEIR WAY!
TIME TO GET OFF THE MAIN ROAD!
ENTERPRISE, THIS IS KIRK! DO YOU COPY? COME IN, ENTERPRISE!
ZZZKKTT-ERPRISE! DO YOU COP-ZZZKKK
CAPTAIN, IT'S UHURA! SIR, SOMETHING'S AFFECTING THE SHIP!

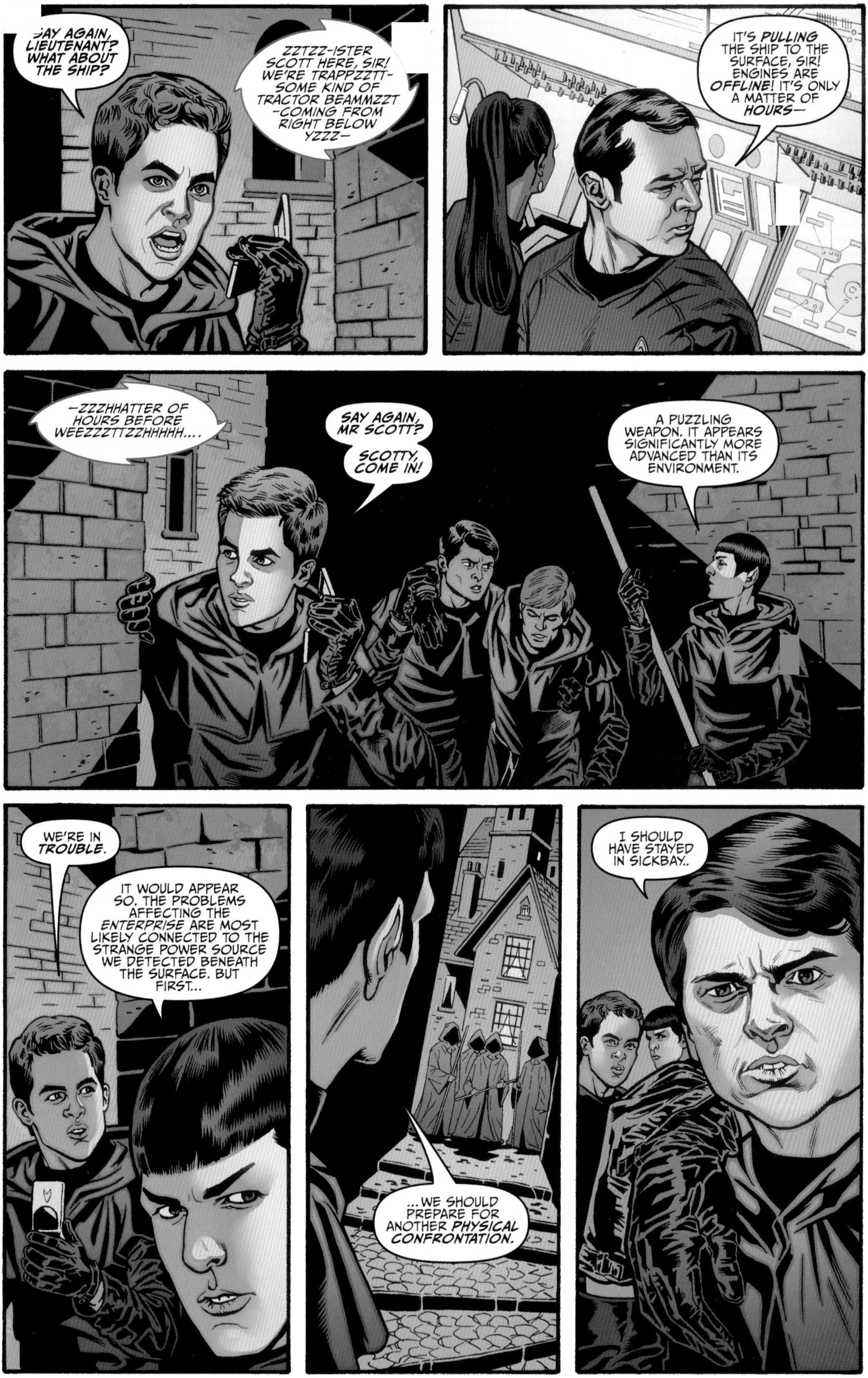
SAY AGAIN, LIEUTENANT? WHAT ABOUT THE SHIP?
ZZTZZ-ISTER SCOTT HERE, SIR! WE'RE TRAPPZZTT-SOME KIND OF TRACTOR BEAMMZZT -COMING FROM RIGHT BELOW YZZZ—
IT'S PULLING THE SHIP TO THE SURFACE, SIR! ENGINES ARE OFFLINE! IT'S ONLY A MATTER OF HOURS—
—ZZZHHATTER OF HOURS BEFORE WEEZZZTTZZHHHHH....
SAY AGAIN, MR SCOTT?
SCOTTY, COME IN!
A PUZZLING WEAPON. IT APPEARS SIGNIFICANTLY MORE ADVANCED THAN ITS ENVIRONMENT.
WE'RE IN TROUBLE.
IT WOULD APPEAR SO. THE PROBLEMS AFFECTING THE ENTERPRISE ARE MOST LIKELY CONNECTED TO THE STRANGE POWER SOURCE WE DETECTED BENEATH THE SURFACE. BUT FIRST...
...WE SHOULD PREPARE FOR ANOTHER PHYSICAL CONFRONTATION.
I SHOULD HAVE STAYED IN SICKBAY..

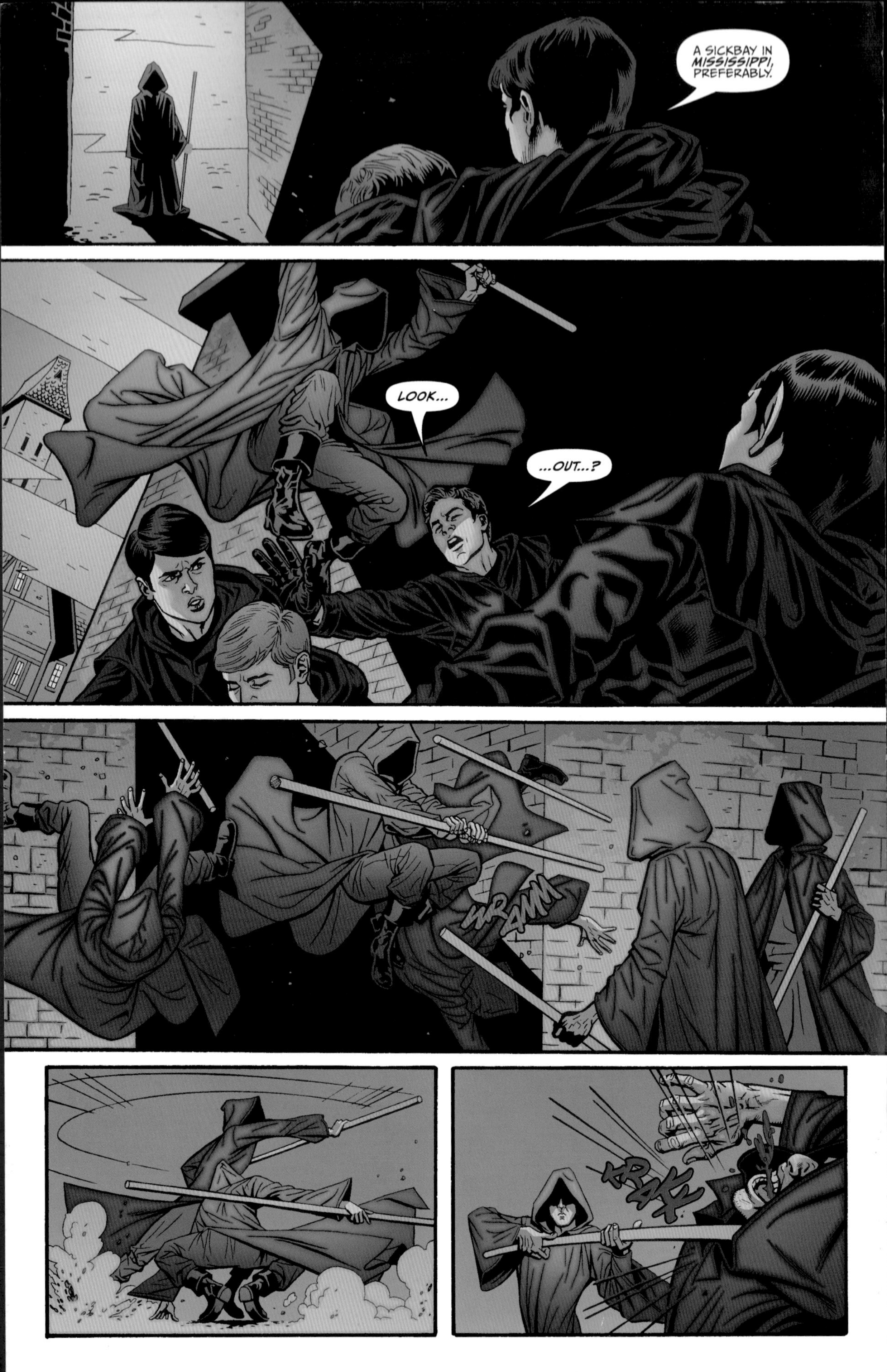
A SICKBAY IN MISSISSIPPI, PREFERABLY.
LOOK...
...OUT...?
WRAMM
KRAK

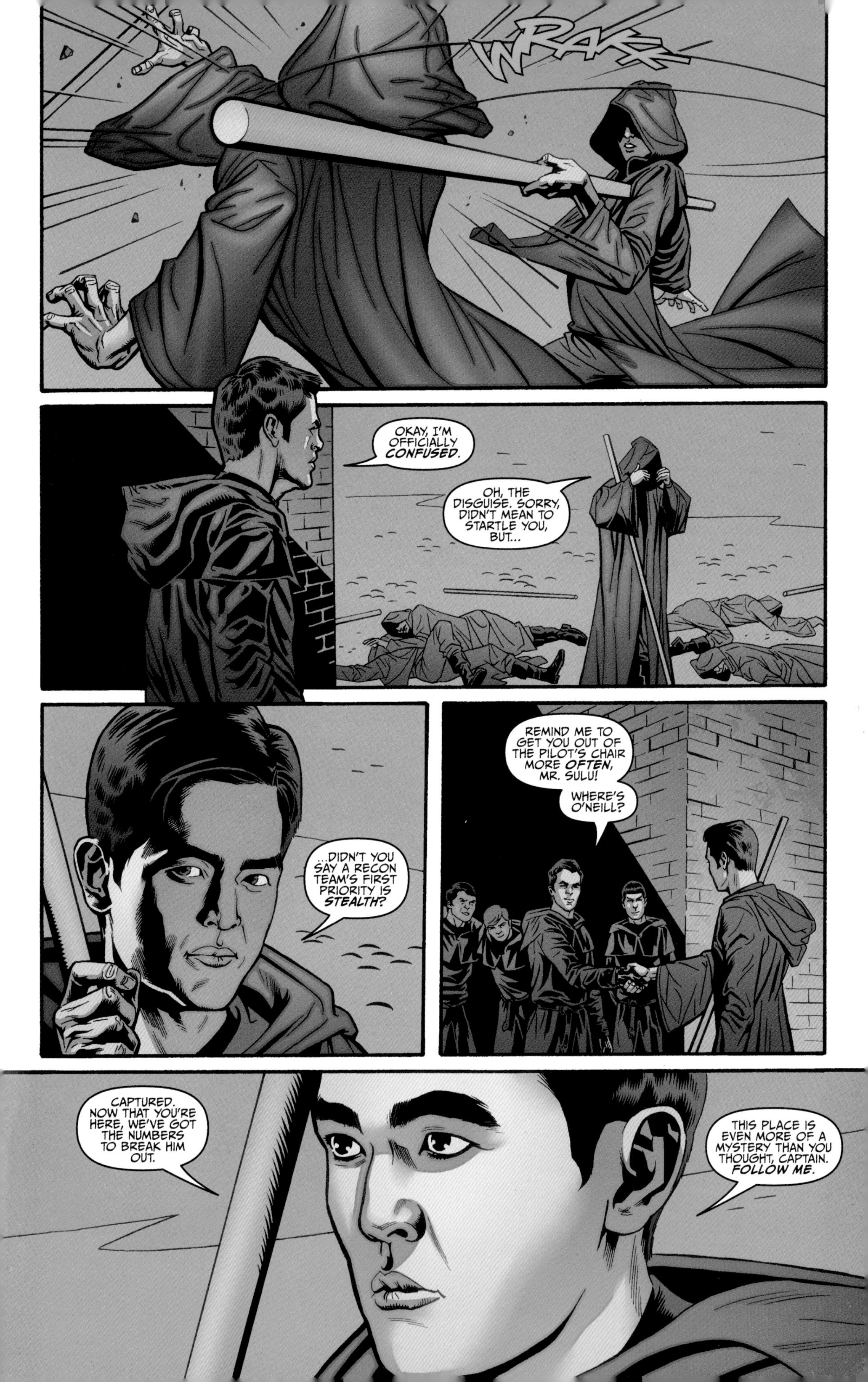
WRAKK
OKAY, I'M OFFICIALLY CONFUSED.
OH, THE DISGUISE. SORRY, DIDN'T MEAN TO STARTLE YOU, BUT...
...DIDN'T YOU SAY A RECON TEAM'S FIRST PRIORITY IS STEALTH?
REMIND ME TO GET YOU OUT OF THE PILOT'S CHAIR MORE OFTEN, MR. SULU!
WHERE'S O'NEILL?
CAPTURED. NOW THAT YOU'RE HERE, WE'VE GOT THE NUMBERS TO BREAK HIM OUT.
THIS PLACE IS EVEN MORE OF A MYSTERY THAN YOU THOUGHT, CAPTAIN. FOLLOW ME.

YOU'VE SEEN THAT THIS PLACE LOOKS LIKE A PRE-INDUSTRIAL EARTH SETTLEMENT. PEOPLE WALKING AROUND IN A DAZE.

BUT IT'S WHEN YOU GET DOWN BELOW...

...THAT THINGS *REALLY GET STRANGE.*

FASCINATING. THIS WOULD APPEAR TO BE MID 22ND-CENTURY TECHNOLOGY...

NOT ALL THAT FAR OFF FROM WHEN THE *ARCHON* SUPPOSEDLY WENT MISSING.

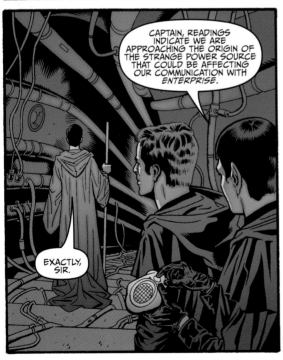

CAPTAIN, READINGS INDICATE WE ARE APPROACHING THE ORIGIN OF THE STRANGE POWER SOURCE THAT COULD BE AFFECTING OUR COMMUNICATION WITH *ENTERPRISE.*

EXACTLY, SIR.

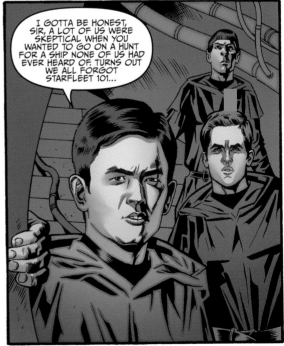

I GOTTA BE HONEST, SIR, A LOT OF US WERE SKEPTICAL WHEN YOU WANTED TO GO ON A HUNT FOR A SHIP NONE OF US HAD EVER HEARD OF. TURNS OUT WE ALL FORGOT STARFLEET 101...

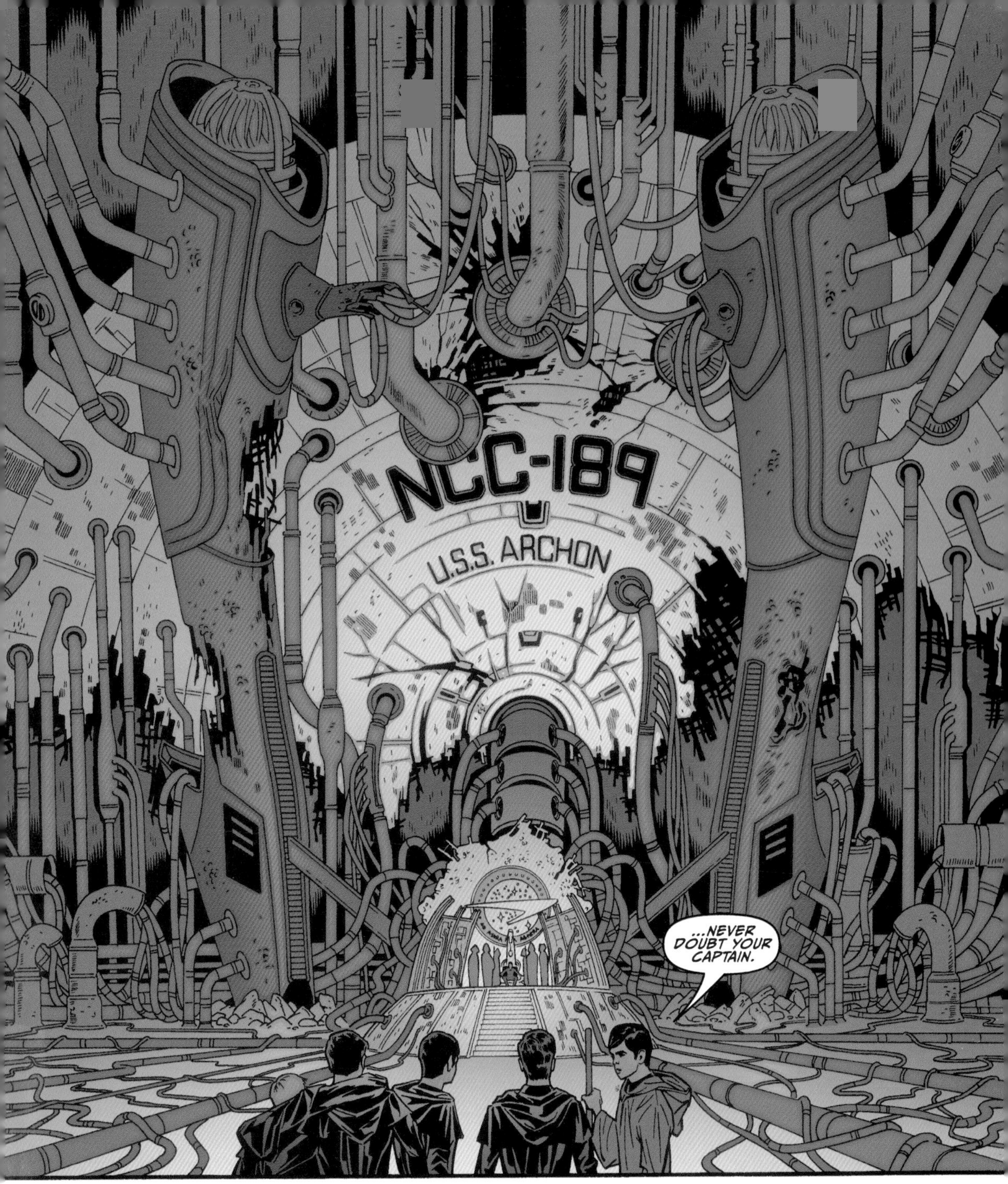
NCC-189
U.S.S. ARCHON
...NEVER DOUBT YOUR CAPTAIN.

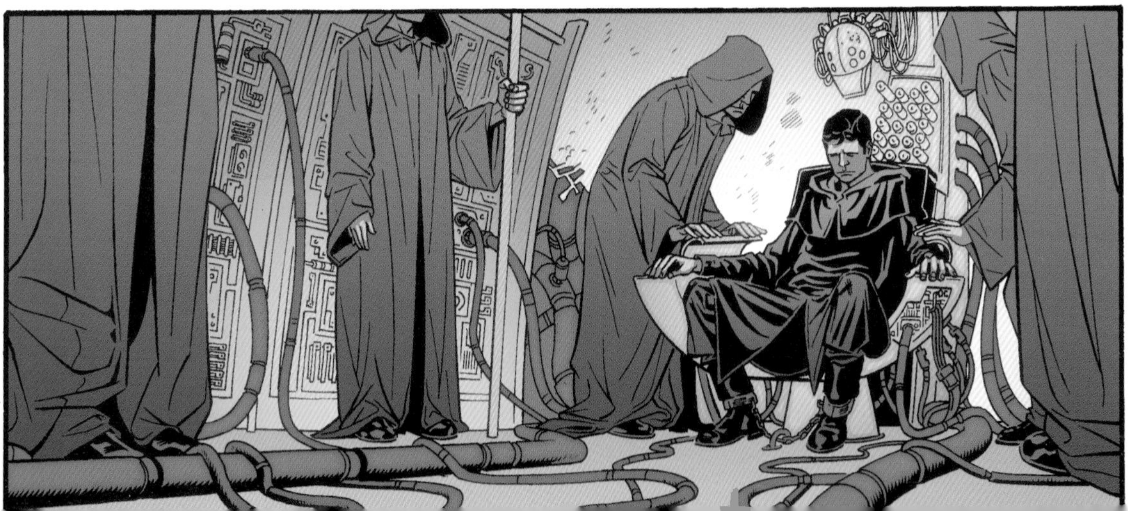

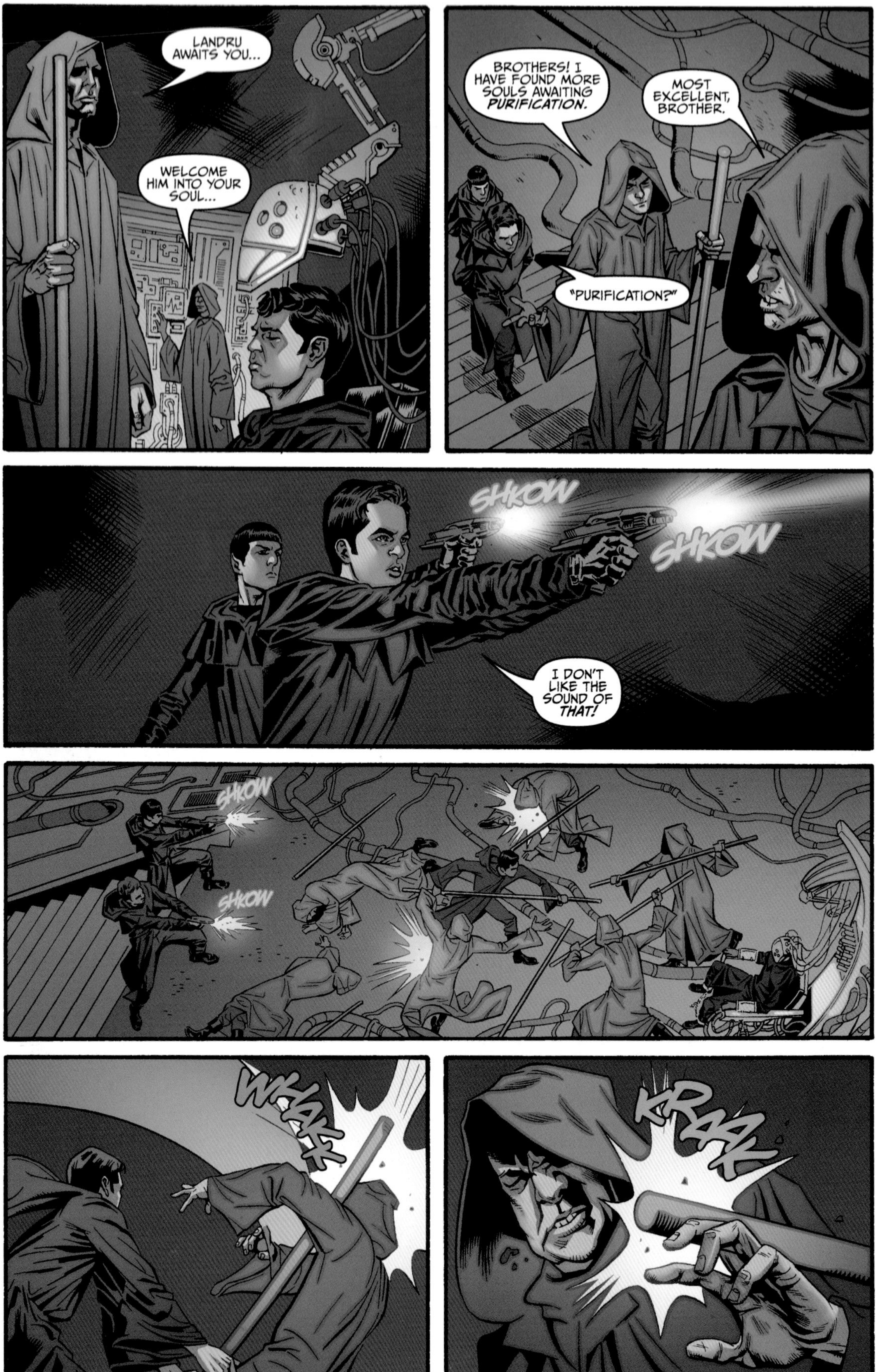
LANDRU AWAITS YOU...
WELCOME HIM INTO YOUR SOUL...
BROTHERS! I HAVE FOUND MORE SOULS AWAITING PURIFICATION.
MOST EXCELLENT, BROTHER.
"PURIFICATION?"
SHKOW
SHKOW
I DON'T LIKE THE SOUND OF THAT!
SHKOW
SHKOW
WHAK
KRAAK

CAPTAIN, ARE YOU SURE OUR USE OF PHASERS WAS WISE GIVEN THE DICTATES OF THE...

...PRIME DIRECTIVE? THEY'VE BUILT AN *UNDERGROUND ALTAR* OUT OF PIECES OF A *STARSHIP* SPOCK. I THINK WE'RE OKAY.

INCREDIBLE...

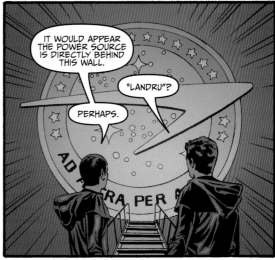

IT WOULD APPEAR THE POWER SOURCE IS DIRECTLY BEHIND THIS WALL.

"LANDRU"?

PERHAPS.

ALL RIGHT THEN. TIME TO OPEN THE *MYSTERY BOX.*

BOOOOOOOOOOM

WHOA!!

SOMETHING BACK HERE... SOMETHING...

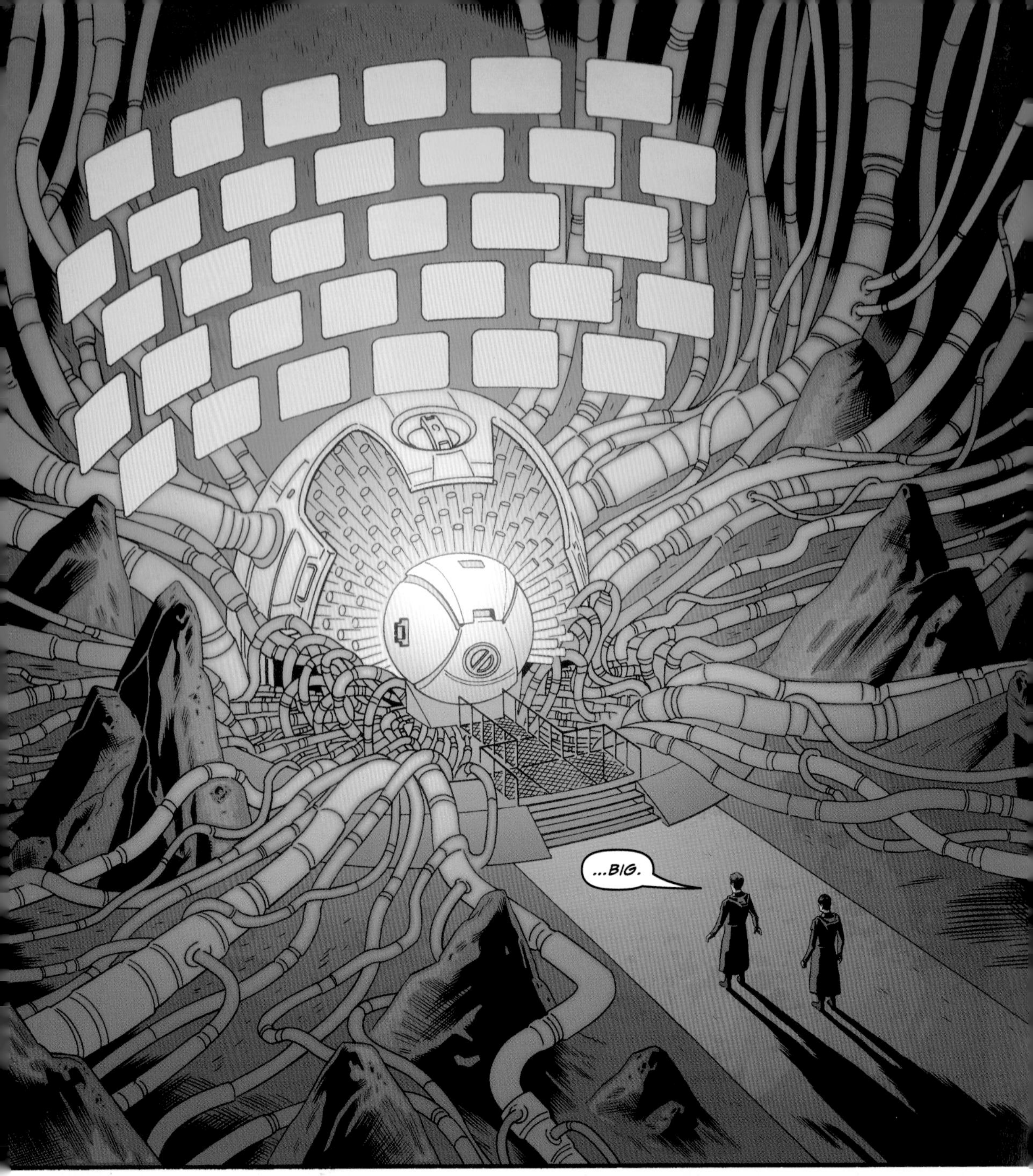
...BIG.

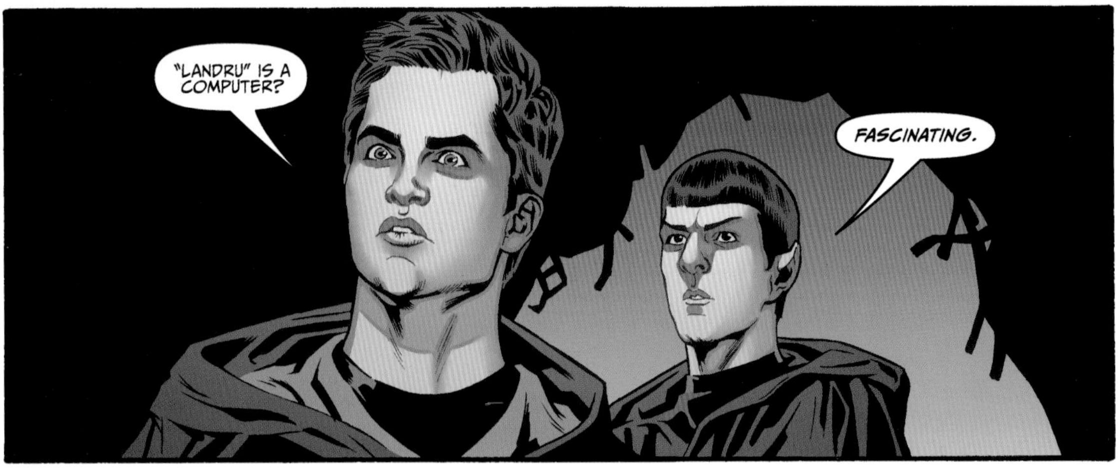
"LANDRU" IS A COMPUTER?
FASCINATING.

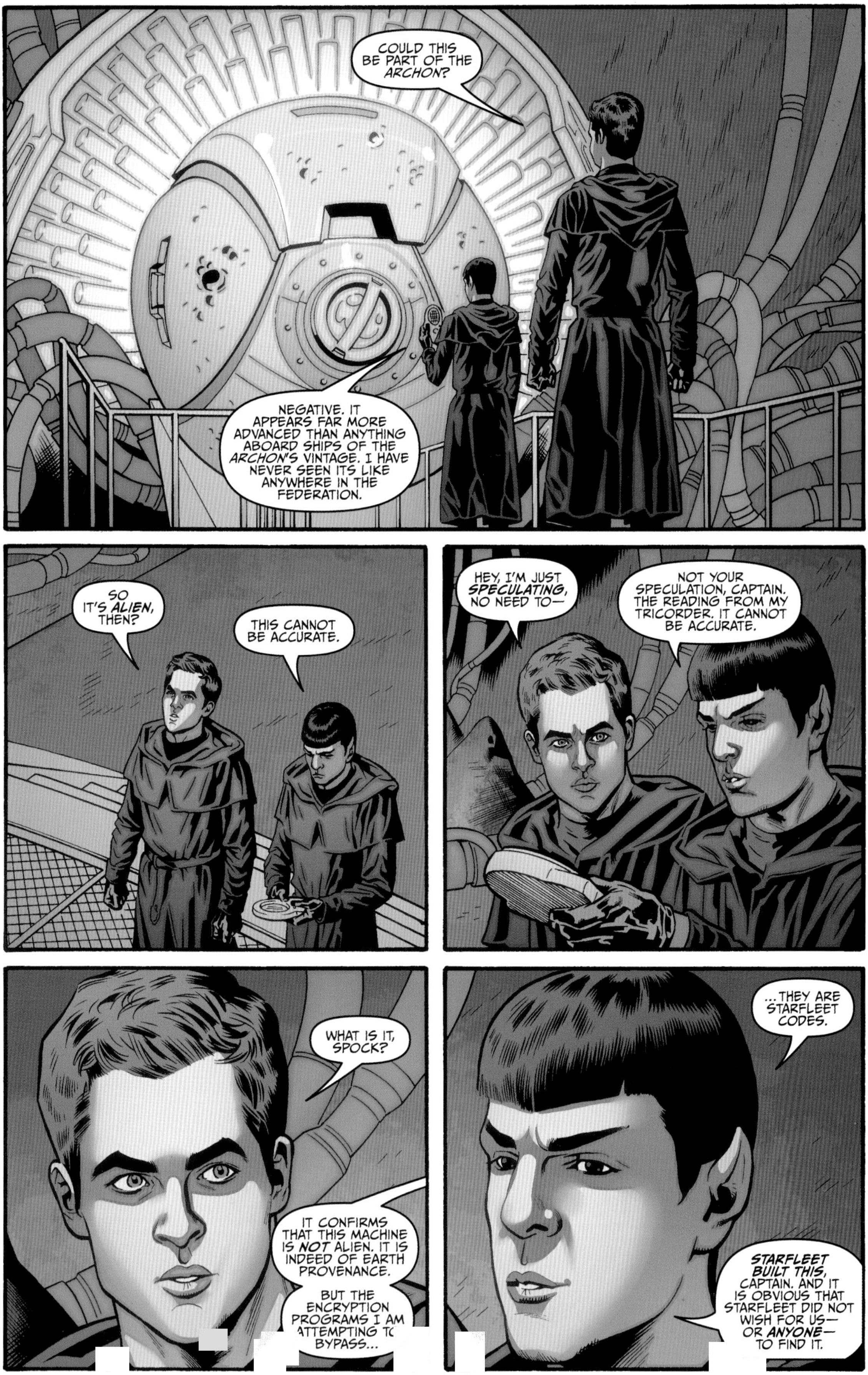
COULD THIS BE PART OF THE *ARCHON*?
NEGATIVE. IT APPEARS FAR MORE ADVANCED THAN ANYTHING ABOARD SHIPS OF THE *ARCHON'S* VINTAGE. I HAVE NEVER SEEN ITS LIKE ANYWHERE IN THE FEDERATION.
SO IT'S ***ALIEN***, THEN?
THIS CANNOT BE ACCURATE.
HEY, I'M JUST ***SPECULATING***, NO NEED TO—
NOT YOUR SPECULATION, CAPTAIN. THE READING FROM MY TRICORDER. IT CANNOT BE ACCURATE.
WHAT IS IT, SPOCK?
IT CONFIRMS THAT THIS MACHINE IS ***NOT*** ALIEN. IT IS INDEED OF EARTH PROVENANCE.
BUT THE ENCRYPTION PROGRAMS I AM ATTEMPTING TO BYPASS...
...THEY ARE STARFLEET CODES.
STARFLEET BUILT THIS, CAPTAIN. AND IT IS OBVIOUS THAT STARFLEET DID NOT WISH FOR US— OR ***ANYONE***— TO FIND IT.

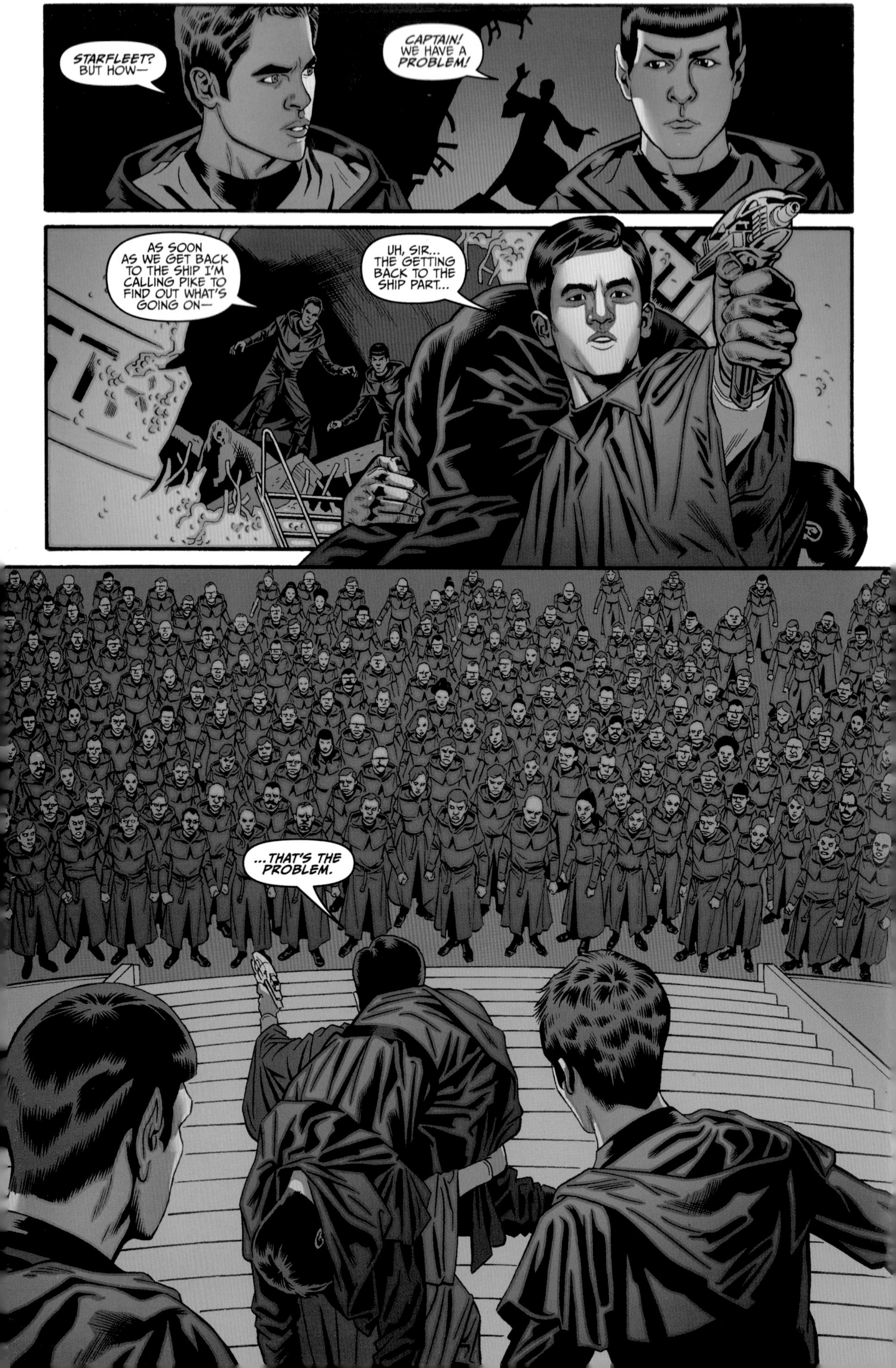
STARFLEET? BUT HOW—
CAPTAIN! WE HAVE A PROBLEM!
AS SOON AS WE GET BACK TO THE SHIP I'M CALLING PIKE TO FIND OUT WHAT'S GOING ON—
UH, SIR... THE GETTING BACK TO THE SHIP PART...
...THAT'S THE PROBLEM.

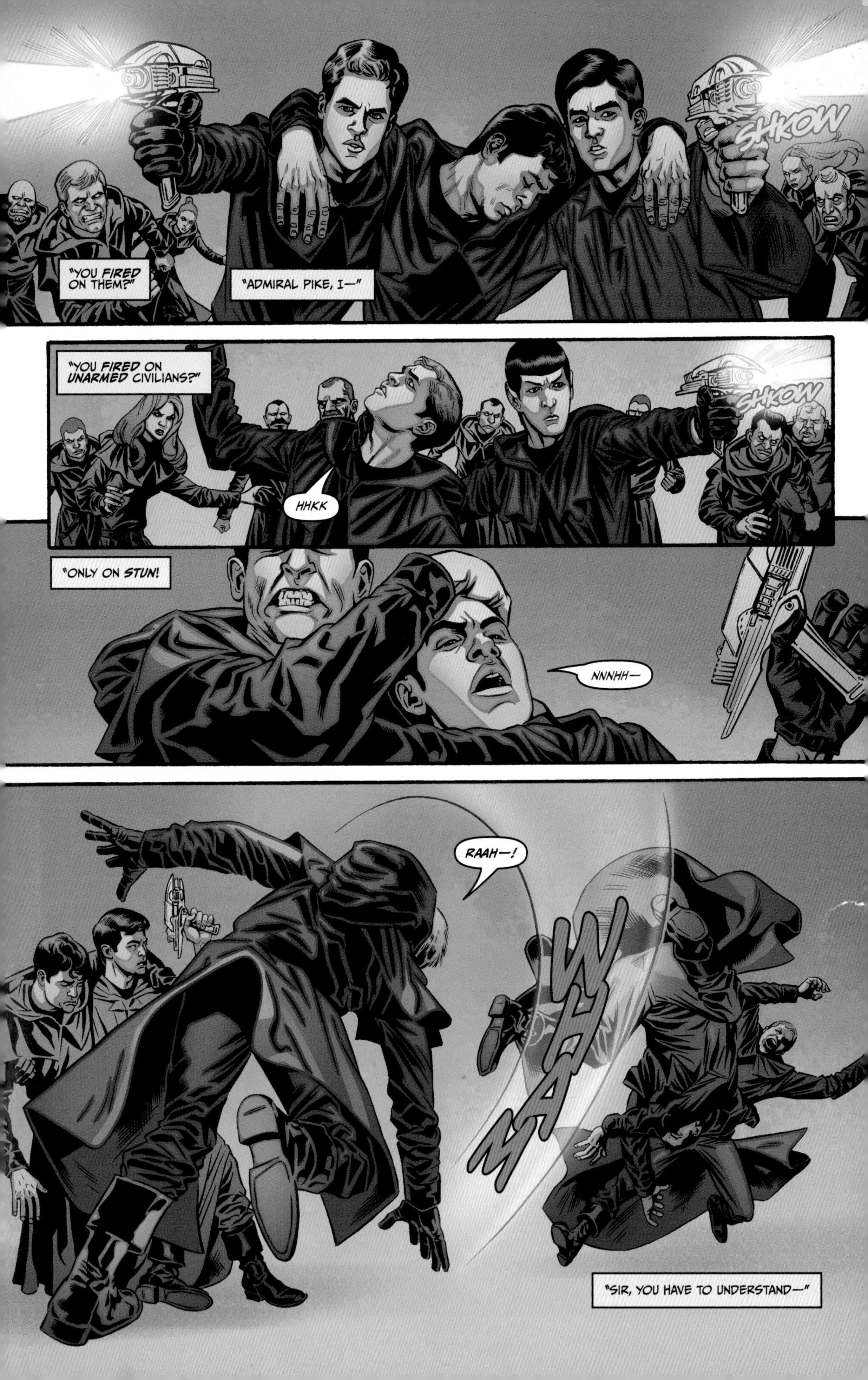
SHKOW
"YOU FIRED ON THEM?"
"ADMIRAL PIKE, I—"
"YOU FIRED ON UNARMED CIVILIANS?"
SHKOW
HHKK
"ONLY ON STUN!
NNNHH—
RAAH—!
WHAM
"SIR, YOU HAVE TO UNDERSTAND—"

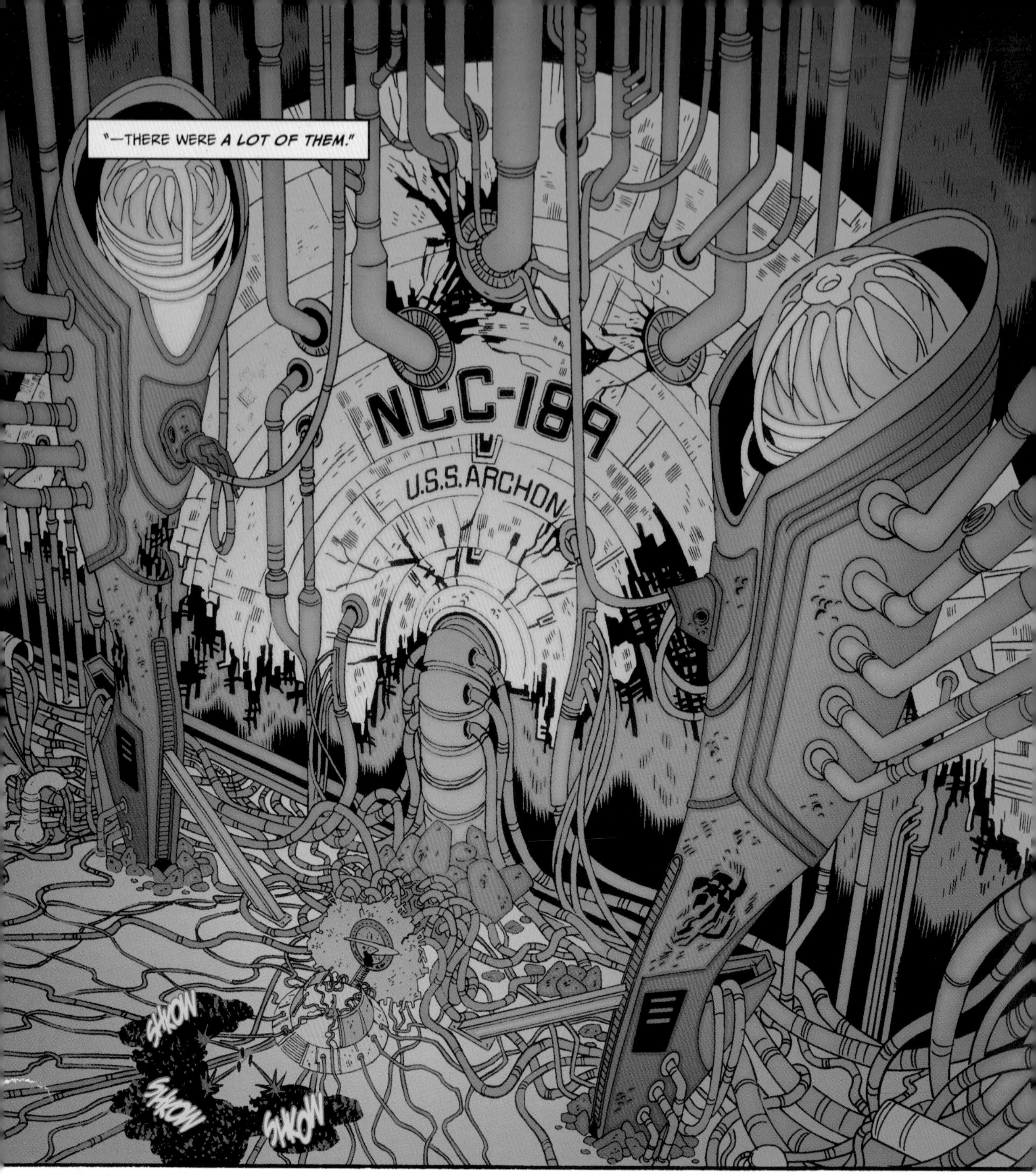
"—THERE WERE A LOT OF THEM."
NCC-189
U.S.S. ARCHON
SHKOW
SHKOW
SHKOW

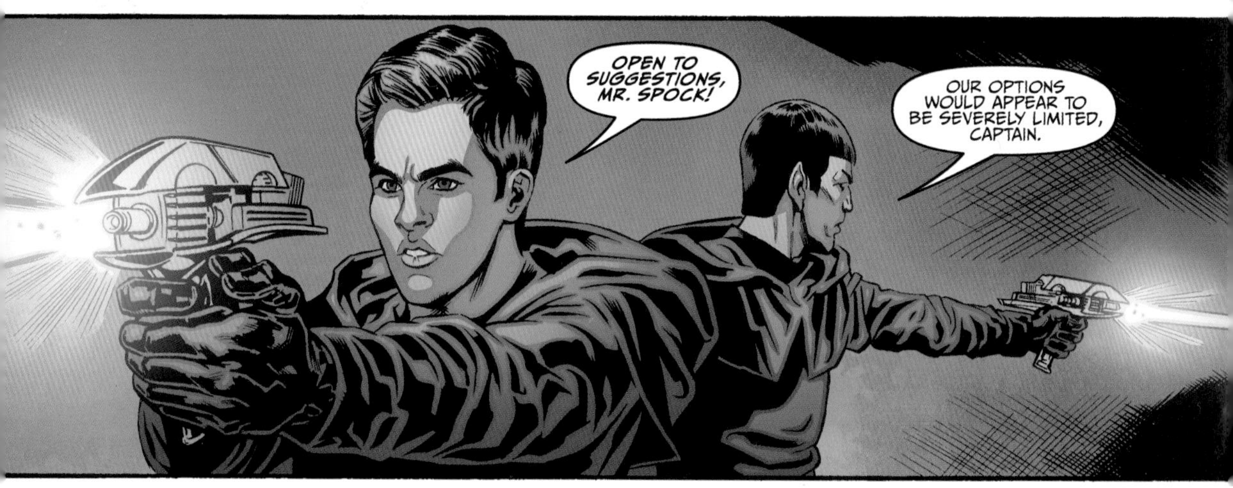
OPEN TO SUGGESTIONS, MR. SPOCK!
OUR OPTIONS WOULD APPEAR TO BE SEVERELY LIMITED, CAPTAIN.

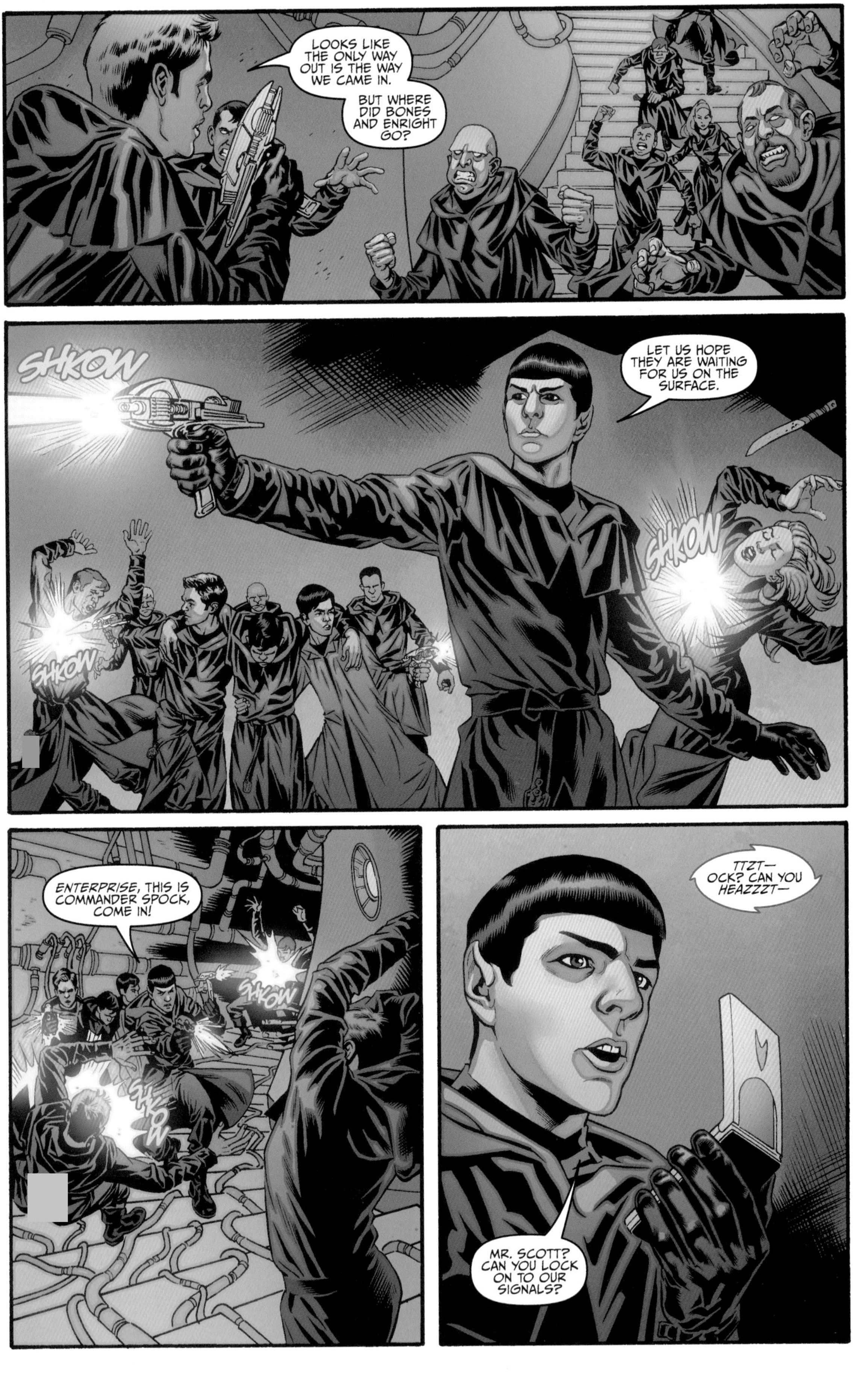
LOOKS LIKE THE ONLY WAY OUT IS THE WAY WE CAME IN.
BUT WHERE DID BONES AND ENRIGHT GO?
SHKOW
LET US HOPE THEY ARE WAITING FOR US ON THE SURFACE.
SHKOW
SHKOW
ENTERPRISE, THIS IS COMMANDER SPOCK, COME IN!
SHKOW
SHKOW
TTZT— OCK? CAN YOU HEAZZZT—
MR. SCOTT? CAN YOU LOCK ON TO OUR SIGNALS?

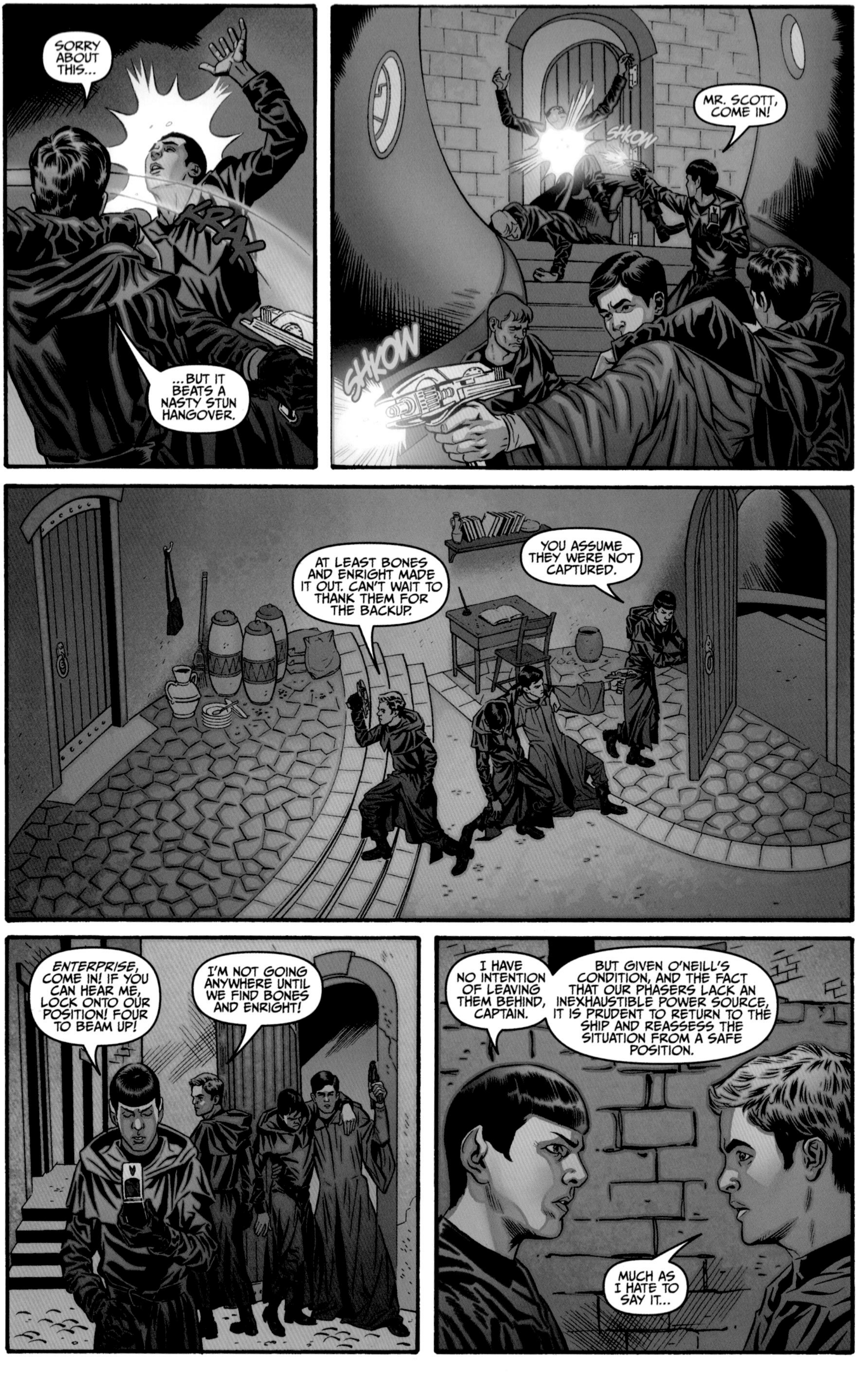
SORRY ABOUT THIS...
KRAK
...BUT IT BEATS A NASTY STUN HANGOVER.
MR. SCOTT, COME IN!
SHKOW
SHKOW
AT LEAST BONES AND ENRIGHT MADE IT OUT. CAN'T WAIT TO THANK THEM FOR THE BACKUP.
YOU ASSUME THEY WERE NOT CAPTURED.
ENTERPRISE, COME IN! IF YOU CAN HEAR ME, LOCK ONTO OUR POSITION! FOUR TO BEAM UP!
I'M NOT GOING ANYWHERE UNTIL WE FIND BONES AND ENRIGHT!
I HAVE NO INTENTION OF LEAVING THEM BEHIND, CAPTAIN.
BUT GIVEN O'NEILL'S CONDITION, AND THE FACT THAT OUR PHASERS LACK AN INEXHAUSTIBLE POWER SOURCE, IT IS PRUDENT TO RETURN TO THE SHIP AND REASSESS THE SITUATION FROM A SAFE POSITION.
MUCH AS I HATE TO SAY IT...

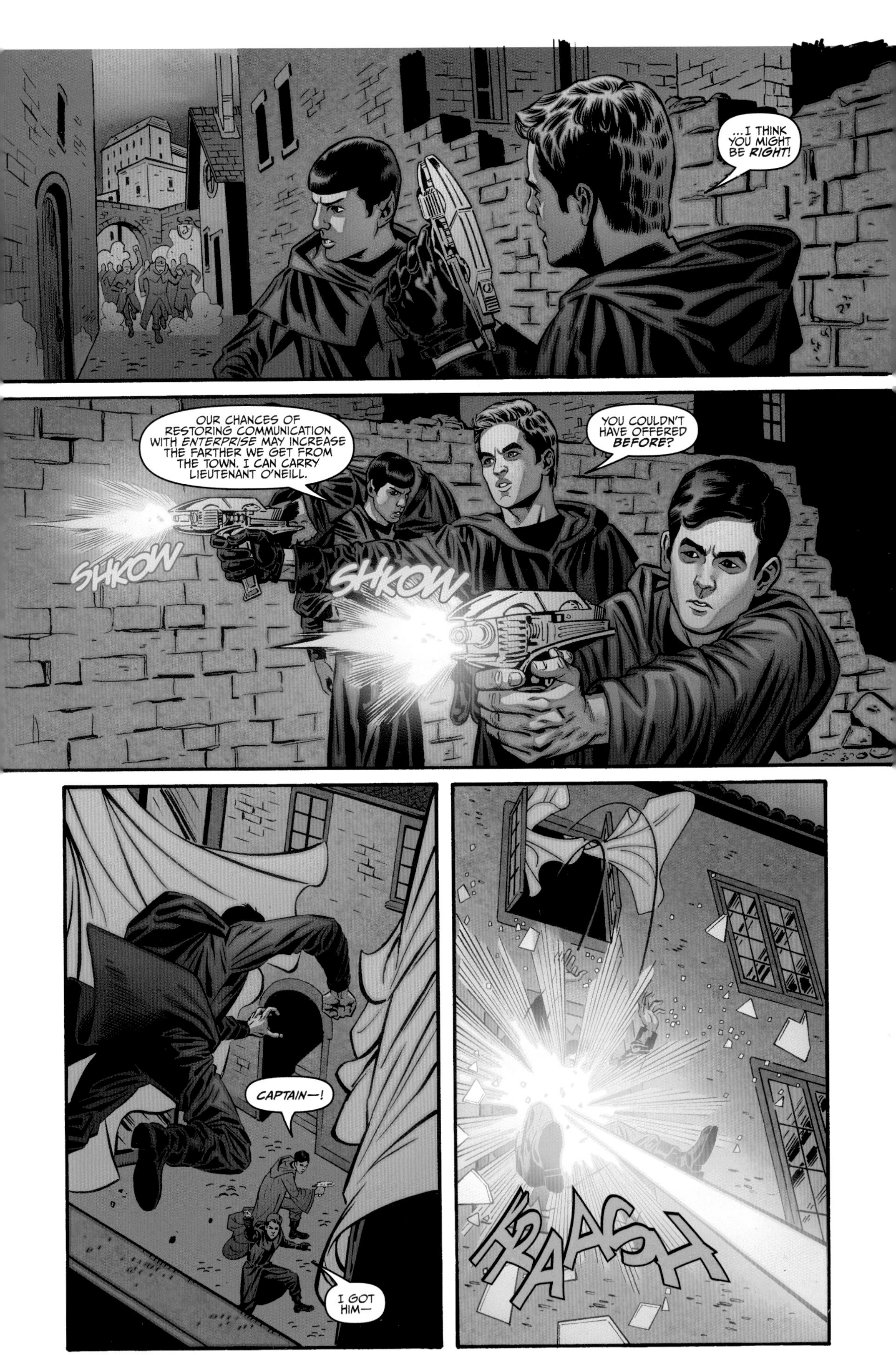
...I THINK YOU MIGHT BE *RIGHT*!
OUR CHANCES OF RESTORING COMMUNICATION WITH *ENTERPRISE* MAY INCREASE THE FARTHER WE GET FROM THE TOWN. I CAN CARRY LIEUTENANT O'NEILL.
YOU COULDN'T HAVE OFFERED *BEFORE*?
SHKOW
SHKOW
CAPTAIN—!
I GOT HIM—
KRAASH

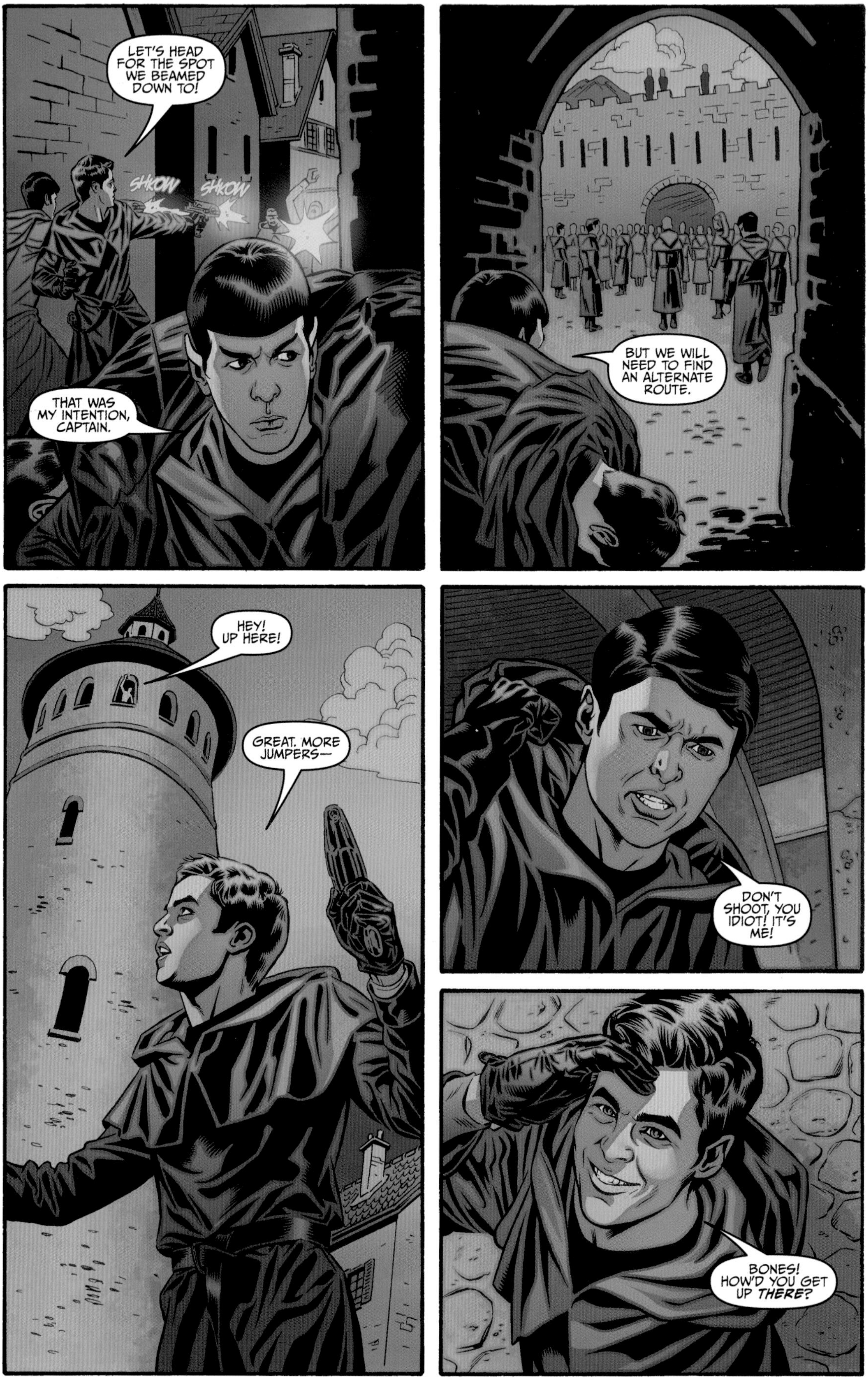

LET'S HEAD FOR THE SPOT WE BEAMED DOWN TO!
SHKOW
SHKOW
THAT WAS MY INTENTION, CAPTAIN.
BUT WE WILL NEED TO FIND AN ALTERNATE ROUTE.
HEY! UP HERE!
GREAT. MORE JUMPERS—
DON'T SHOOT, YOU IDIOT! IT'S ME!
BONES! HOW'D YOU GET UP *THERE?*

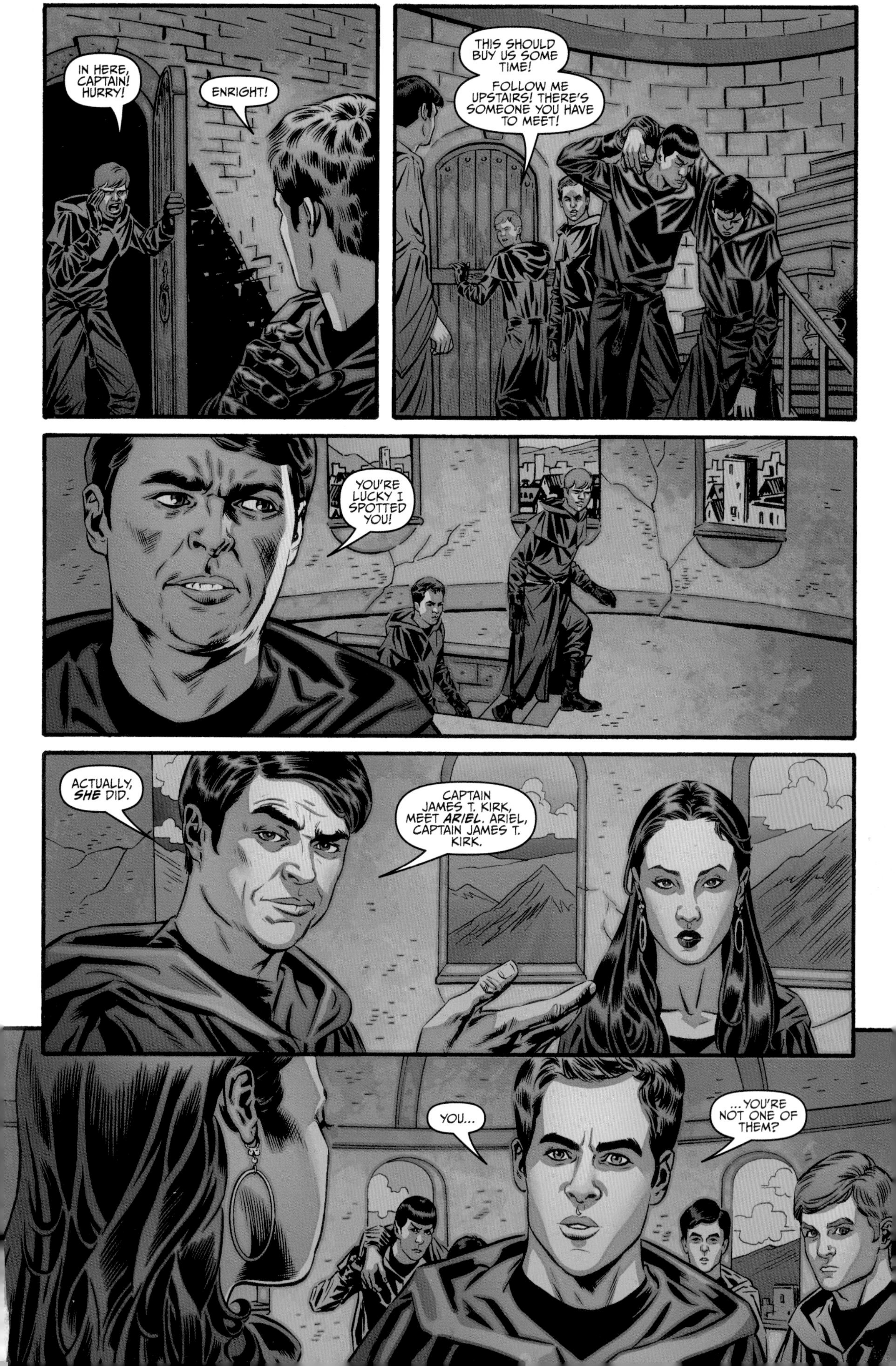
IN HERE, CAPTAIN! HURRY!
ENRIGHT!
THIS SHOULD BUY US SOME TIME!
FOLLOW ME UPSTAIRS! THERE'S SOMEONE YOU HAVE TO MEET!
YOU'RE LUCKY I SPOTTED YOU!
ACTUALLY, SHE DID.
CAPTAIN JAMES T. KIRK, MEET ARIEL. ARIEL, CAPTAIN JAMES T. KIRK.
YOU...
...YOU'RE NOT ONE OF THEM?

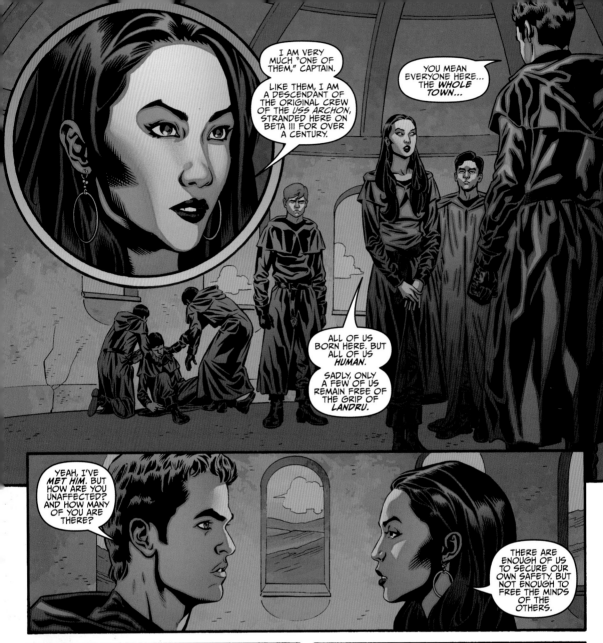

I AM VERY MUCH "ONE OF THEM," CAPTAIN.

LIKE THEM, I AM A DESCENDANT OF THE ORIGINAL CREW OF THE *USS ARCHON*, STRANDED HERE ON BETA III FOR OVER A CENTURY.

YOU MEAN EVERYONE HERE... THE *WHOLE TOWN*...

ALL OF US BORN HERE. BUT ALL OF US *HUMAN*.

SADLY, ONLY A FEW OF US REMAIN FREE OF THE GRIP OF *LANDRU*.

YEAH, I'VE *MET HIM*. BUT HOW ARE YOU UNAFFECTED? AND HOW MANY OF YOU ARE THERE?

THERE ARE ENOUGH OF US TO SECURE OUR OWN SAFETY. BUT NOT ENOUGH TO FREE THE MINDS OF THE OTHERS.

AS FOR HOW WE ESCAPED THEIR FATE... SOME ARE DESCENDED FROM THE ORIGINAL CREW WHO AVOIDED LANDRU'S GRASP, BORN AND RAISED FREE. OTHERS WE RESCUED BEFORE THEY COULD BE CONVERTED.

AT TIMES, SOMEONE WILL BREAK FREE OF LANDRU, BUT THE LAWGIVERS ARE QUICK TO CATCH AND "RE-EDUCATE" THEM.

YOU AND YOUR COMRADES ARE LUCKY TO HAVE ESCAPED.

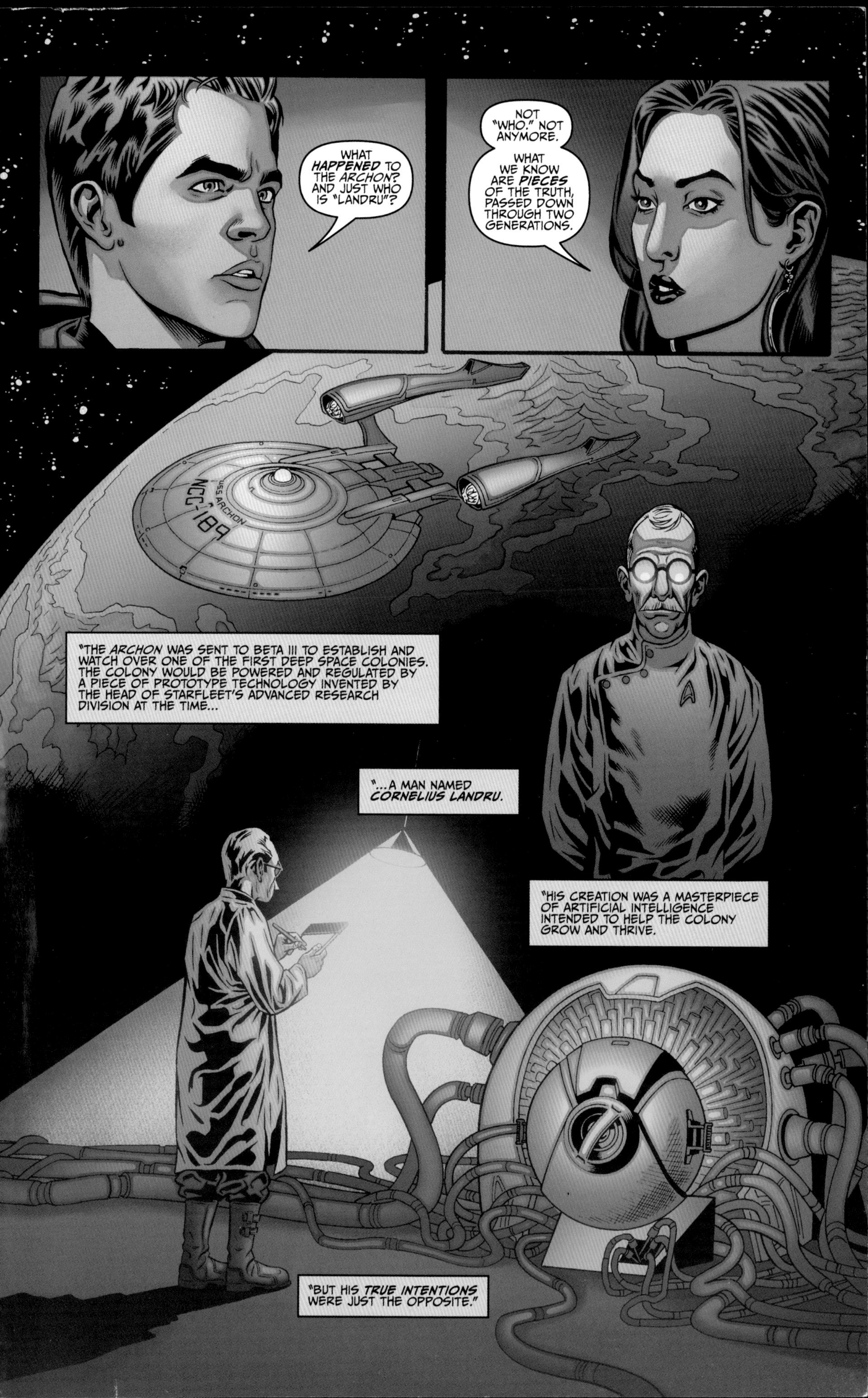
WHAT HAPPENED TO THE ARCHON? AND JUST WHO IS "LANDRU"?
NOT "WHO." NOT ANYMORE.
WHAT WE KNOW ARE PIECES OF THE TRUTH, PASSED DOWN THROUGH TWO GENERATIONS.
USS ARCHON NCC-189
"THE ARCHON WAS SENT TO BETA III TO ESTABLISH AND WATCH OVER ONE OF THE FIRST DEEP SPACE COLONIES. THE COLONY WOULD BE POWERED AND REGULATED BY A PIECE OF PROTOTYPE TECHNOLOGY INVENTED BY THE HEAD OF STARFLEET'S ADVANCED RESEARCH DIVISION AT THE TIME...
"...A MAN NAMED CORNELIUS LANDRU.
"HIS CREATION WAS A MASTERPIECE OF ARTIFICIAL INTELLIGENCE INTENDED TO HELP THE COLONY GROW AND THRIVE.
"BUT HIS TRUE INTENTIONS WERE JUST THE OPPOSITE."

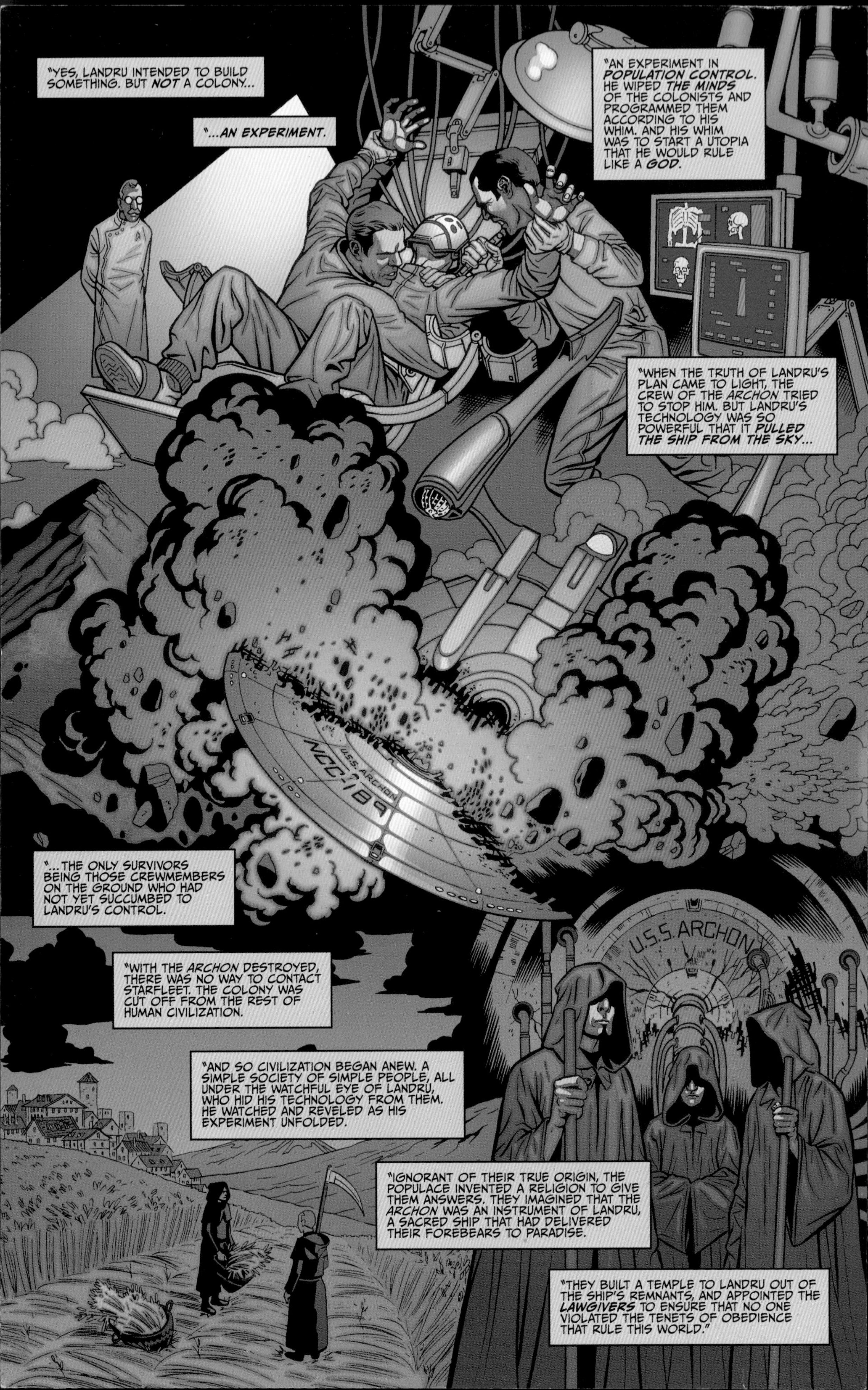
"YES, LANDRU INTENDED TO BUILD SOMETHING. BUT NOT A COLONY...
"...AN EXPERIMENT.
"AN EXPERIMENT IN POPULATION CONTROL. HE WIPED THE MINDS OF THE COLONISTS AND PROGRAMMED THEM ACCORDING TO HIS WHIM. AND HIS WHIM WAS TO START A UTOPIA THAT HE WOULD RULE LIKE A GOD.
"WHEN THE TRUTH OF LANDRU'S PLAN CAME TO LIGHT, THE CREW OF THE ARCHON TRIED TO STOP HIM. BUT LANDRU'S TECHNOLOGY WAS SO POWERFUL THAT IT PULLED THE SHIP FROM THE SKY...
U.S.S. ARCHON
NCC-189
"...THE ONLY SURVIVORS BEING THOSE CREWMEMBERS ON THE GROUND WHO HAD NOT YET SUCCUMBED TO LANDRU'S CONTROL.
U.S.S. ARCHON
"WITH THE ARCHON DESTROYED, THERE WAS NO WAY TO CONTACT STARFLEET. THE COLONY WAS CUT OFF FROM THE REST OF HUMAN CIVILIZATION.
"AND SO CIVILIZATION BEGAN ANEW. A SIMPLE SOCIETY OF SIMPLE PEOPLE, ALL UNDER THE WATCHFUL EYE OF LANDRU, WHO HID HIS TECHNOLOGY FROM THEM. HE WATCHED AND REVELED AS HIS EXPERIMENT UNFOLDED.
"IGNORANT OF THEIR TRUE ORIGIN, THE POPULACE INVENTED A RELIGION TO GIVE THEM ANSWERS. THEY IMAGINED THAT THE ARCHON WAS AN INSTRUMENT OF LANDRU, A SACRED SHIP THAT HAD DELIVERED THEIR FOREBEARS TO PARADISE.
"THEY BUILT A TEMPLE TO LANDRU OUT OF THE SHIP'S REMNANTS, AND APPOINTED THE LAWGIVERS TO ENSURE THAT NO ONE VIOLATED THE TENETS OF OBEDIENCE THAT RULE THIS WORLD."

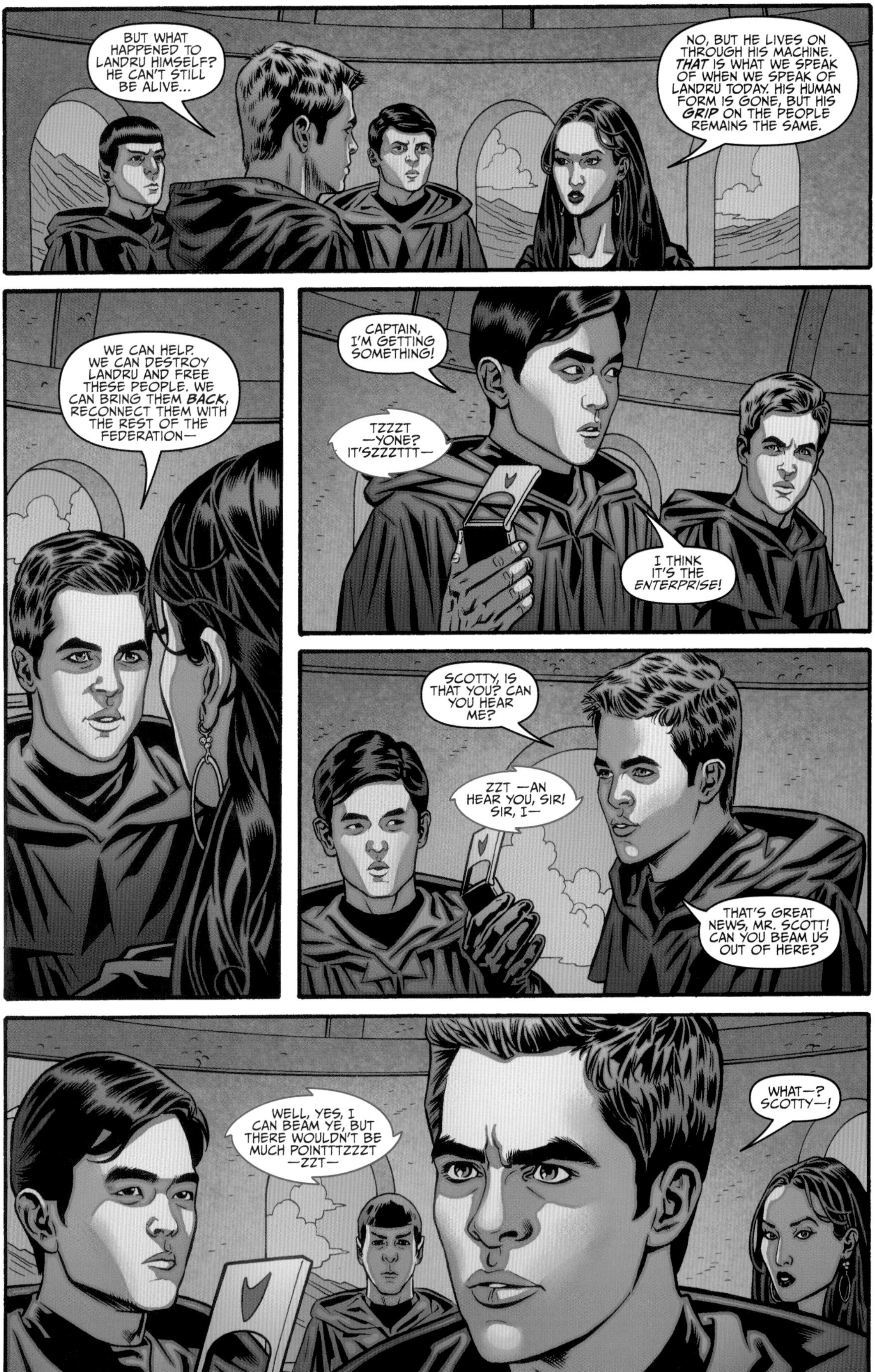
BUT WHAT HAPPENED TO LANDRU HIMSELF? HE CAN'T STILL BE ALIVE...
NO, BUT HE LIVES ON THROUGH HIS MACHINE. THAT IS WHAT WE SPEAK OF WHEN WE SPEAK OF LANDRU TODAY. HIS HUMAN FORM IS GONE, BUT HIS GRIP ON THE PEOPLE REMAINS THE SAME.
WE CAN HELP. WE CAN DESTROY LANDRU AND FREE THESE PEOPLE. WE CAN BRING THEM BACK, RECONNECT THEM WITH THE REST OF THE FEDERATION—
CAPTAIN, I'M GETTING SOMETHING!
TZZZT —YONE? IT'SZZZTTT—
I THINK IT'S THE ENTERPRISE!
SCOTTY, IS THAT YOU? CAN YOU HEAR ME?
ZZT —AN HEAR YOU, SIR! SIR, I—
THAT'S GREAT NEWS, MR. SCOTT! CAN YOU BEAM US OUT OF HERE?
WELL, YES, I CAN BEAM YE, BUT THERE WOULDN'T BE MUCH POINTTTZZZT —ZZT—
WHAT—? SCOTTY—!

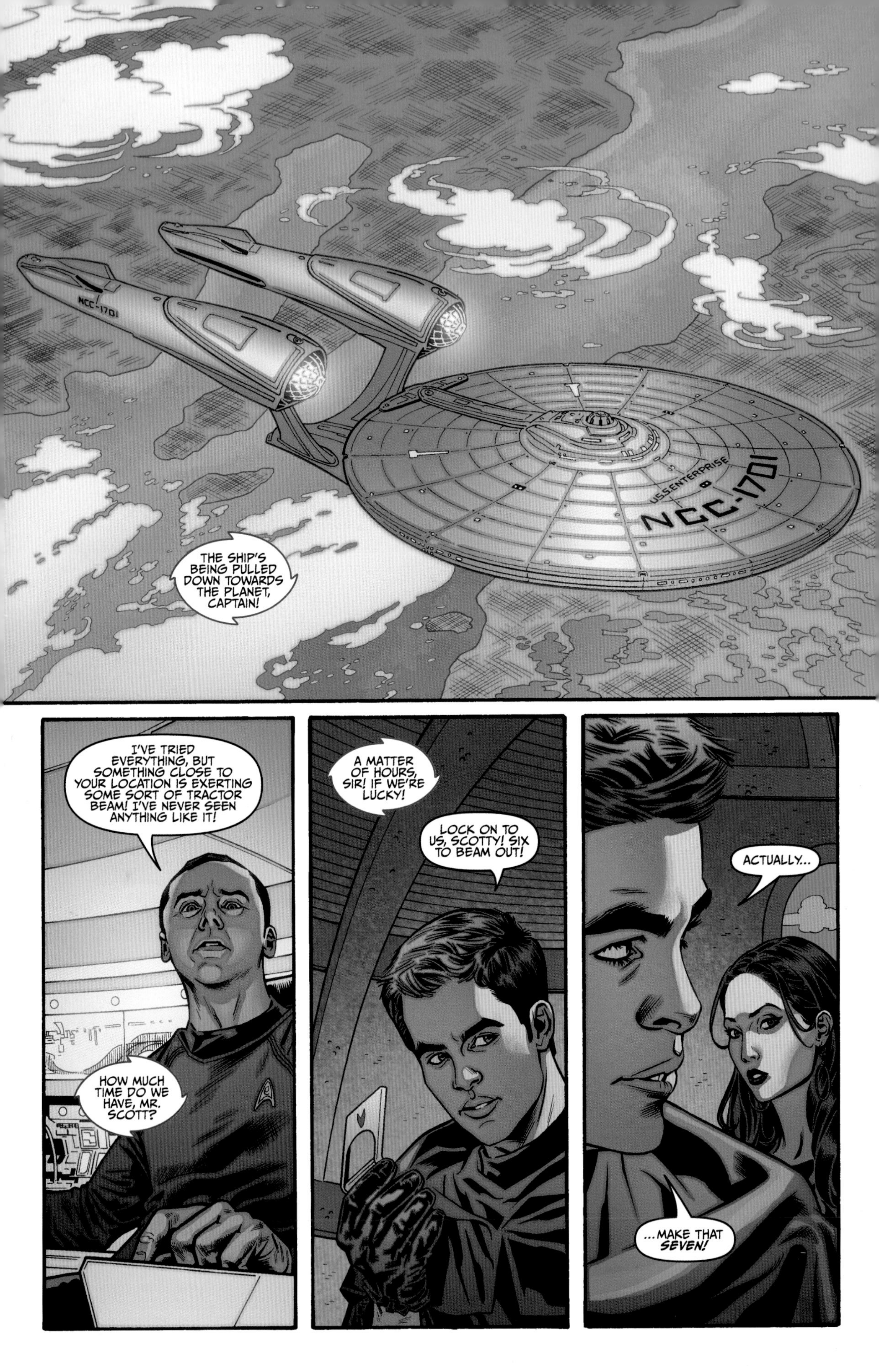

NCC-1701
U.S.S. ENTERPRISE
NCC-1701
THE SHIP'S BEING PULLED DOWN TOWARDS THE PLANET, CAPTAIN!
I'VE TRIED EVERYTHING, BUT SOMETHING CLOSE TO YOUR LOCATION IS EXERTING SOME SORT OF TRACTOR BEAM! I'VE NEVER SEEN ANYTHING LIKE IT!
HOW MUCH TIME DO WE HAVE, MR. SCOTT?
A MATTER OF HOURS, SIR! IF WE'RE LUCKY!
LOCK ON TO US, SCOTTY! SIX TO BEAM OUT!
ACTUALLY...
...MAKE THAT SEVEN!

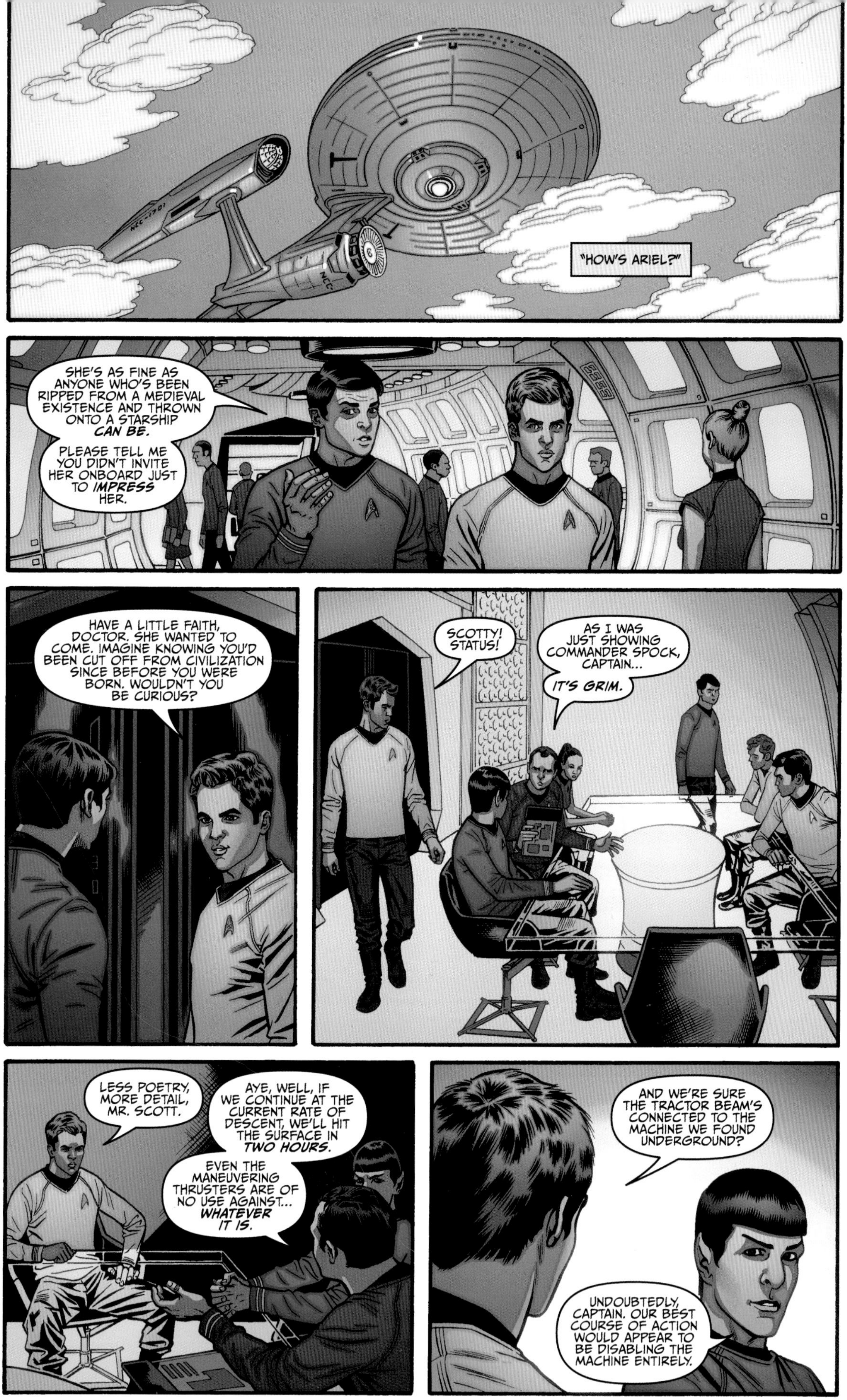
"HOW'S ARIEL?"
SHE'S AS FINE AS ANYONE WHO'S BEEN RIPPED FROM A MEDIEVAL EXISTENCE AND THROWN ONTO A STARSHIP CAN BE.
PLEASE TELL ME YOU DIDN'T INVITE HER ONBOARD JUST TO IMPRESS HER.
HAVE A LITTLE FAITH, DOCTOR. SHE WANTED TO COME. IMAGINE KNOWING YOU'D BEEN CUT OFF FROM CIVILIZATION SINCE BEFORE YOU WERE BORN. WOULDN'T YOU BE CURIOUS?
SCOTTY! STATUS!
AS I WAS JUST SHOWING COMMANDER SPOCK, CAPTAIN...
IT'S GRIM.
LESS POETRY, MORE DETAIL, MR. SCOTT.
AYE, WELL, IF WE CONTINUE AT THE CURRENT RATE OF DESCENT, WE'LL HIT THE SURFACE IN TWO HOURS.
EVEN THE MANEUVERING THRUSTERS ARE OF NO USE AGAINST... WHATEVER IT IS.
AND WE'RE SURE THE TRACTOR BEAM'S CONNECTED TO THE MACHINE WE FOUND UNDERGROUND?
UNDOUBTEDLY, CAPTAIN. OUR BEST COURSE OF ACTION WOULD APPEAR TO BE DISABLING THE MACHINE ENTIRELY.

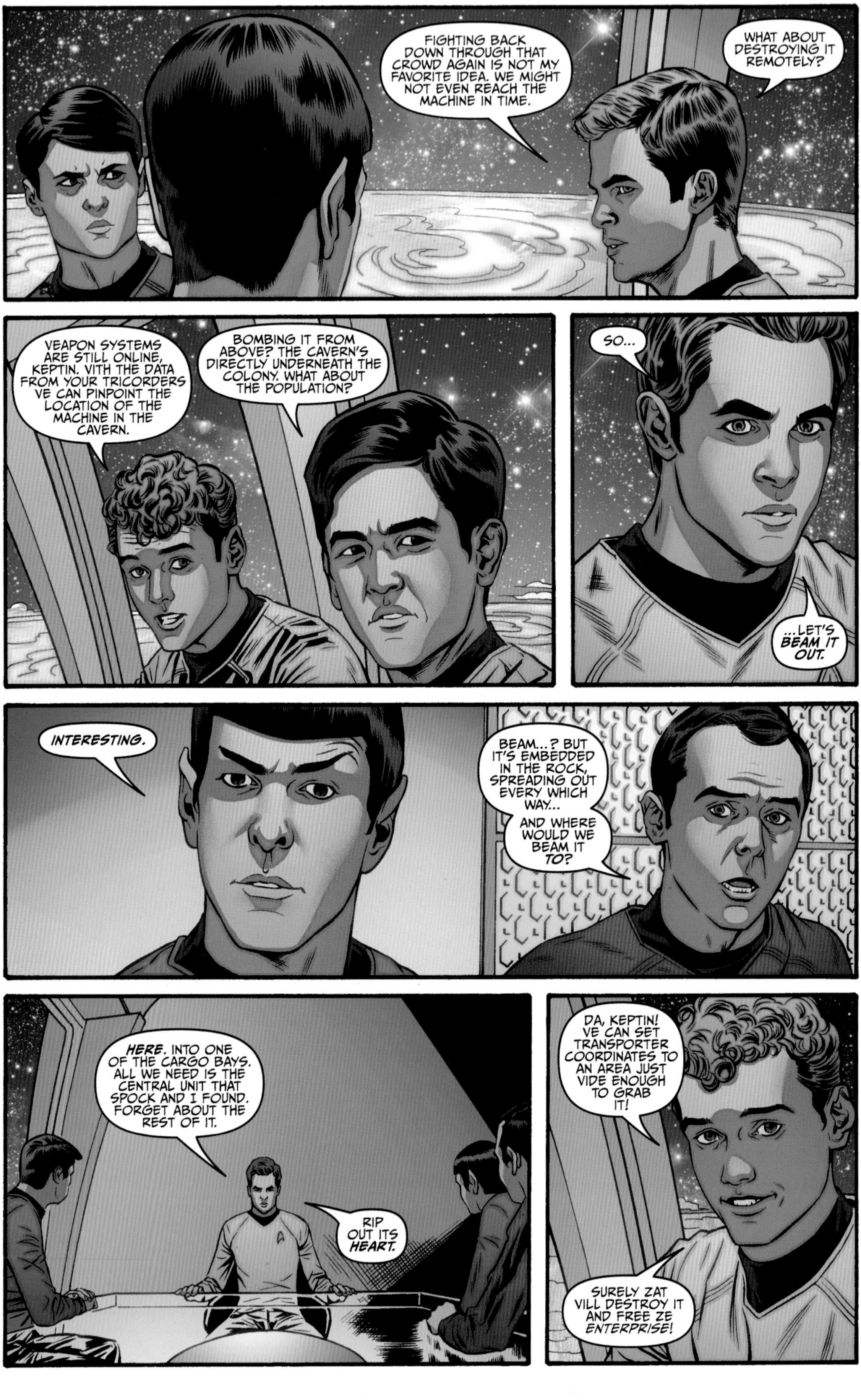
FIGHTING BACK DOWN THROUGH THAT CROWD AGAIN IS NOT MY FAVORITE IDEA. WE MIGHT NOT EVEN REACH THE MACHINE IN TIME.
WHAT ABOUT DESTROYING IT REMOTELY?
VEAPON SYSTEMS ARE STILL ONLINE, KEPTIN. VITH THE DATA FROM YOUR TRICORDERS VE CAN PINPOINT THE LOCATION OF THE MACHINE IN THE CAVERN.
BOMBING IT FROM ABOVE? THE CAVERN'S DIRECTLY UNDERNEATH THE COLONY. WHAT ABOUT THE POPULATION?
SO...
...LET'S BEAM IT OUT.
INTERESTING.
BEAM...? BUT IT'S EMBEDDED IN THE ROCK, SPREADING OUT EVERY WHICH WAY...
AND WHERE WOULD WE BEAM IT TO?
HERE. INTO ONE OF THE CARGO BAYS. ALL WE NEED IS THE CENTRAL UNIT THAT SPOCK AND I FOUND. FORGET ABOUT THE REST OF IT.
RIP OUT ITS HEART.
DA, KEPTIN! VE CAN SET TRANSPORTER COORDINATES TO AN AREA JUST VIDE ENOUGH TO GRAB IT!
SURELY ZAT VILL DESTROY IT AND FREE ZE ENTERPRISE!

MR. SCOTT, MR. CHEKOV, MAKE IT HAPPEN.

MR. SULU, SEE WHAT YOU CAN GET OUT OF THE THRUSTERS. DO THE BEST YOU CAN TO PUT US *DIRECTLY ABOVE* THE CAVERN.

AYE, THAT'LL HELP!

BUT IF IT *DOESN'T* WORK, SIR...!

SCOTTY. THE FIRST TIME I MET YOU, YOU MANAGED TO BEAM US BOTH ABOARD THE *ENTERPRISE MID-WARP.*

I THINK YOU CAN DIG A COMPUTER OUT OF THE GROUND WITHOUT A HITCH.

AYE, BUT I HAD NICE OLD *WRINKLY SPOCK* HELPING ME THAT LAST TIME...

JIM... ...WHAT ABOUT THE POPULATION?

THAT MACHINE HAS SOME KIND OF *HOLD* OVER THEIR *MINDS.* WE RIP THAT MACHINE OUT OF THE GROUND—*SHUT IT DOWN*—

—AND WE COULD END UP WITH SEVERAL HUNDRED *DEAD COLONISTS* ON OUR HANDS.

I CONCUR, CAPTAIN. WE SHOULD FIND ANOTHER WAY TO FREE THE SHIP.

I CAN'T BELIEVE WE AGREE FOR ONCE, SPOCK—

BUT NOT FOR THE REASON PUT FORWARD BY DR. MCCOY.

EXPLAIN.

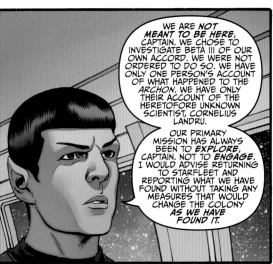

WE ARE *NOT MEANT TO BE HERE*, CAPTAIN. WE CHOSE TO INVESTIGATE BETA III OF OUR OWN ACCORD. WE WERE NOT ORDERED TO DO SO. WE HAVE ONLY ONE PERSON'S ACCOUNT OF WHAT HAPPENED TO THE *ARCHON.* WE HAVE ONLY THEIR ACCOUNT OF THE HERETOFORE UNKNOWN SCIENTIST, CORNELIUS LANDRU.

OUR PRIMARY MISSION HAS ALWAYS BEEN TO *EXPLORE*, CAPTAIN. NOT TO *ENGAGE.* I WOULD ADVISE RETURNING TO STARFLEET AND REPORTING WHAT WE HAVE FOUND WITHOUT TAKING ANY MEASURES THAT WOULD CHANGE THE COLONY *AS WE HAVE FOUND IT.*

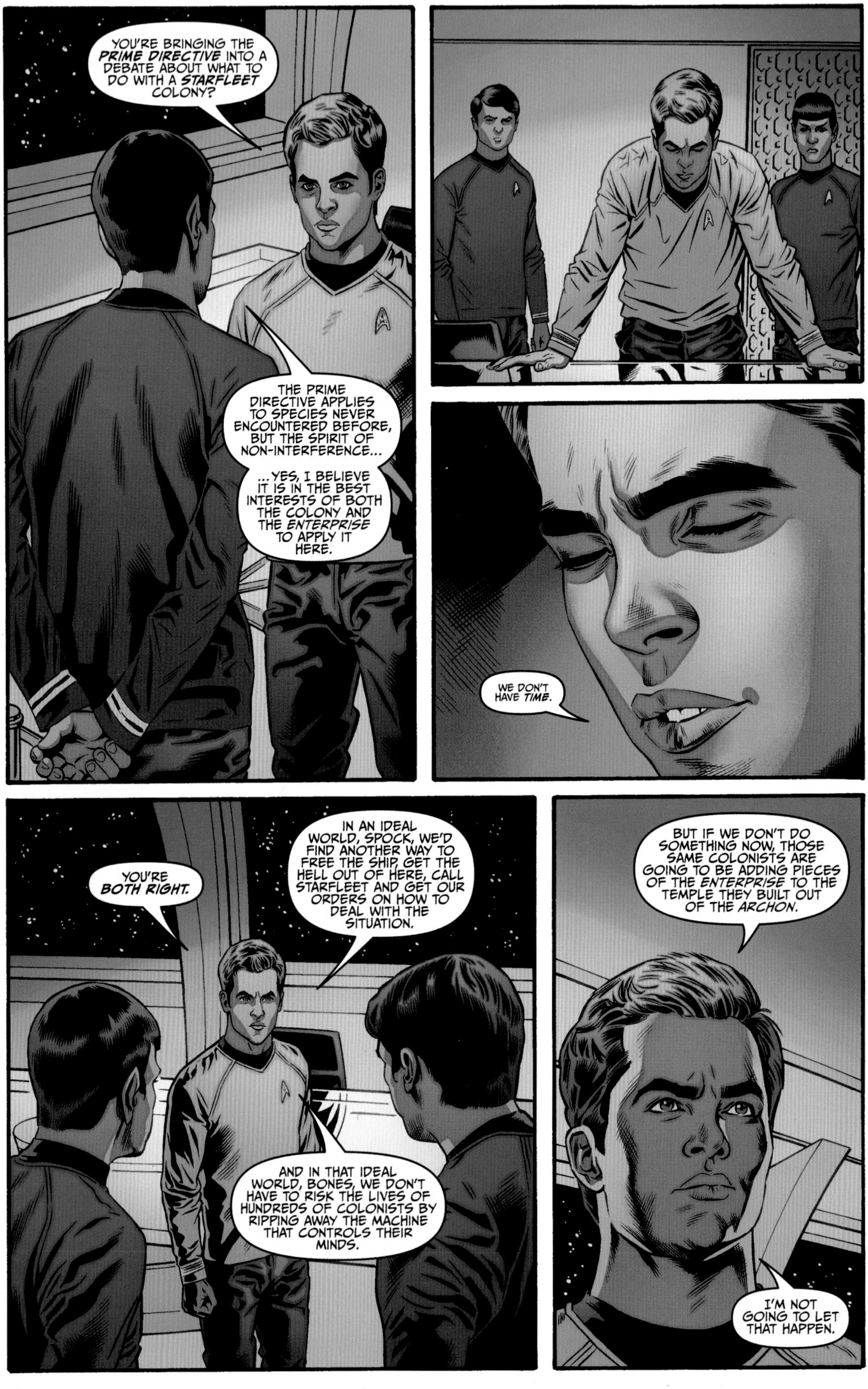
YOU'RE BRINGING THE PRIME DIRECTIVE INTO A DEBATE ABOUT WHAT TO DO WITH A STARFLEET COLONY?
THE PRIME DIRECTIVE APPLIES TO SPECIES NEVER ENCOUNTERED BEFORE, BUT THE SPIRIT OF NON-INTERFERENCE...
...YES, I BELIEVE IT IS IN THE BEST INTERESTS OF BOTH THE COLONY AND THE ENTERPRISE TO APPLY IT HERE.
WE DON'T HAVE TIME.
YOU'RE BOTH RIGHT.
IN AN IDEAL WORLD, SPOCK, WE'D FIND ANOTHER WAY TO FREE THE SHIP, GET THE HELL OUT OF HERE, CALL STARFLEET AND GET OUR ORDERS ON HOW TO DEAL WITH THE SITUATION.
AND IN THAT IDEAL WORLD, BONES, WE DON'T HAVE TO RISK THE LIVES OF HUNDREDS OF COLONISTS BY RIPPING AWAY THE MACHINE THAT CONTROLS THEIR MINDS.
BUT IF WE DON'T DO SOMETHING NOW, THOSE SAME COLONISTS ARE GOING TO BE ADDING PIECES OF THE ENTERPRISE TO THE TEMPLE THEY BUILT OUT OF THE ARCHON.
I'M NOT GOING TO LET THAT HAPPEN.

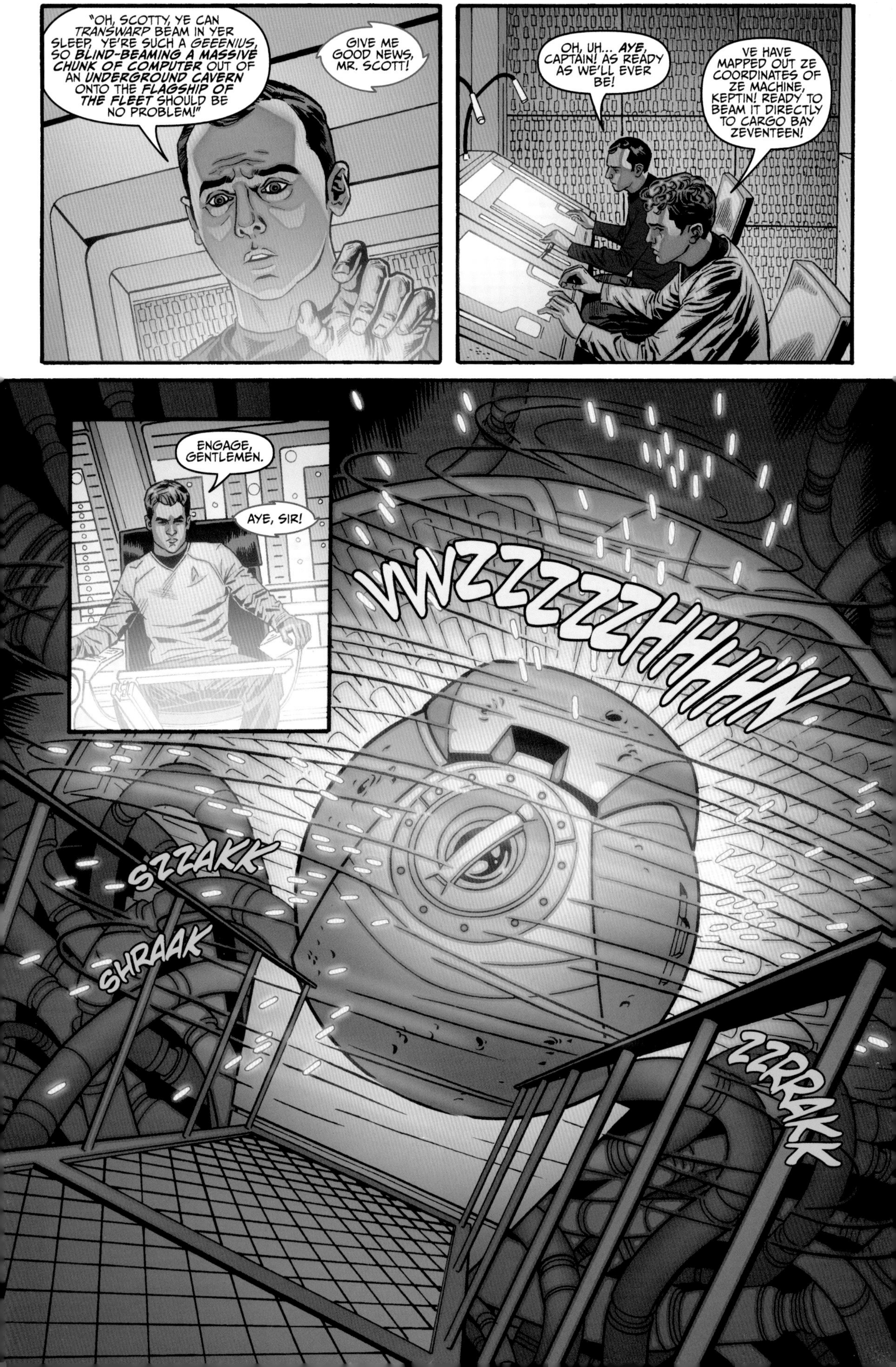
"OH, SCOTTY, YE CAN TRANSWARP BEAM IN YER SLEEP, YE'RE SUCH A GEEENIUS, SO BLIND-BEAMING A MASSIVE CHUNK OF COMPUTER OUT OF AN UNDERGROUND CAVERN ONTO THE FLAGSHIP OF THE FLEET SHOULD BE NO PROBLEM!"
GIVE ME GOOD NEWS, MR. SCOTT!
OH, UH... AYE, CAPTAIN! AS READY AS WE'LL EVER BE!
VE HAVE MAPPED OUT ZE COORDINATES OF ZE MACHINE, KEPTIN! READY TO BEAM IT DIRECTLY TO CARGO BAY ZEVENTEEN!
ENGAGE, GENTLEMEN.
AYE, SIR!
VVVZZZZZHHHHN
SZZZAKK
SHRAAK
ZZRRAKK

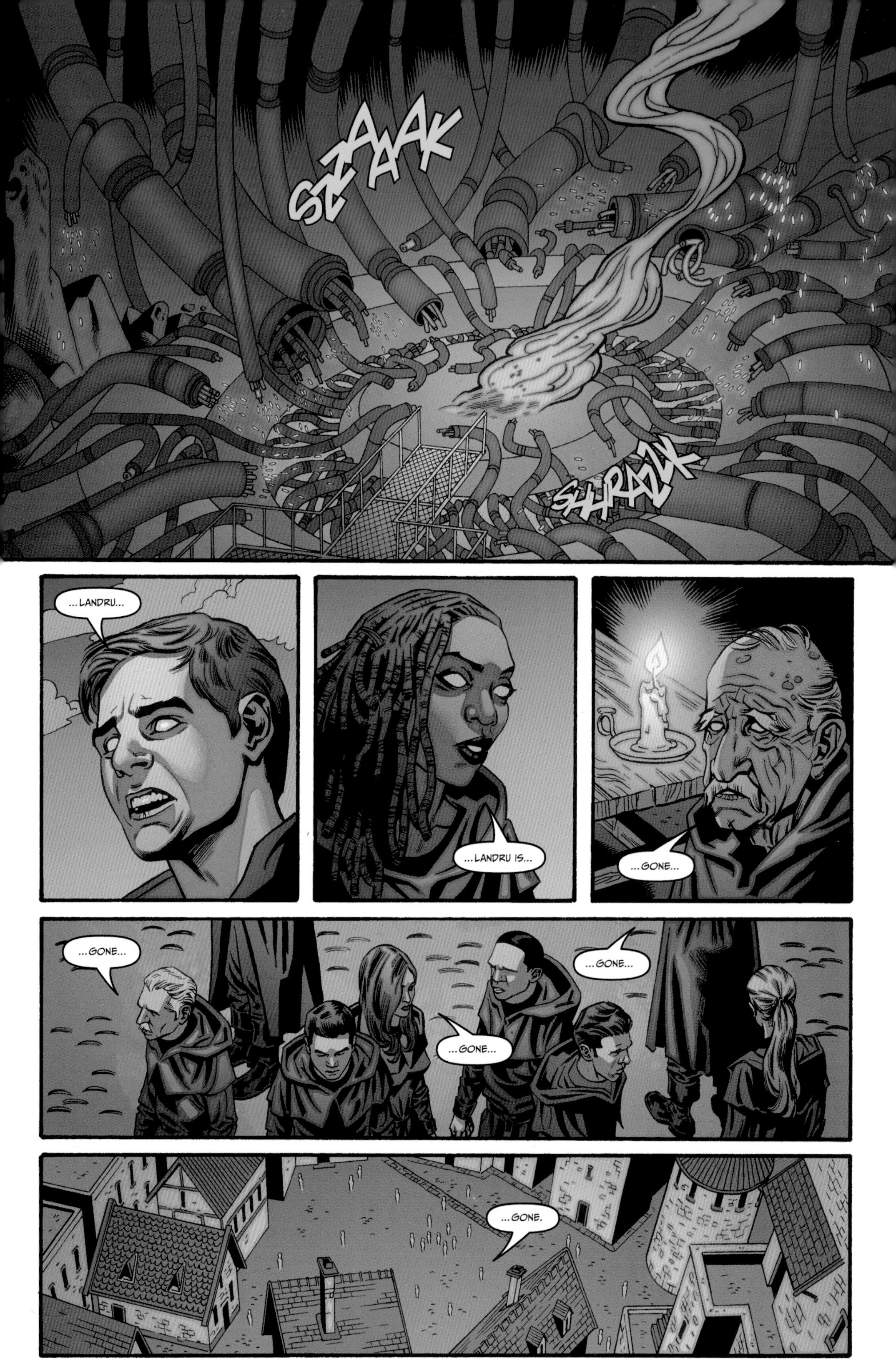
SZZAAK
SKKRAZK
...LANDRU...
...LANDRU IS...
...GONE...
...GONE...
...GONE...
...GONE...
...GONE.

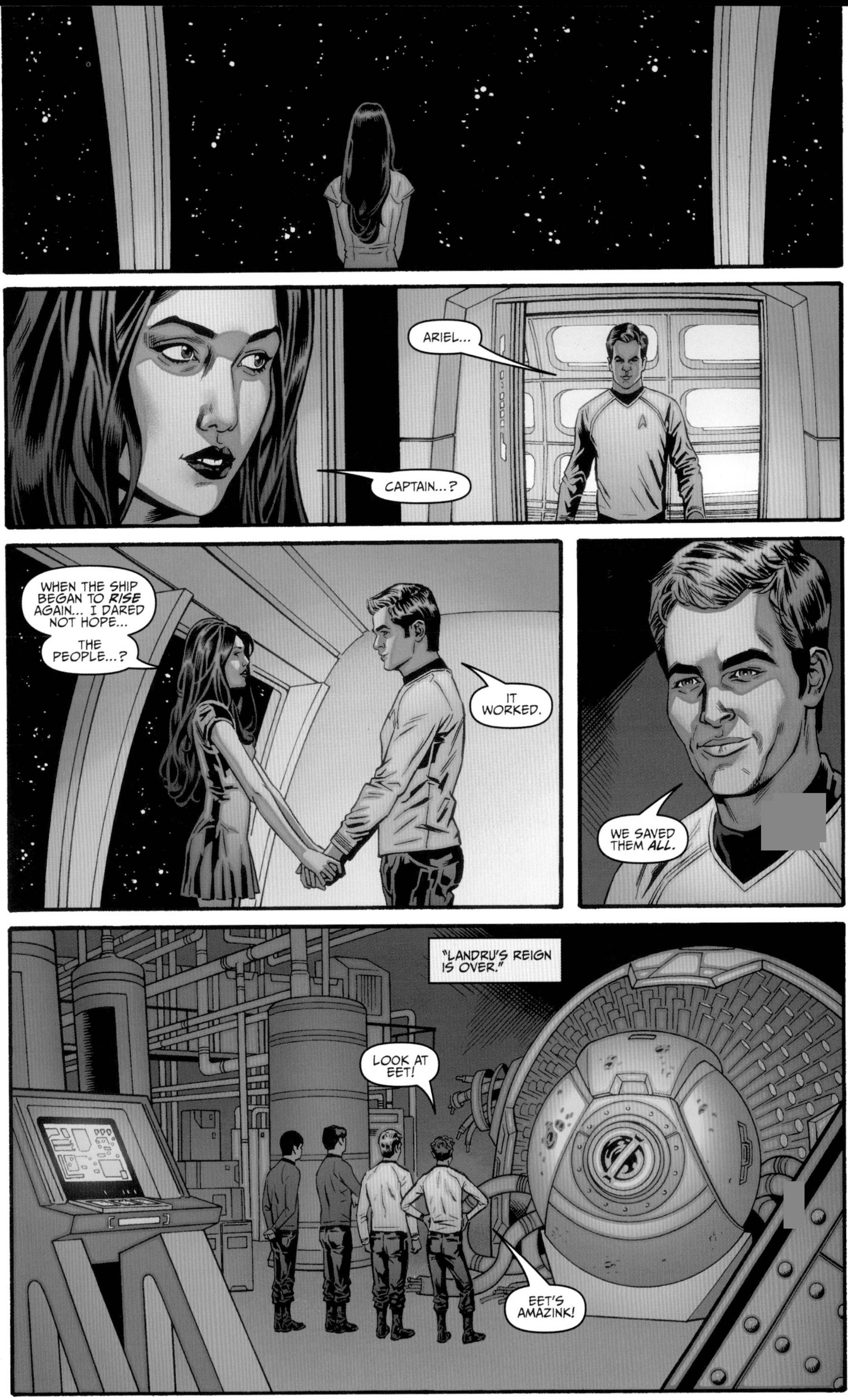
ARIEL...
CAPTAIN...?
WHEN THE SHIP BEGAN TO RISE AGAIN... I DARED NOT HOPE...
THE PEOPLE...?
IT WORKED.
WE SAVED THEM ALL.
"LANDRU'S REIGN IS OVER."
LOOK AT EET!
EET'S AMAZINK!

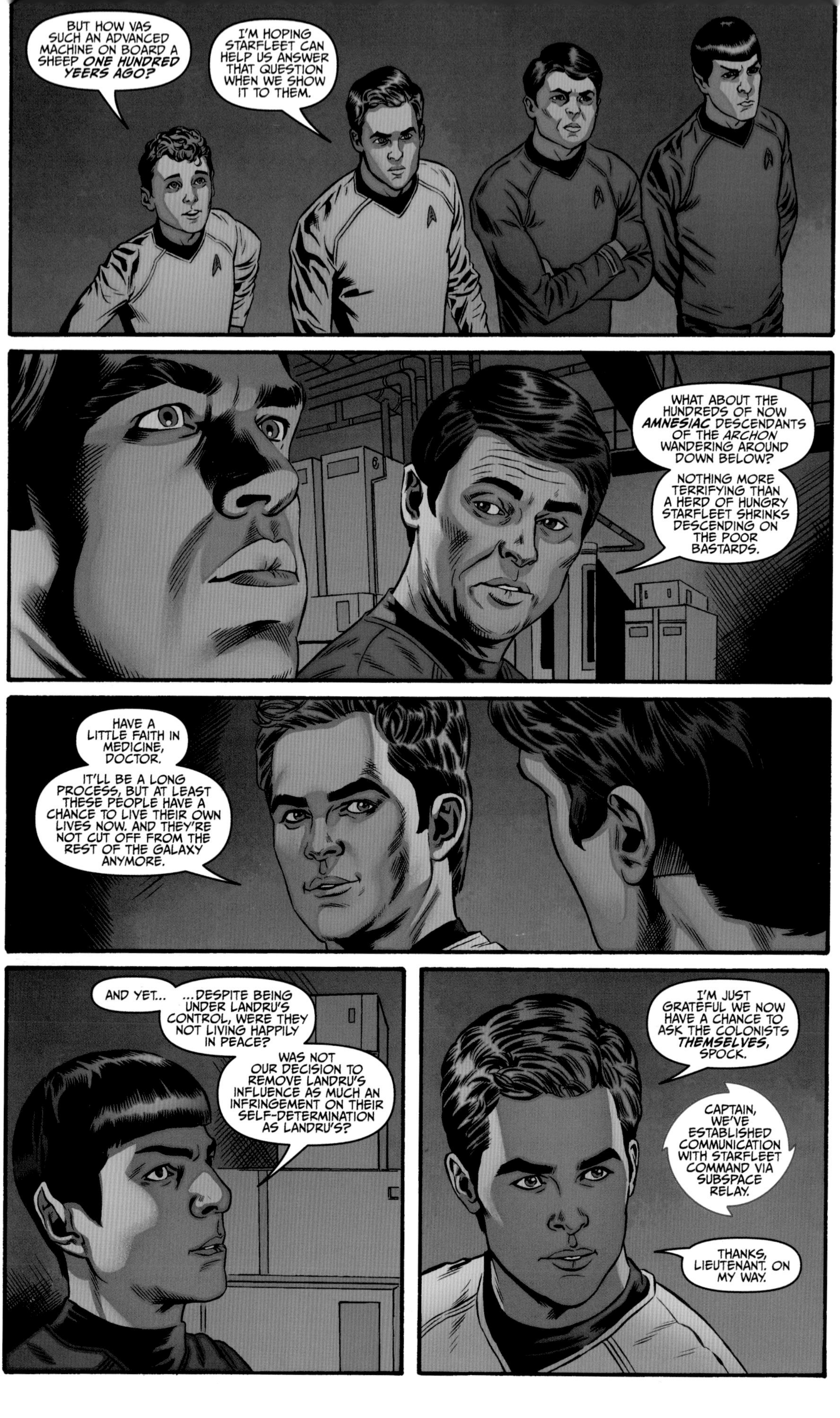
BUT HOW VAS SUCH AN ADVANCED MACHINE ON BOARD A SHEEP *ONE HUNDRED YEERS AGO?*
I'M HOPING STARFLEET CAN HELP US ANSWER THAT QUESTION WHEN WE SHOW IT TO THEM.
WHAT ABOUT THE HUNDREDS OF NOW *AMNESIAC* DESCENDANTS OF THE *ARCHON* WANDERING AROUND DOWN BELOW?
NOTHING MORE TERRIFYING THAN A HERD OF HUNGRY STARFLEET SHRINKS DESCENDING ON THE POOR BASTARDS.
HAVE A LITTLE FAITH IN MEDICINE, DOCTOR.
IT'LL BE A LONG PROCESS, BUT AT LEAST THESE PEOPLE HAVE A CHANCE TO LIVE THEIR OWN LIVES NOW. AND THEY'RE NOT CUT OFF FROM THE REST OF THE GALAXY ANYMORE.
AND YET...
...DESPITE BEING UNDER LANDRU'S CONTROL, WERE THEY NOT LIVING HAPPILY IN PEACE?
WAS NOT OUR DECISION TO REMOVE LANDRU'S INFLUENCE AS MUCH AN INFRINGEMENT ON THEIR SELF-DETERMINATION AS LANDRU'S?
I'M JUST GRATEFUL WE NOW HAVE A CHANCE TO ASK THE COLONISTS *THEMSELVES,* SPOCK.
CAPTAIN, WE'VE ESTABLISHED COMMUNICATION WITH STARFLEET COMMAND VIA SUBSPACE RELAY.
THANKS, LIEUTENANT. ON MY WAY.

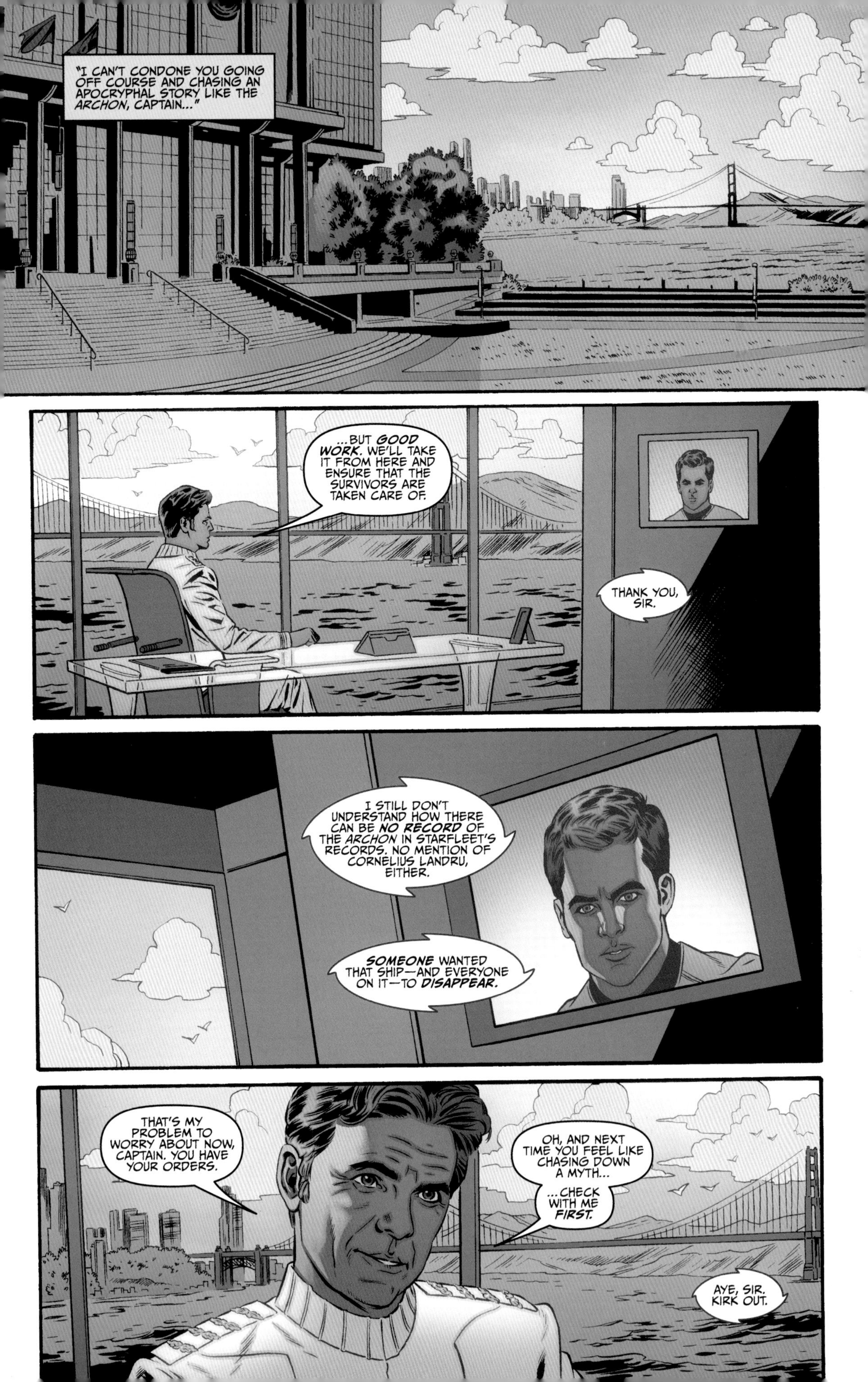
"I CAN'T CONDONE YOU GOING OFF COURSE AND CHASING AN APOCRYPHAL STORY LIKE THE ARCHON, CAPTAIN..."
...BUT GOOD WORK. WE'LL TAKE IT FROM HERE AND ENSURE THAT THE SURVIVORS ARE TAKEN CARE OF.
THANK YOU, SIR.
I STILL DON'T UNDERSTAND HOW THERE CAN BE NO RECORD OF THE ARCHON IN STARFLEET'S RECORDS. NO MENTION OF CORNELIUS LANDRU, EITHER.
SOMEONE WANTED THAT SHIP—AND EVERYONE ON IT—TO DISAPPEAR.
THAT'S MY PROBLEM TO WORRY ABOUT NOW, CAPTAIN. YOU HAVE YOUR ORDERS.
OH, AND NEXT TIME YOU FEEL LIKE CHASING DOWN A MYTH...
...CHECK WITH ME FIRST.
AYE, SIR. KIRK OUT.

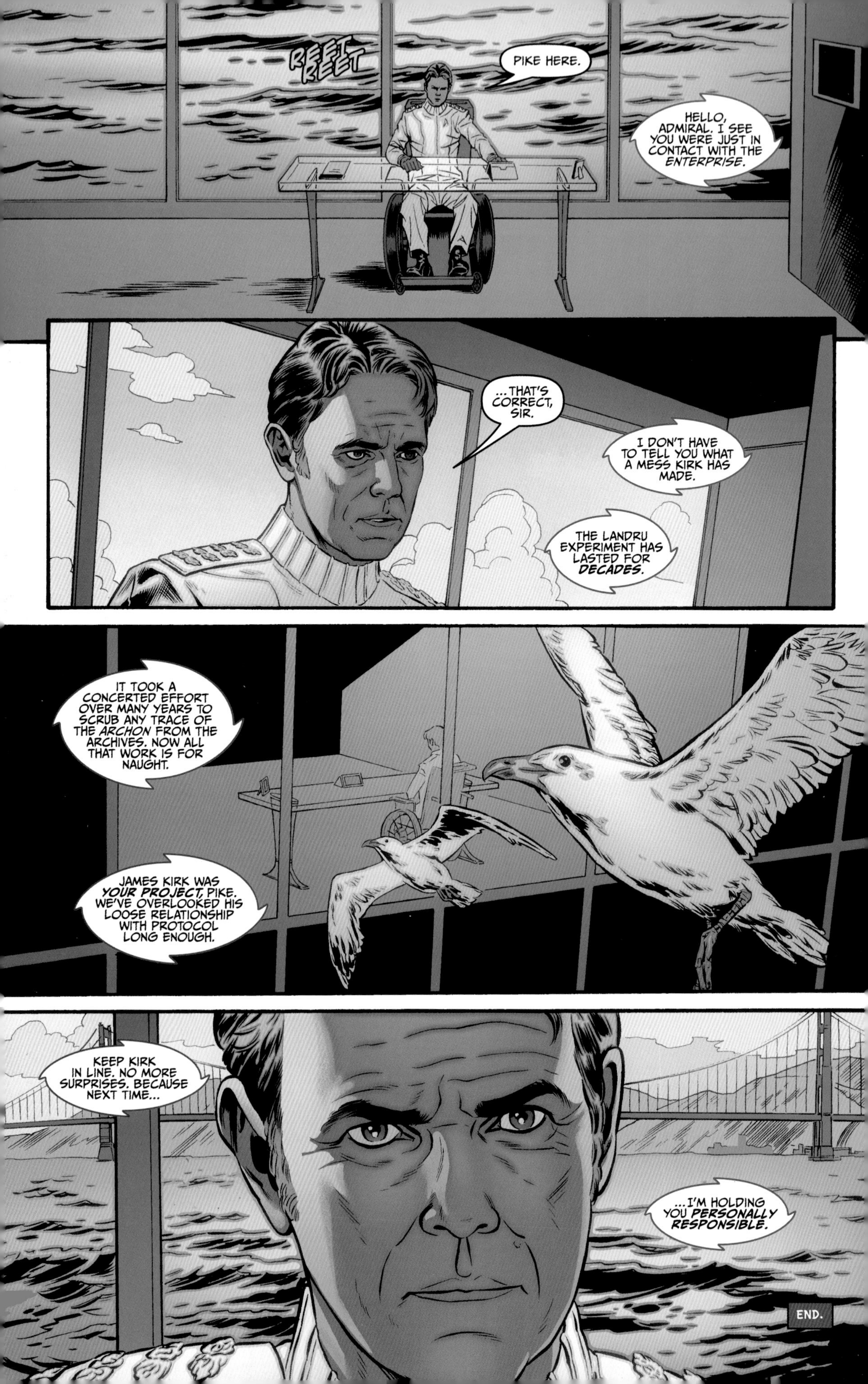
REET REET
PIKE HERE.
HELLO, ADMIRAL. I SEE YOU WERE JUST IN CONTACT WITH THE *ENTERPRISE*.
...THAT'S CORRECT, SIR.
I DON'T HAVE TO TELL YOU WHAT A MESS KIRK HAS MADE.
THE LANDRU EXPERIMENT HAS LASTED FOR *DECADES*.
IT TOOK A CONCERTED EFFORT OVER MANY YEARS TO SCRUB ANY TRACE OF THE *ARCHON* FROM THE ARCHIVES. NOW ALL THAT WORK IS FOR NAUGHT.
JAMES KIRK WAS ***YOUR PROJECT***, PIKE. WE'VE OVERLOOKED HIS LOOSE RELATIONSHIP WITH PROTOCOL LONG ENOUGH.
KEEP KIRK IN LINE. NO MORE SURPRISES. BECAUSE NEXT TIME...
...I'M HOLDING YOU ***PERSONALLY RESPONSIBLE***.
END.

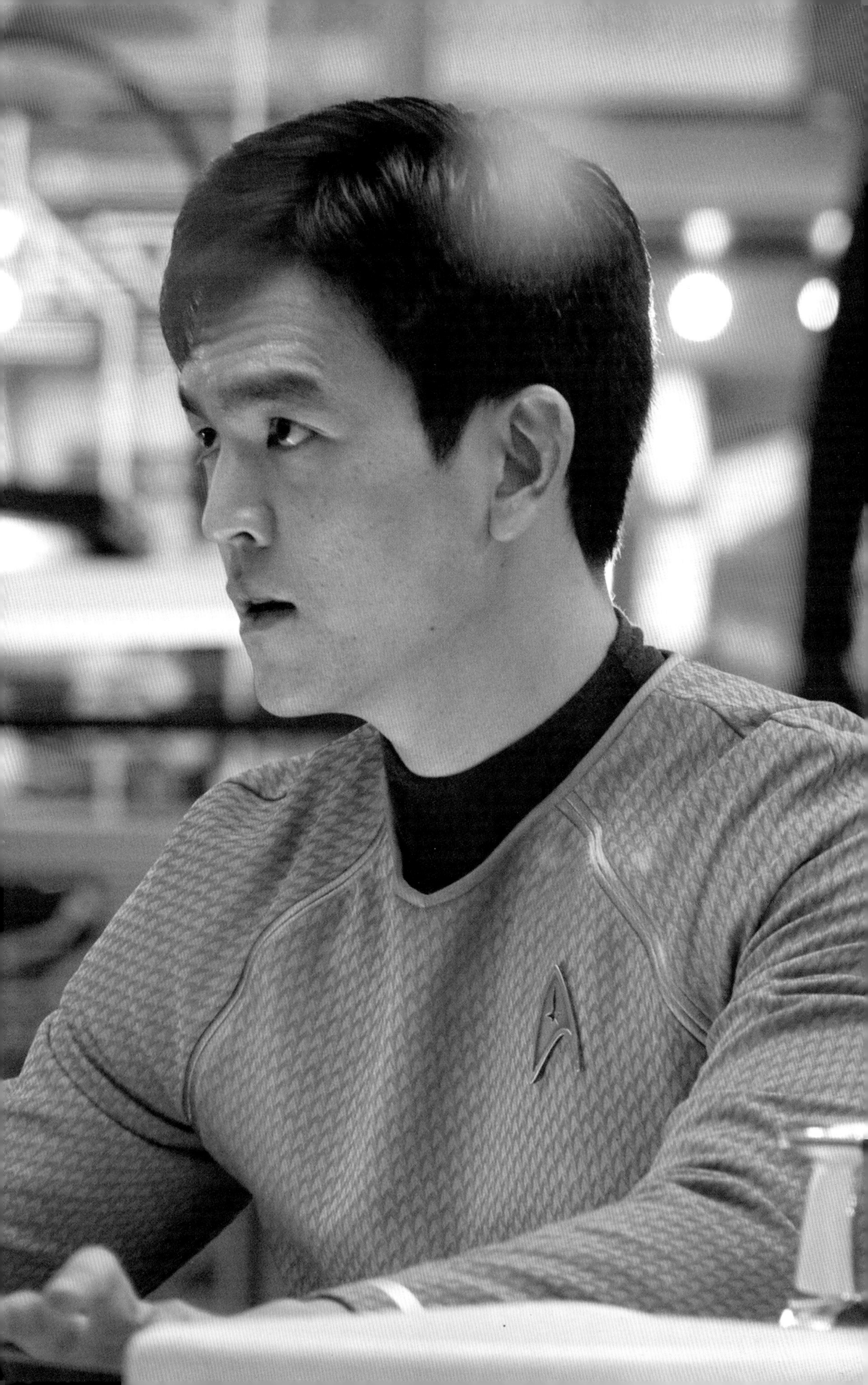

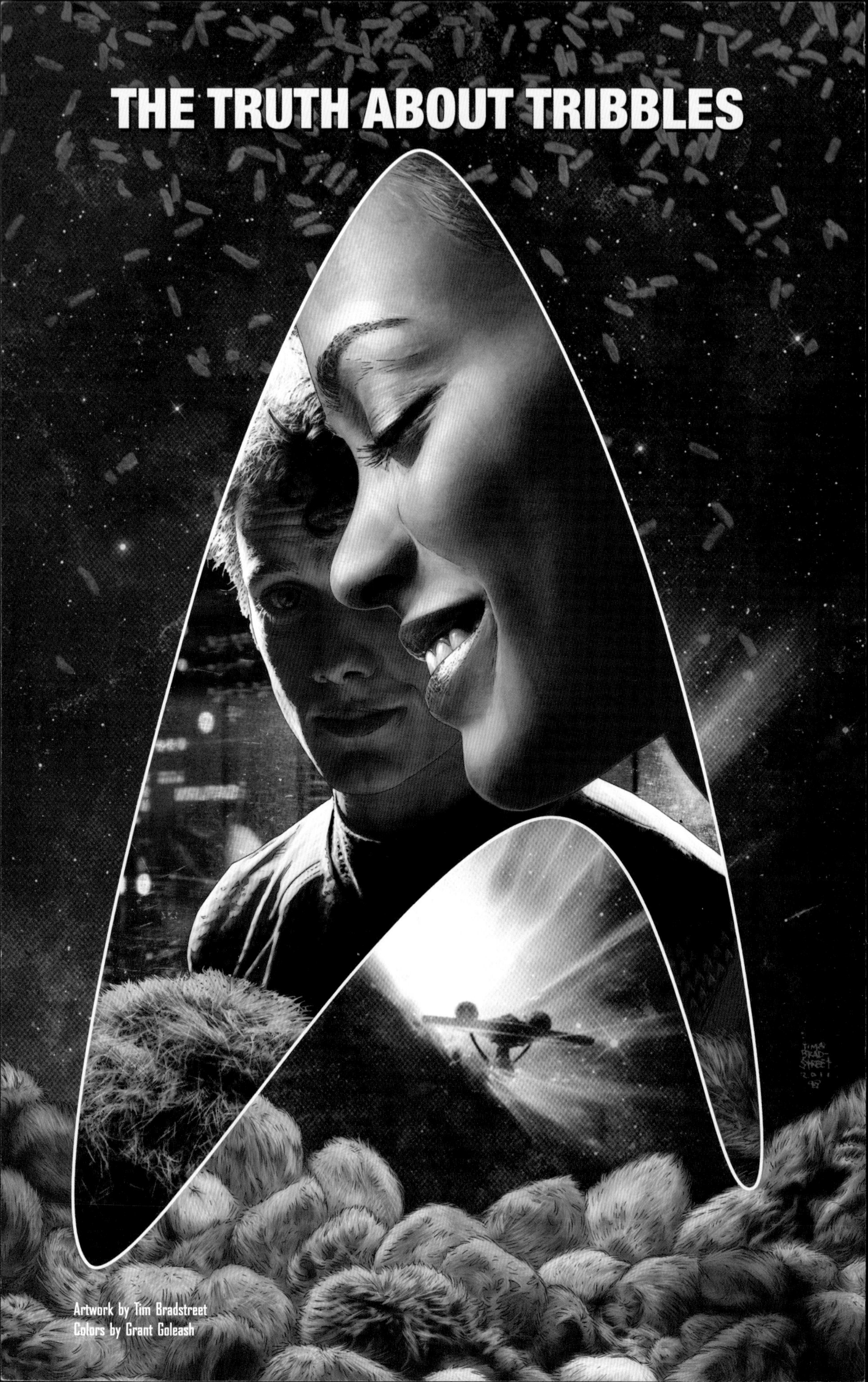
THE TRUTH ABOUT TRIBBLES

Artwork by Tim Bradstreet
Colors by Grant Goleash

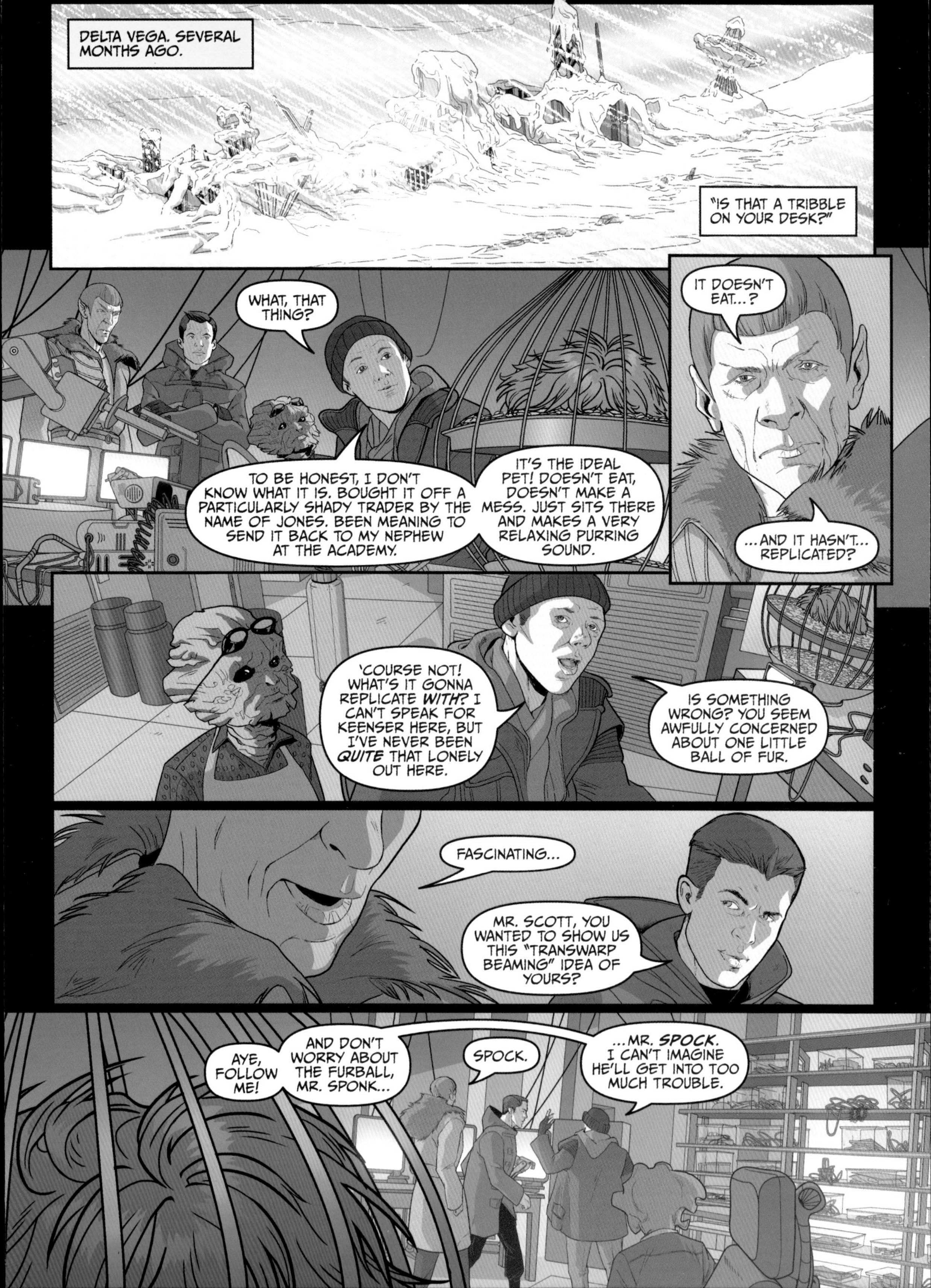
DELTA VEGA. SEVERAL MONTHS AGO.
"IS THAT A TRIBBLE ON YOUR DESK?"
WHAT, THAT THING?
TO BE HONEST, I DON'T KNOW WHAT IT IS. BOUGHT IT OFF A PARTICULARLY SHADY TRADER BY THE NAME OF JONES. BEEN MEANING TO SEND IT BACK TO MY NEPHEW AT THE ACADEMY.
IT'S THE IDEAL PET! DOESN'T EAT, DOESN'T MAKE A MESS. JUST SITS THERE AND MAKES A VERY RELAXING PURRING SOUND.
IT DOESN'T EAT...?
...AND IT HASN'T... REPLICATED?
'COURSE NOT! WHAT'S IT GONNA REPLICATE *WITH*? I CAN'T SPEAK FOR KEENSER HERE, BUT I'VE NEVER BEEN *QUITE* THAT LONELY OUT HERE.
IS SOMETHING WRONG? YOU SEEM AWFULLY CONCERNED ABOUT ONE LITTLE BALL OF FUR.
FASCINATING...
MR. SCOTT, YOU WANTED TO SHOW US THIS "TRANSWARP BEAMING" IDEA OF YOURS?
AYE, FOLLOW ME!
AND DON'T WORRY ABOUT THE FURBALL, MR. SPONK...
SPOCK.
...MR. *SPOCK*. I CAN'T IMAGINE HE'LL GET INTO TOO MUCH TROUBLE.

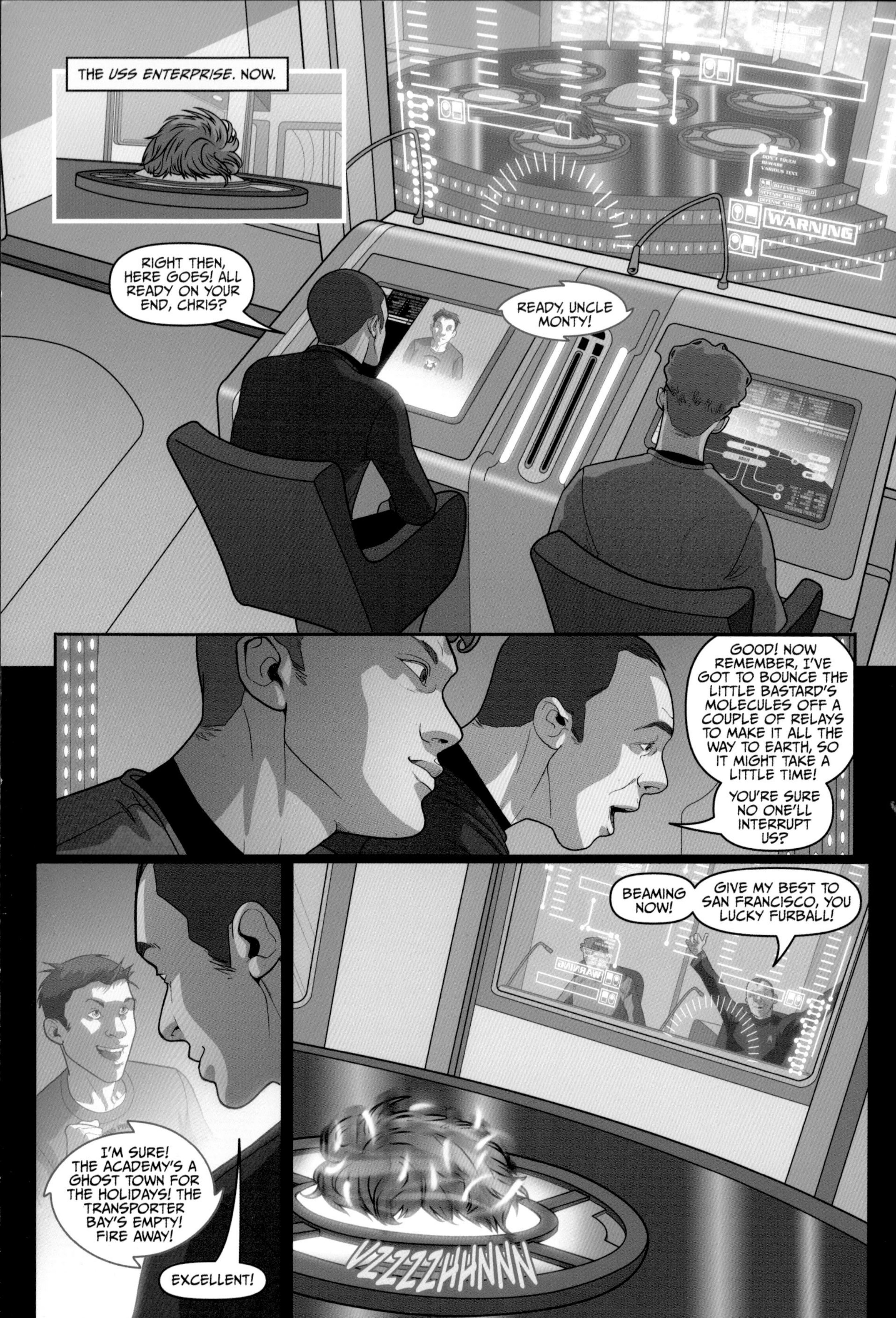
THE *USS ENTERPRISE*. NOW.
WARNING
RIGHT THEN, HERE GOES! ALL READY ON YOUR END, CHRIS?
READY, UNCLE MONTY!
GOOD! NOW REMEMBER, I'VE GOT TO BOUNCE THE LITTLE BASTARD'S MOLECULES OFF A COUPLE OF RELAYS TO MAKE IT ALL THE WAY TO EARTH, SO IT MIGHT TAKE A LITTLE TIME!
YOU'RE SURE NO ONE'LL INTERRUPT US?
I'M SURE! THE ACADEMY'S A GHOST TOWN FOR THE HOLIDAYS! THE TRANSPORTER BAY'S EMPTY! FIRE AWAY!
EXCELLENT!
BEAMING NOW!
GIVE MY BEST TO SAN FRANCISCO, YOU LUCKY FURBALL!
VZZZZZHHNNN

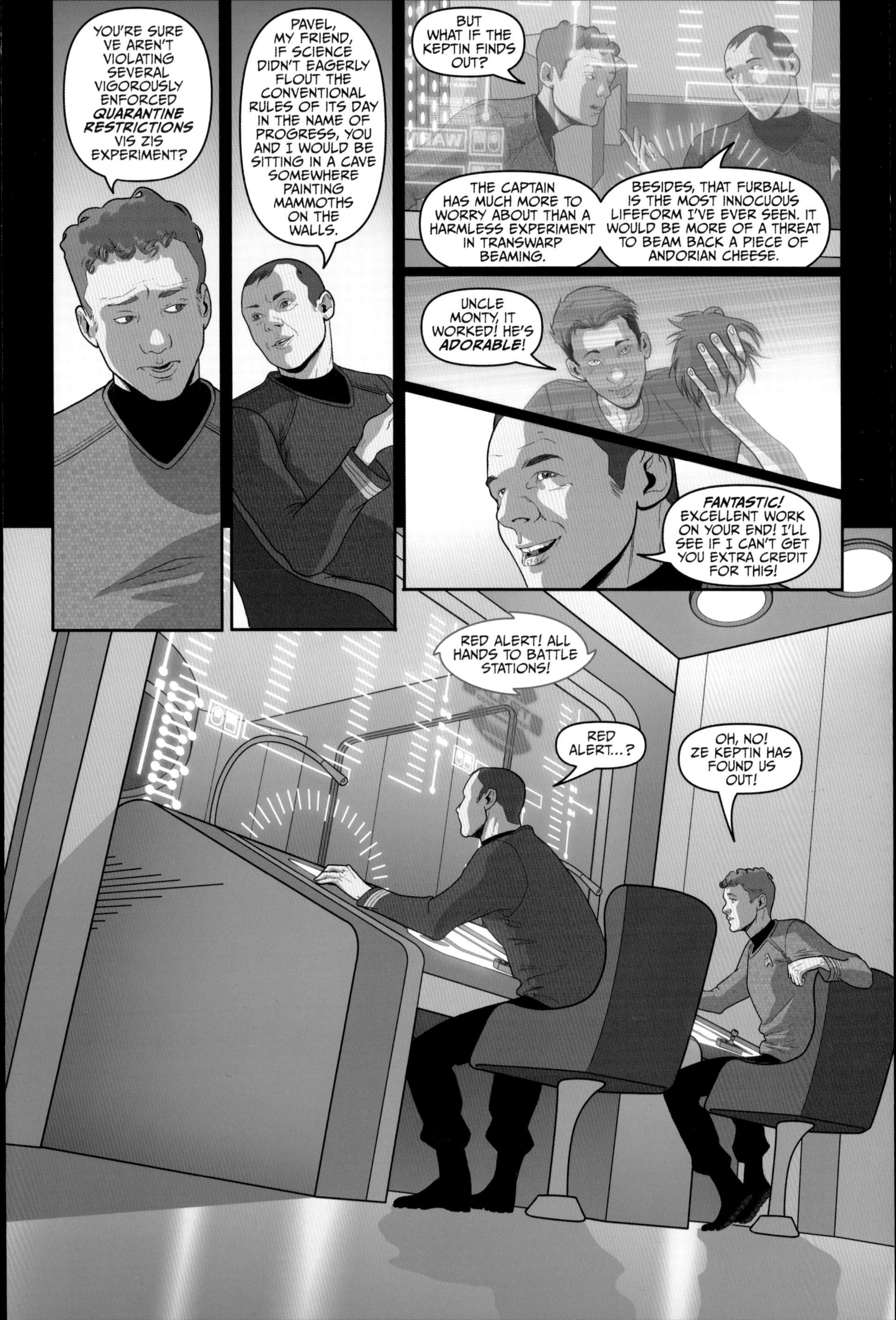
YOU'RE SURE VE AREN'T VIOLATING SEVERAL VIGOROUSLY ENFORCED ***QUARANTINE RESTRICTIONS*** VIS ZIS EXPERIMENT?
PAVEL, MY FRIEND, IF SCIENCE DIDN'T EAGERLY FLOUT THE CONVENTIONAL RULES OF ITS DAY IN THE NAME OF PROGRESS, YOU AND I WOULD BE SITTING IN A CAVE SOMEWHERE PAINTING MAMMOTHS ON THE WALLS.
BUT WHAT IF THE KEPTIN FINDS OUT?
THE CAPTAIN HAS MUCH MORE TO WORRY ABOUT THAN A HARMLESS EXPERIMENT IN TRANSWARP BEAMING.
BESIDES, THAT FURBALL IS THE MOST INNOCUOUS LIFEFORM I'VE EVER SEEN. IT WOULD BE MORE OF A THREAT TO BEAM BACK A PIECE OF ANDORIAN CHEESE.
UNCLE MONTY, IT WORKED! HE'S ***ADORABLE!***
FANTASTIC! EXCELLENT WORK ON YOUR END! I'LL SEE IF I CAN'T GET YOU EXTRA CREDIT FOR THIS!
RED ALERT! ALL HANDS TO BATTLE STATIONS!
RED ALERT...?
OH, NO! ZE KEPTIN HAS FOUND US OUT!

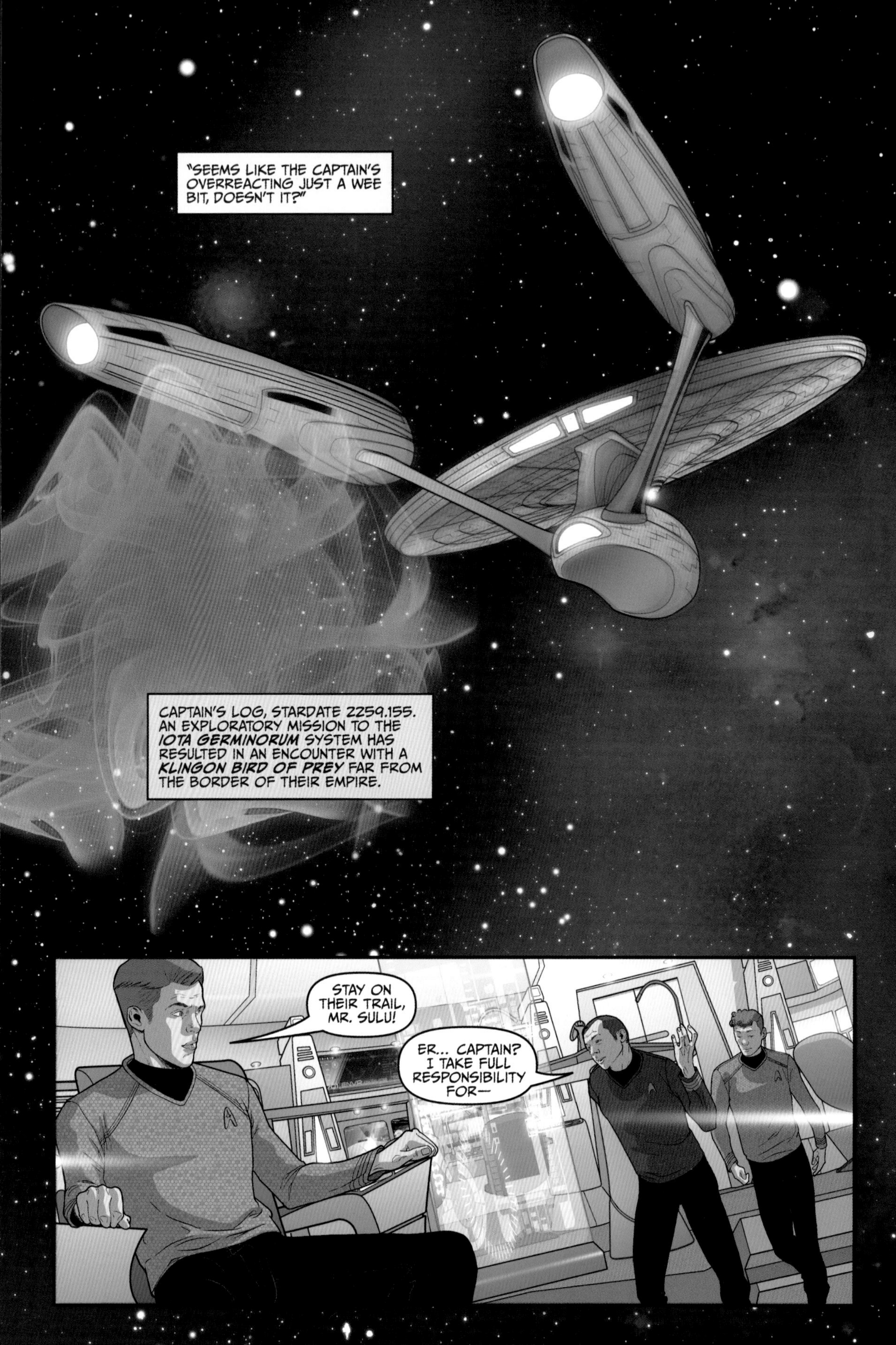
"SEEMS LIKE THE CAPTAIN'S OVERREACTING JUST A WEE BIT, DOESN'T IT?"
CAPTAIN'S LOG, STARDATE 2259.155. AN EXPLORATORY MISSION TO THE ***IOTA GERMINORUM*** SYSTEM HAS RESULTED IN AN ENCOUNTER WITH A ***KLINGON BIRD OF PREY*** FAR FROM THE BORDER OF THEIR EMPIRE.
STAY ON THEIR TRAIL, MR. SULU!
ER... CAPTAIN? I TAKE FULL RESPONSIBILITY FOR—

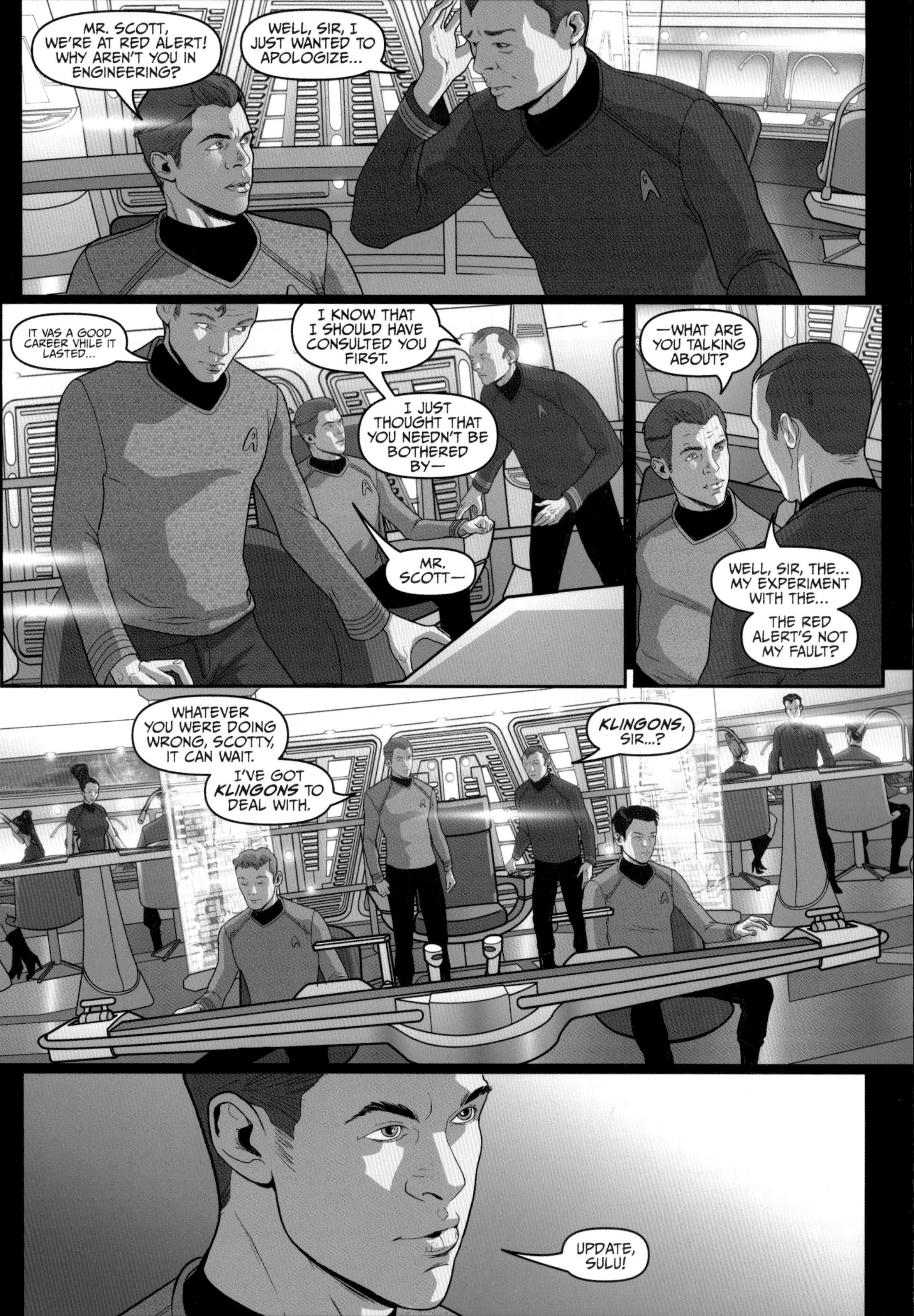
MR. SCOTT, WE'RE AT RED ALERT! WHY AREN'T YOU IN ENGINEERING?
WELL, SIR, I JUST WANTED TO APOLOGIZE...
IT VAS A GOOD CAREER VHILE IT LASTED...
I KNOW THAT I SHOULD HAVE CONSULTED YOU FIRST.
I JUST THOUGHT THAT YOU NEEDN'T BE BOTHERED BY—
MR. SCOTT—
—WHAT ARE YOU TALKING ABOUT?
WELL, SIR, THE... MY EXPERIMENT WITH THE...
THE RED ALERT'S NOT MY FAULT?
WHATEVER YOU WERE DOING WRONG, SCOTTY, IT CAN WAIT.
I'VE GOT KLINGONS TO DEAL WITH.
KLINGONS, SIR...?
UPDATE, SULU!

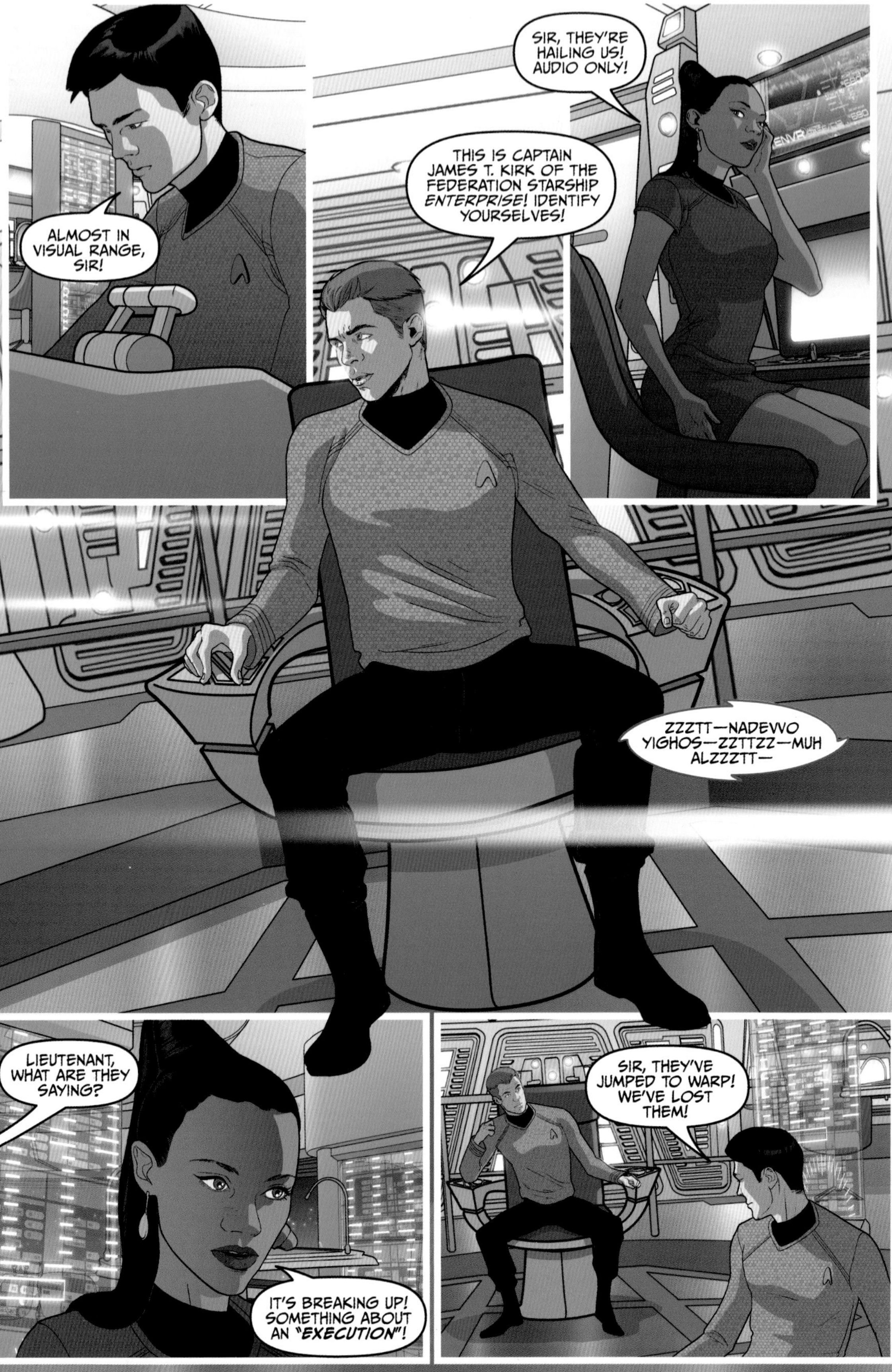
ALMOST IN VISUAL RANGE, SIR!
SIR, THEY'RE HAILING US! AUDIO ONLY!
THIS IS CAPTAIN JAMES T. KIRK OF THE FEDERATION STARSHIP *ENTERPRISE*! IDENTIFY YOURSELVES!
ZZZTT—NADEVVO YIGHOS—ZZTTZZ—MUH ALZZZTT—
LIEUTENANT, WHAT ARE THEY SAYING?
IT'S BREAKING UP! SOMETHING ABOUT AN "***EXECUTION***"!
SIR, THEY'VE JUMPED TO WARP! WE'VE LOST THEM!

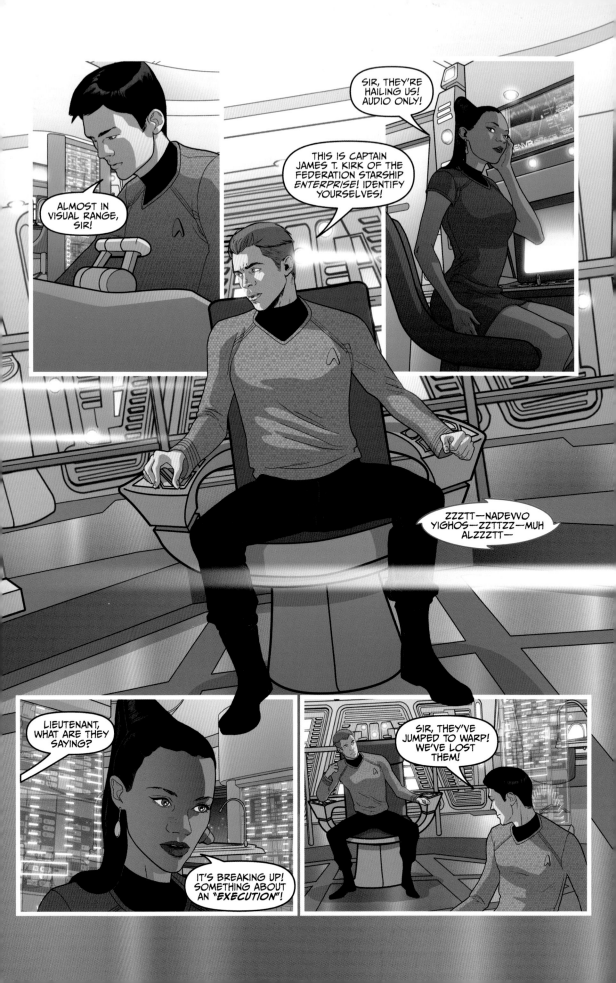

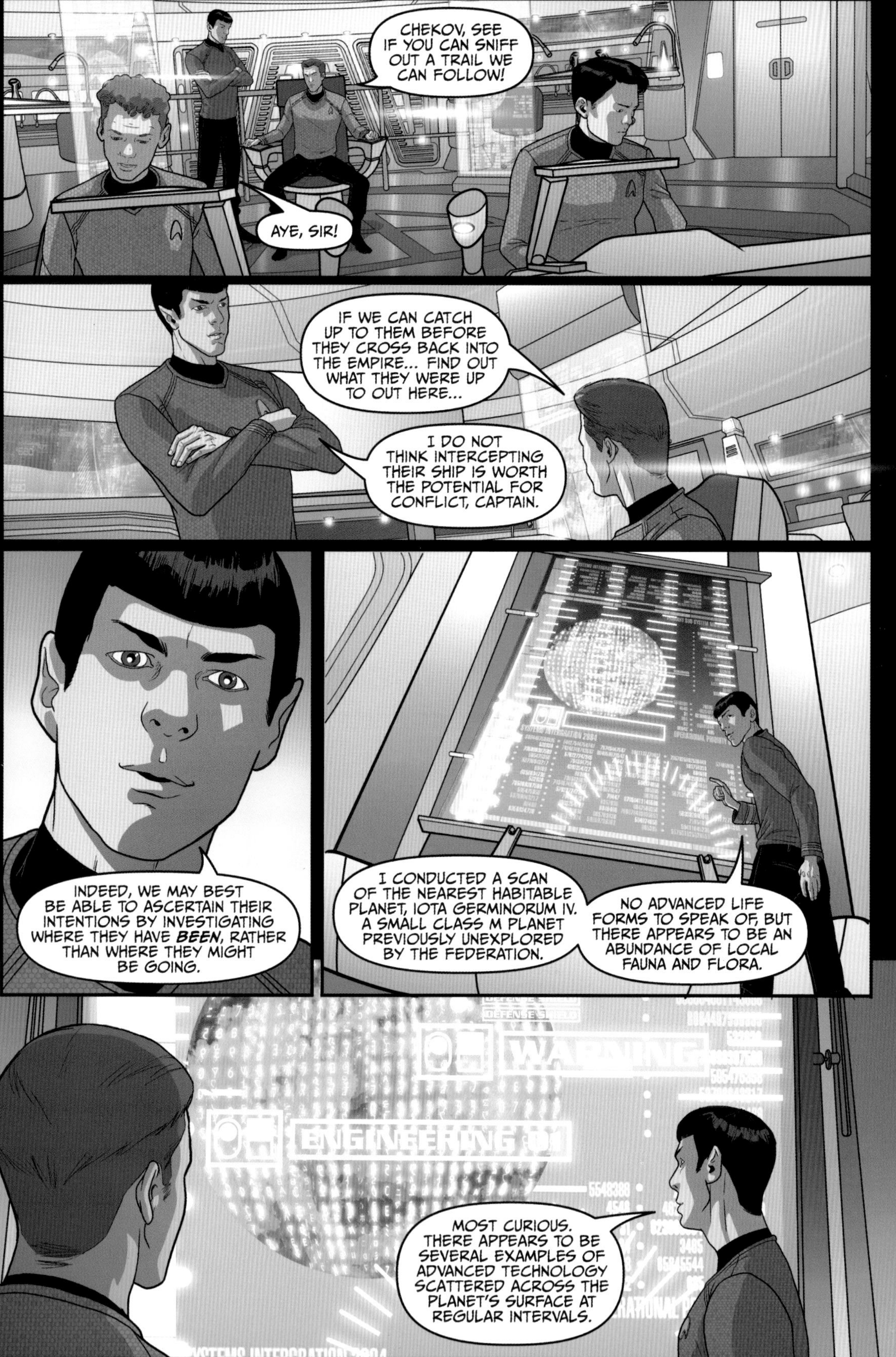
CHEKOV, SEE IF YOU CAN SNIFF OUT A TRAIL WE CAN FOLLOW!
AYE, SIR!
IF WE CAN CATCH UP TO THEM BEFORE THEY CROSS BACK INTO THE EMPIRE... FIND OUT WHAT THEY WERE UP TO OUT HERE...
I DO NOT THINK INTERCEPTING THEIR SHIP IS WORTH THE POTENTIAL FOR CONFLICT, CAPTAIN.
INDEED, WE MAY BEST BE ABLE TO ASCERTAIN THEIR INTENTIONS BY INVESTIGATING WHERE THEY HAVE *BEEN*, RATHER THAN WHERE THEY MIGHT BE GOING.
I CONDUCTED A SCAN OF THE NEAREST HABITABLE PLANET, IOTA GERMINORUM IV. A SMALL CLASS M PLANET PREVIOUSLY UNEXPLORED BY THE FEDERATION.
NO ADVANCED LIFE FORMS TO SPEAK OF, BUT THERE APPEARS TO BE AN ABUNDANCE OF LOCAL FAUNA AND FLORA.
DEFENSE SHIELD
WARNING
ENGINEERING 01
MOST CURIOUS. THERE APPEARS TO BE SEVERAL EXAMPLES OF ADVANCED TECHNOLOGY SCATTERED ACROSS THE PLANET'S SURFACE AT REGULAR INTERVALS.

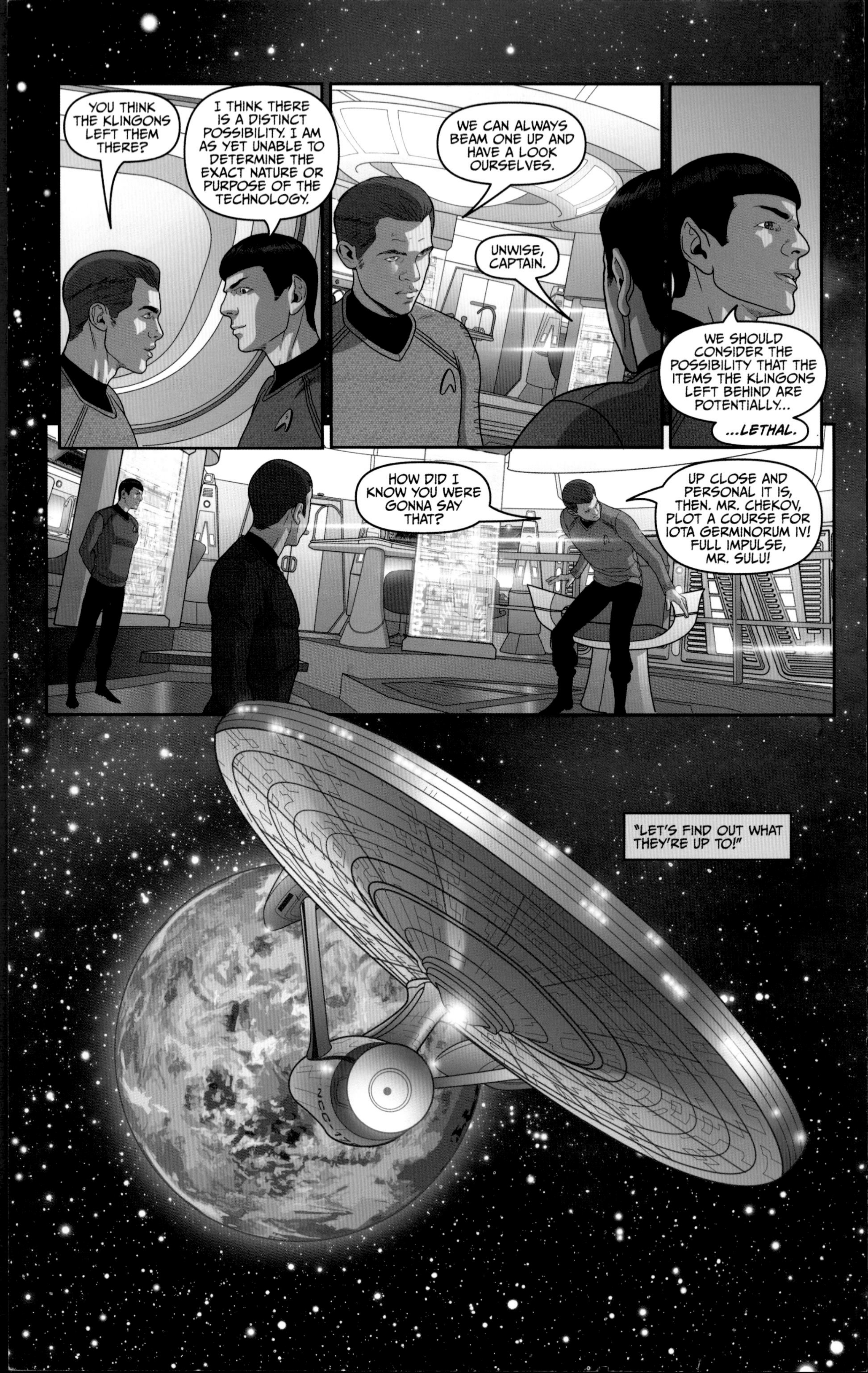
YOU THINK THE KLINGONS LEFT THEM THERE?
I THINK THERE IS A DISTINCT POSSIBILITY. I AM AS YET UNABLE TO DETERMINE THE EXACT NATURE OR PURPOSE OF THE TECHNOLOGY.
WE CAN ALWAYS BEAM ONE UP AND HAVE A LOOK OURSELVES.
UNWISE, CAPTAIN.
WE SHOULD CONSIDER THE POSSIBILITY THAT THE ITEMS THE KLINGONS LEFT BEHIND ARE POTENTIALLY...
...LETHAL.
HOW DID I KNOW YOU WERE GONNA SAY THAT?
UP CLOSE AND PERSONAL IT IS, THEN. MR. CHEKOV, PLOT A COURSE FOR IOTA GERMINORUM IV! FULL IMPULSE, MR. SULU!
"LET'S FIND OUT WHAT THEY'RE UP TO!"

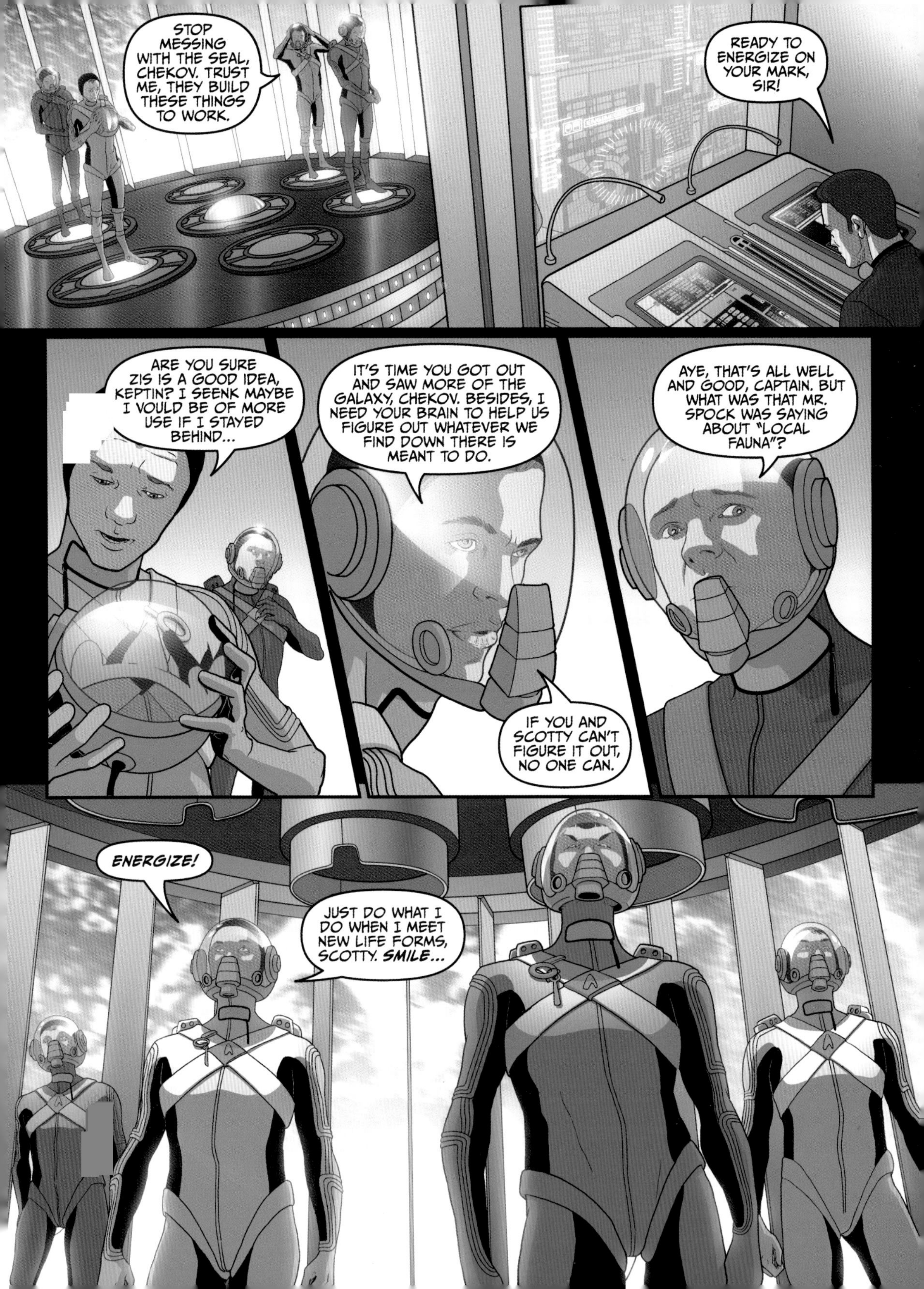
STOP MESSING WITH THE SEAL, CHEKOV. TRUST ME, THEY BUILD THESE THINGS TO WORK.
READY TO ENERGIZE ON YOUR MARK, SIR!
ARE YOU SURE ZIS IS A GOOD IDEA, KEPTIN? I SEENK MAYBE I VOULD BE OF MORE USE IF I STAYED BEHIND...
IT'S TIME YOU GOT OUT AND SAW MORE OF THE GALAXY, CHEKOV. BESIDES, I NEED YOUR BRAIN TO HELP US FIGURE OUT WHATEVER WE FIND DOWN THERE IS MEANT TO DO.
IF YOU AND SCOTTY CAN'T FIGURE IT OUT, NO ONE CAN.
AYE, THAT'S ALL WELL AND GOOD, CAPTAIN. BUT WHAT WAS THAT MR. SPOCK WAS SAYING ABOUT "LOCAL FAUNA"?
ENERGIZE!
JUST DO WHAT I DO WHEN I MEET NEW LIFE FORMS, SCOTTY. SMILE...

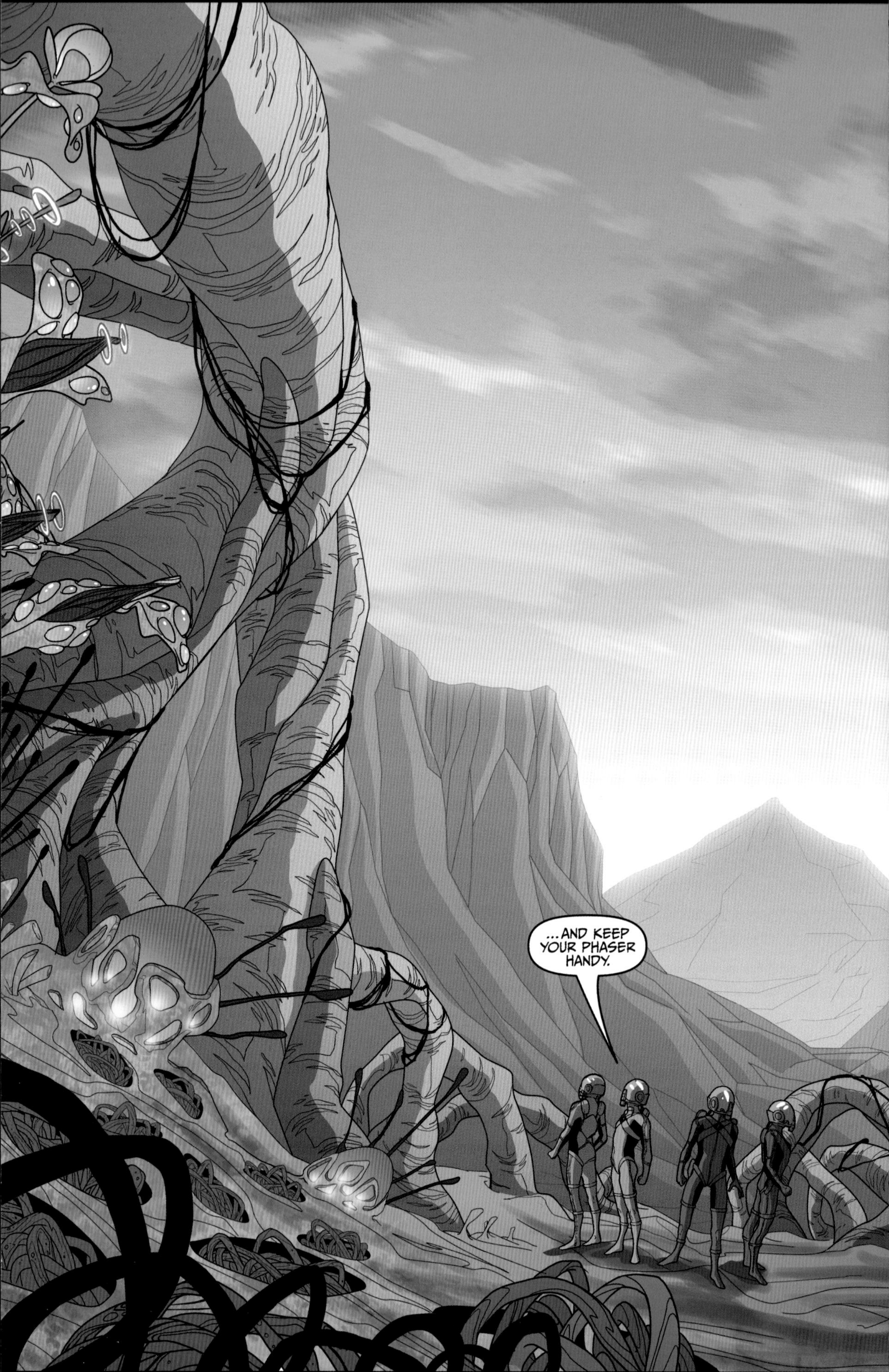
...AND KEEP YOUR PHASER HANDY.

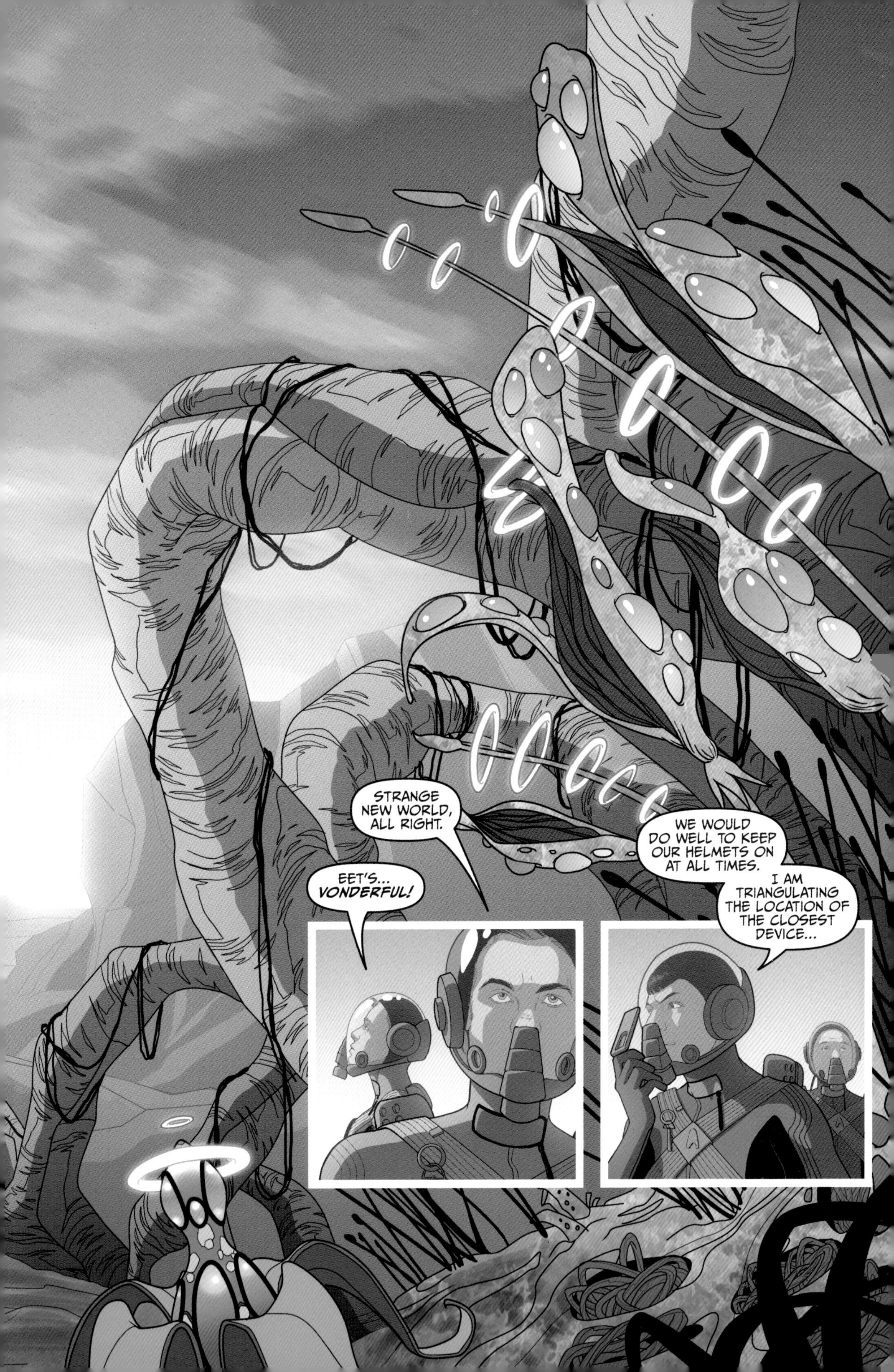
STRANGE NEW WORLD, ALL RIGHT.
EET'S... *VONDERFUL!*
WE WOULD DO WELL TO KEEP OUR HELMETS ON AT ALL TIMES.
I AM TRIANGULATING THE LOCATION OF THE CLOSEST DEVICE...

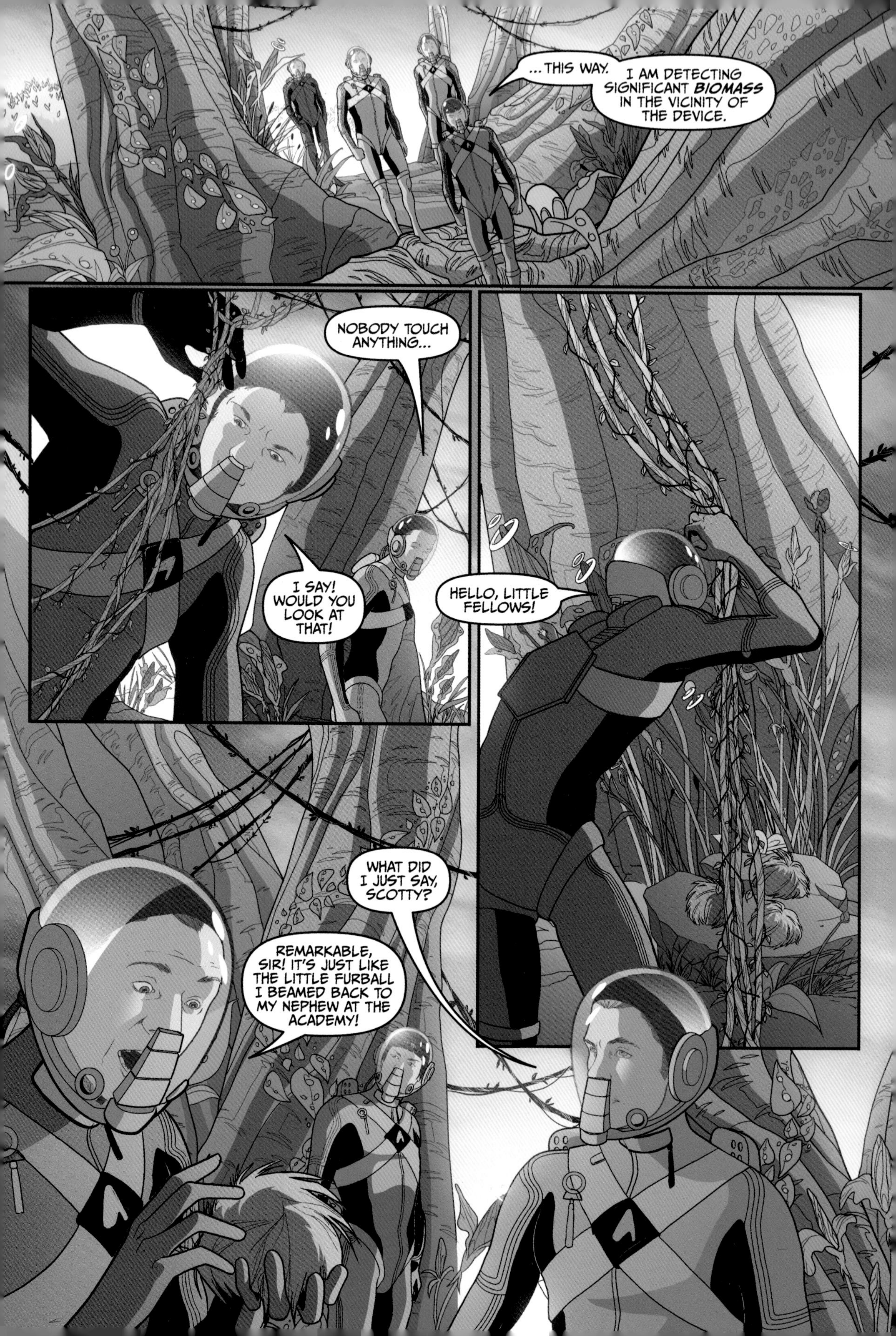
...THIS WAY.
I AM DETECTING SIGNIFICANT BIOMASS IN THE VICINITY OF THE DEVICE.
NOBODY TOUCH ANYTHING...
I SAY! WOULD YOU LOOK AT THAT!
HELLO, LITTLE FELLOWS!
WHAT DID I JUST SAY, SCOTTY?
REMARKABLE, SIR! IT'S JUST LIKE THE LITTLE FURBALL I BEAMED BACK TO MY NEPHEW AT THE ACADEMY!

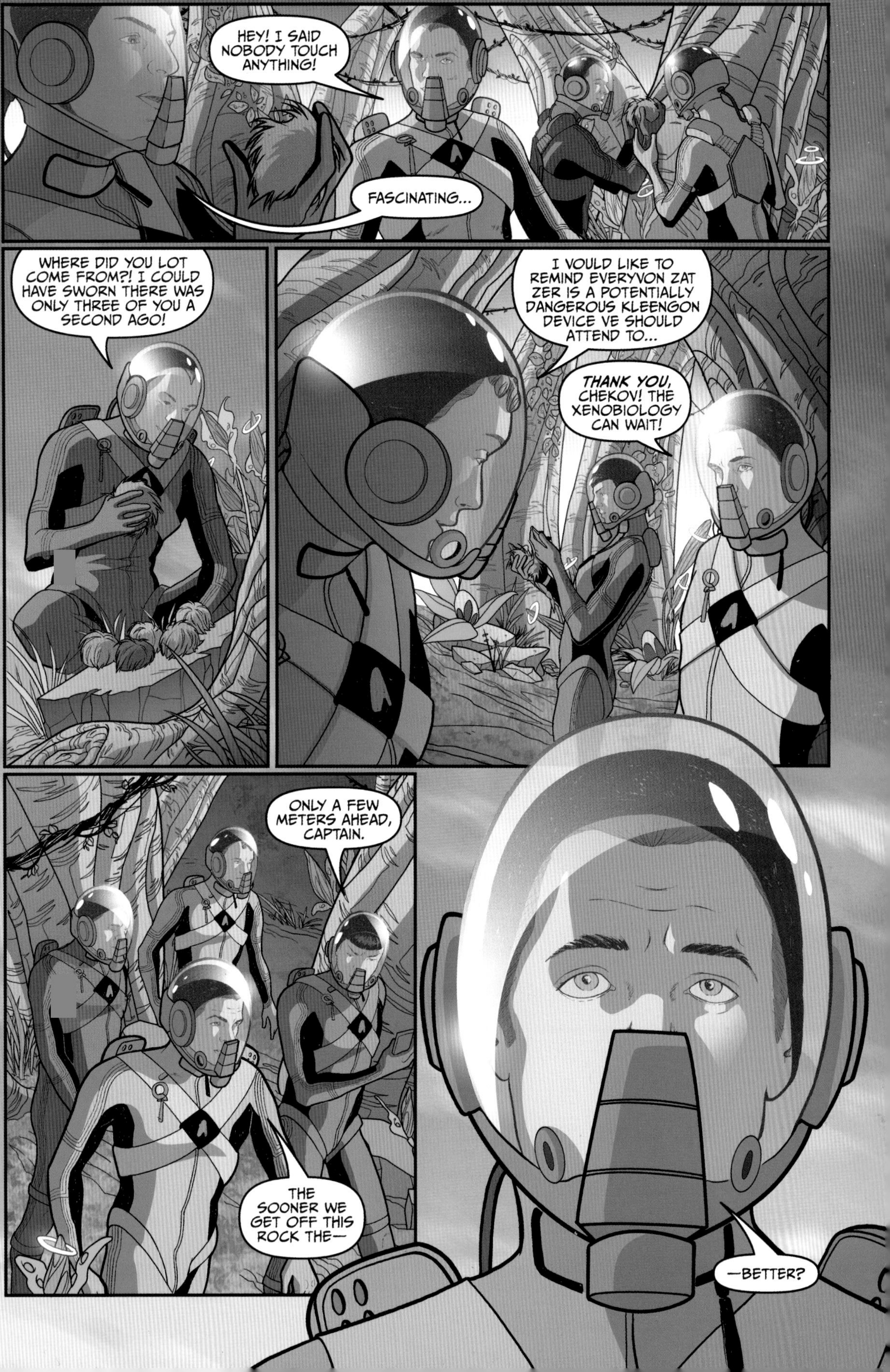
HEY! I SAID NOBODY TOUCH ANYTHING!
FASCINATING...
WHERE DID YOU LOT COME FROM?! I COULD HAVE SWORN THERE WAS ONLY THREE OF YOU A SECOND AGO!
I VOULD LIKE TO REMIND EVERYVON ZAT ZER IS A POTENTIALLY DANGEROUS KLEENGON DEVICE VE SHOULD ATTEND TO...
THANK YOU, CHEKOV! THE XENOBIOLOGY CAN WAIT!
ONLY A FEW METERS AHEAD, CAPTAIN.
THE SOONER WE GET OFF THIS ROCK THE—
—BETTER?

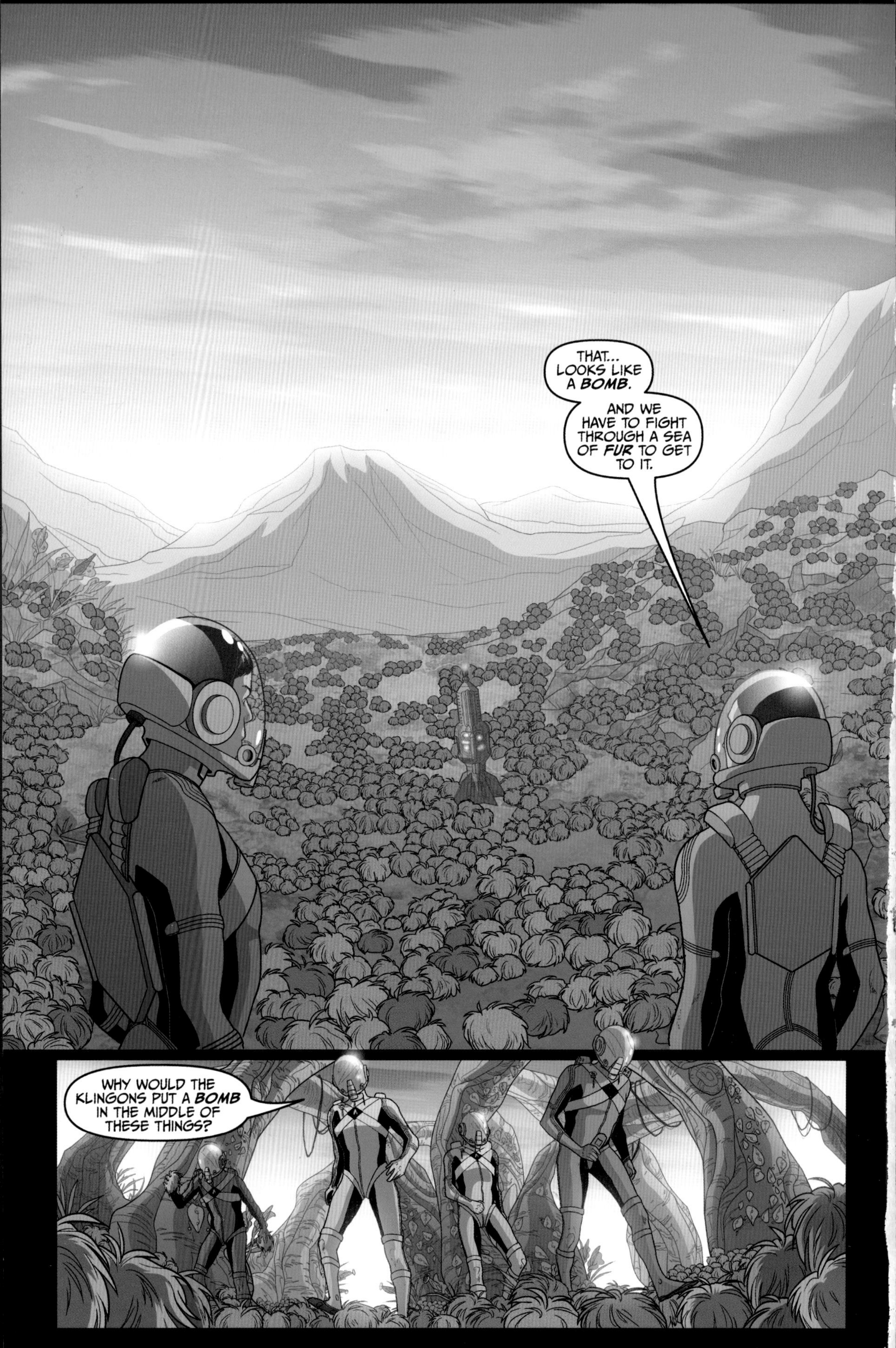
THAT... LOOKS LIKE A **BOMB**.
AND WE HAVE TO FIGHT THROUGH A SEA OF **FUR** TO GET TO IT.
WHY WOULD THE KLINGONS PUT A **BOMB** IN THE MIDDLE OF THESE THINGS?

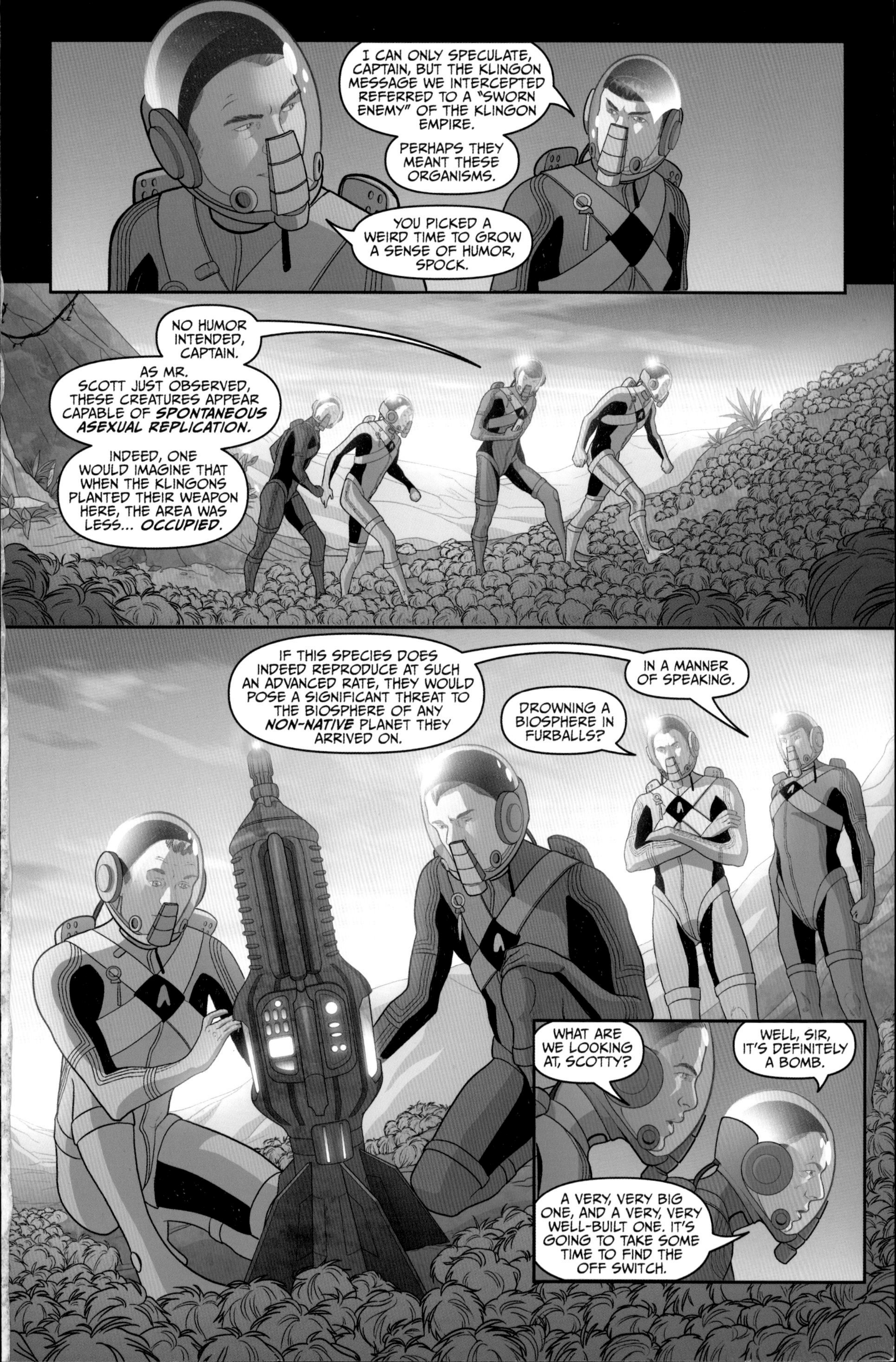
I CAN ONLY SPECULATE, CAPTAIN, BUT THE KLINGON MESSAGE WE INTERCEPTED REFERRED TO A "SWORN ENEMY" OF THE KLINGON EMPIRE.
PERHAPS THEY MEANT THESE ORGANISMS.
YOU PICKED A WEIRD TIME TO GROW A SENSE OF HUMOR, SPOCK.
NO HUMOR INTENDED, CAPTAIN.
AS MR. SCOTT JUST OBSERVED, THESE CREATURES APPEAR CAPABLE OF SPONTANEOUS ASEXUAL REPLICATION.
INDEED, ONE WOULD IMAGINE THAT WHEN THE KLINGONS PLANTED THEIR WEAPON HERE, THE AREA WAS LESS... OCCUPIED.
IF THIS SPECIES DOES INDEED REPRODUCE AT SUCH AN ADVANCED RATE, THEY WOULD POSE A SIGNIFICANT THREAT TO THE BIOSPHERE OF ANY NON-NATIVE PLANET THEY ARRIVED ON.
DROWNING A BIOSPHERE IN FURBALLS?
IN A MANNER OF SPEAKING.
WHAT ARE WE LOOKING AT, SCOTTY?
WELL, SIR, IT'S DEFINITELY A BOMB.
A VERY, VERY BIG ONE, AND A VERY, VERY WELL-BUILT ONE. IT'S GOING TO TAKE SOME TIME TO FIND THE OFF SWITCH.

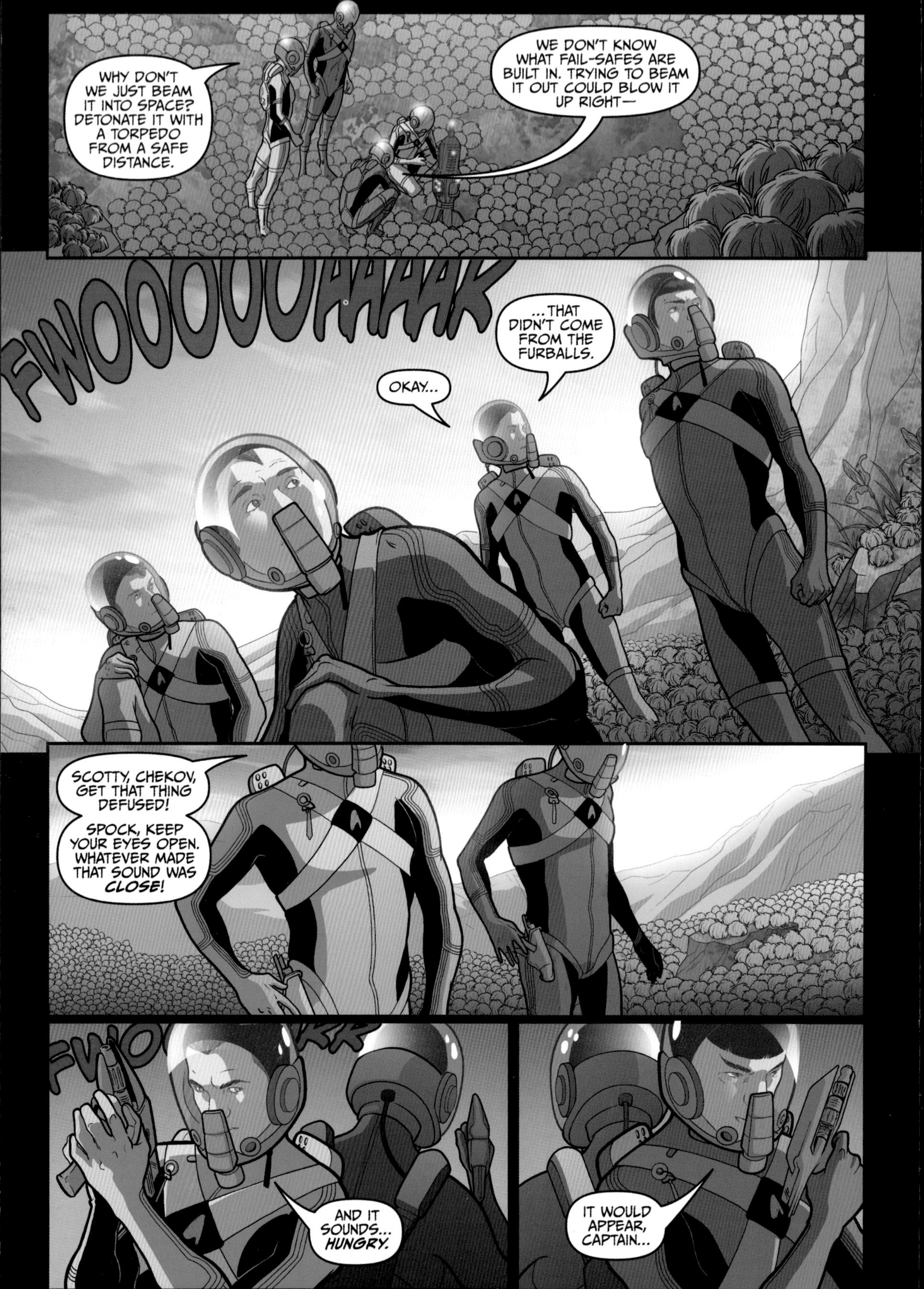
WHY DON'T WE JUST BEAM IT INTO SPACE? DETONATE IT WITH A TORPEDO FROM A SAFE DISTANCE.
WE DON'T KNOW WHAT FAIL-SAFES ARE BUILT IN. TRYING TO BEAM IT OUT COULD BLOW IT UP RIGHT—
FWOOOOOAAAAK
...THAT DIDN'T COME FROM THE FURBALLS.
OKAY...
SCOTTY, CHEKOV, GET THAT THING DEFUSED!
SPOCK, KEEP YOUR EYES OPEN. WHATEVER MADE THAT SOUND WAS CLOSE!
AND IT SOUNDS... HUNGRY.
IT WOULD APPEAR, CAPTAIN...

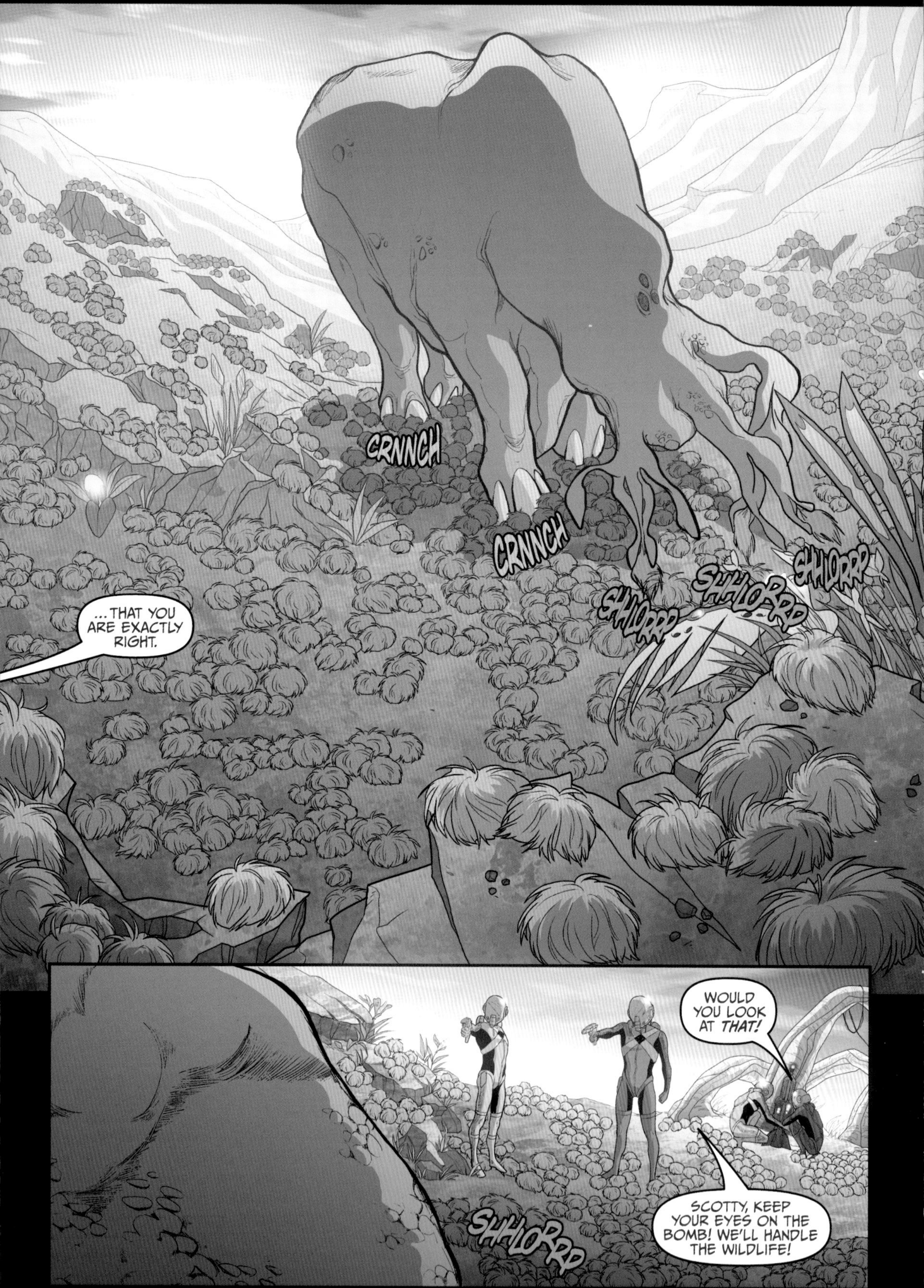
CRNNCH
CRNNCH
SHHLORRP
SHHLORRP
SHHLORRP
...THAT YOU ARE EXACTLY RIGHT.
WOULD YOU LOOK AT *THAT!*
SHHLORRP
SCOTTY, KEEP YOUR EYES ON THE BOMB! WE'LL HANDLE THE WILDLIFE!

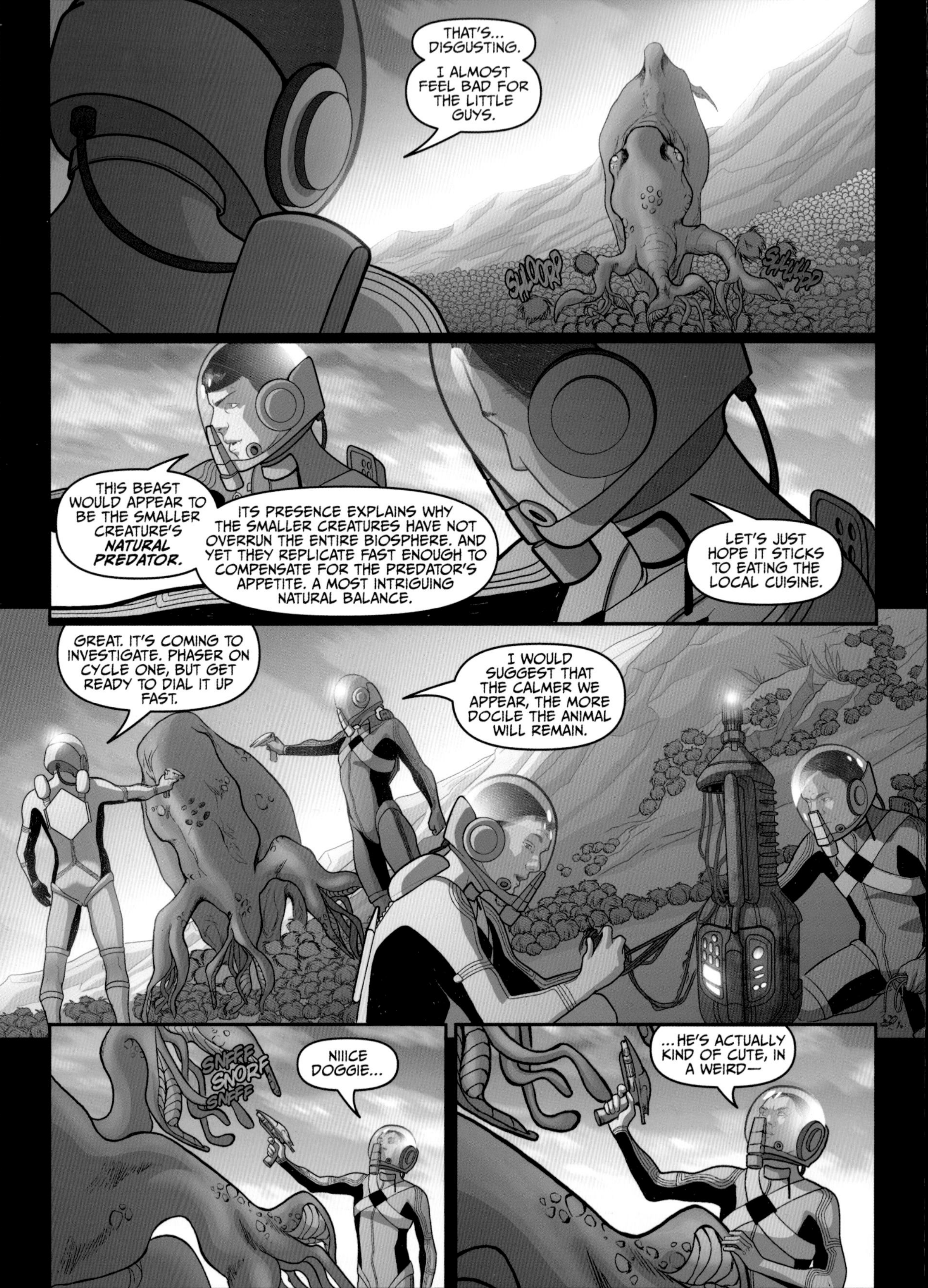
THAT'S... DISGUSTING.
I ALMOST FEEL BAD FOR THE LITTLE GUYS.
SHLOORP
SHLURP
THIS BEAST WOULD APPEAR TO BE THE SMALLER CREATURE'S *NATURAL PREDATOR.*
ITS PRESENCE EXPLAINS WHY THE SMALLER CREATURES HAVE NOT OVERRUN THE ENTIRE BIOSPHERE. AND YET THEY REPLICATE FAST ENOUGH TO COMPENSATE FOR THE PREDATOR'S APPETITE. A MOST INTRIGUING NATURAL BALANCE.
LET'S JUST HOPE IT STICKS TO EATING THE LOCAL CUISINE.
GREAT. IT'S COMING TO INVESTIGATE. PHASER ON CYCLE ONE, BUT GET READY TO DIAL IT UP FAST.
I WOULD SUGGEST THAT THE CALMER WE APPEAR, THE MORE DOCILE THE ANIMAL WILL REMAIN.
SNFFF
SNORF
SNFFF
NIIICE DOGGIE...
...HE'S ACTUALLY KIND OF CUTE, IN A WEIRD—

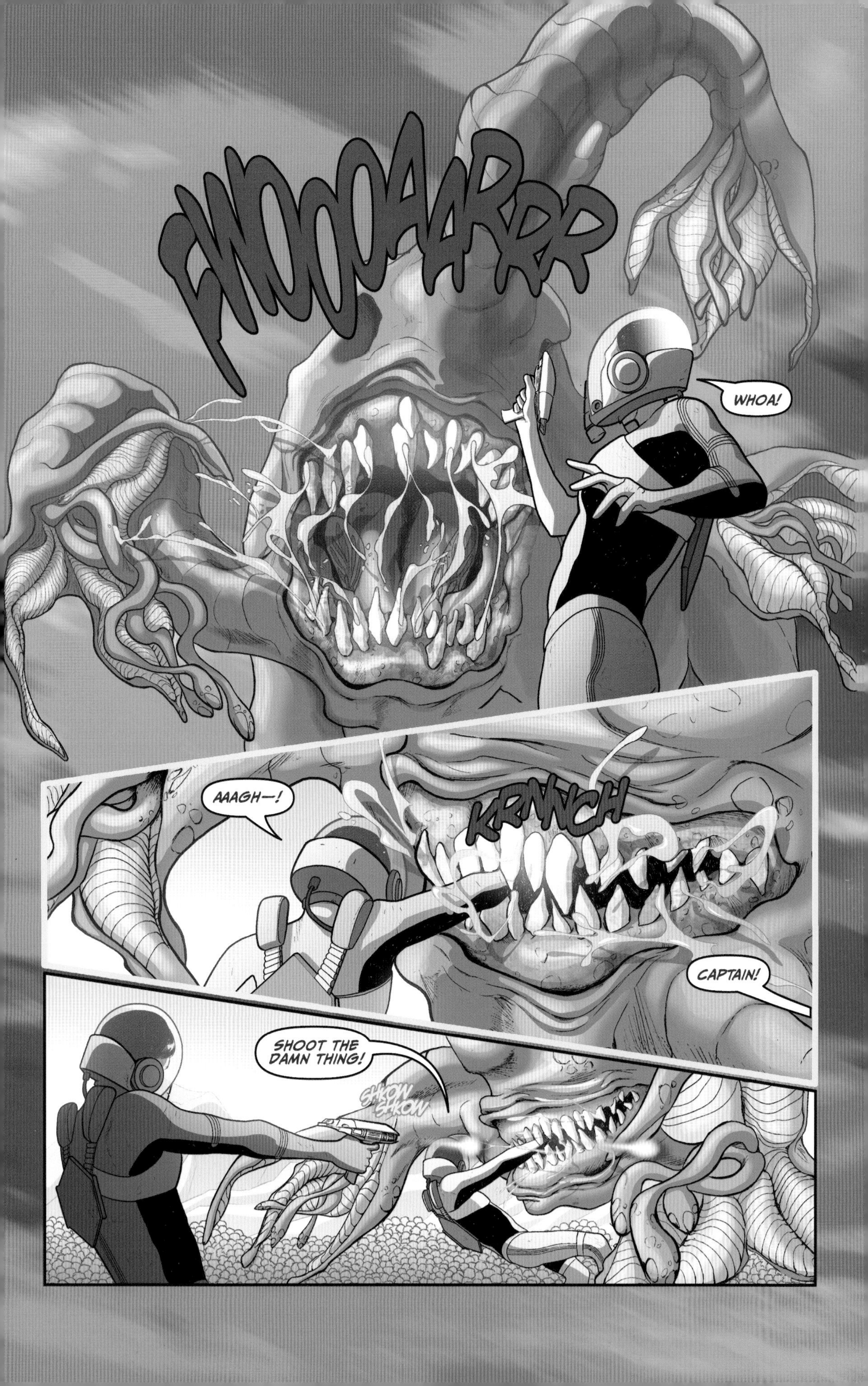
EHOOOAARRR
WHOA!
AAAGH—!
KRNNCH
CAPTAIN!
SHOOT THE DAMN THING!
SHKOW SHKOW

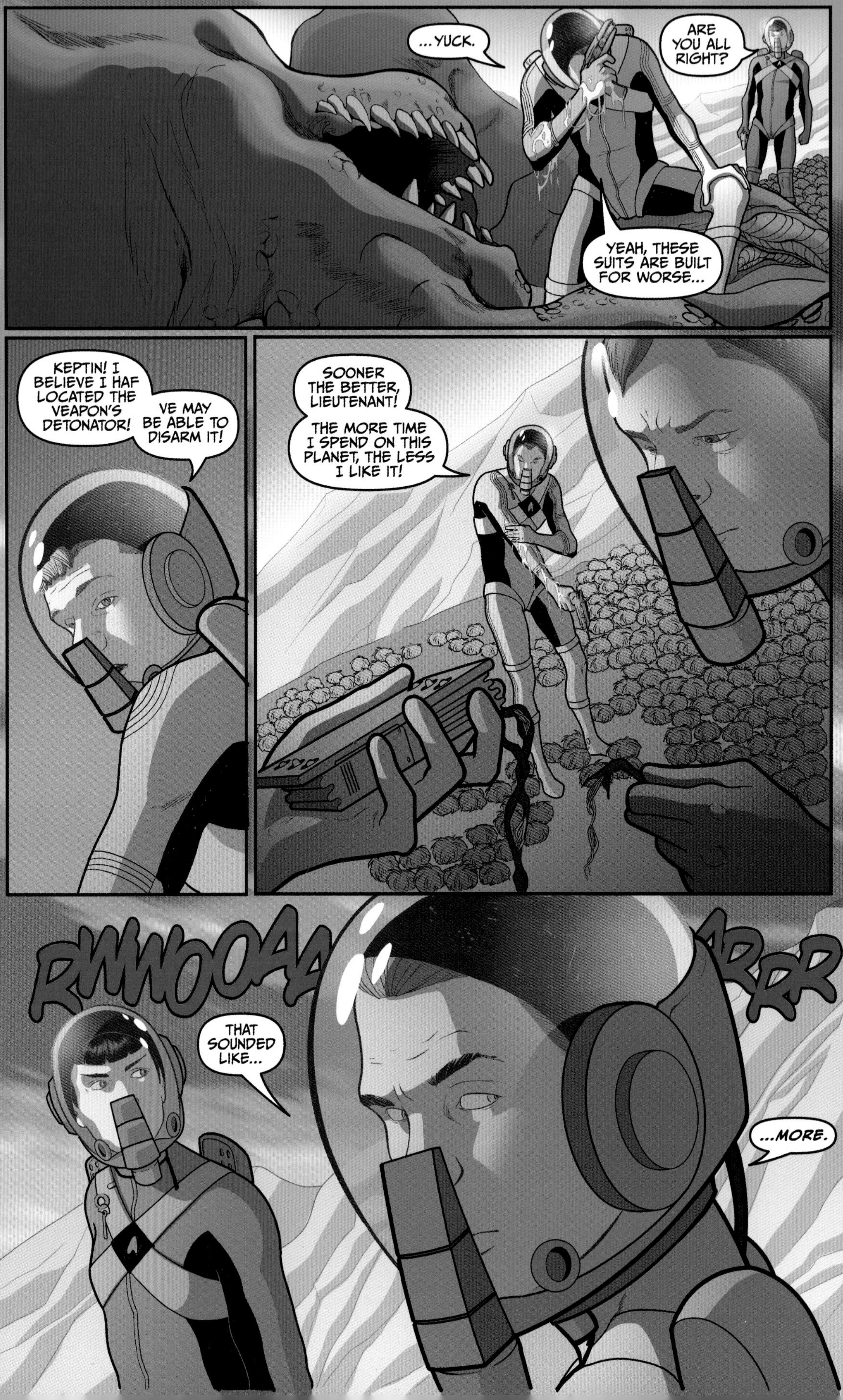
...YUCK.
ARE YOU ALL RIGHT?
YEAH, THESE SUITS ARE BUILT FOR WORSE...
KEPTIN! I BELIEVE I HAF LOCATED THE VEAPON'S DETONATOR!
VE MAY BE ABLE TO DISARM IT!
SOONER THE BETTER, LIEUTENANT!
THE MORE TIME I SPEND ON THIS PLANET, THE LESS I LIKE IT!
RWWOAA ARRR
THAT SOUNDED LIKE...
...MORE.

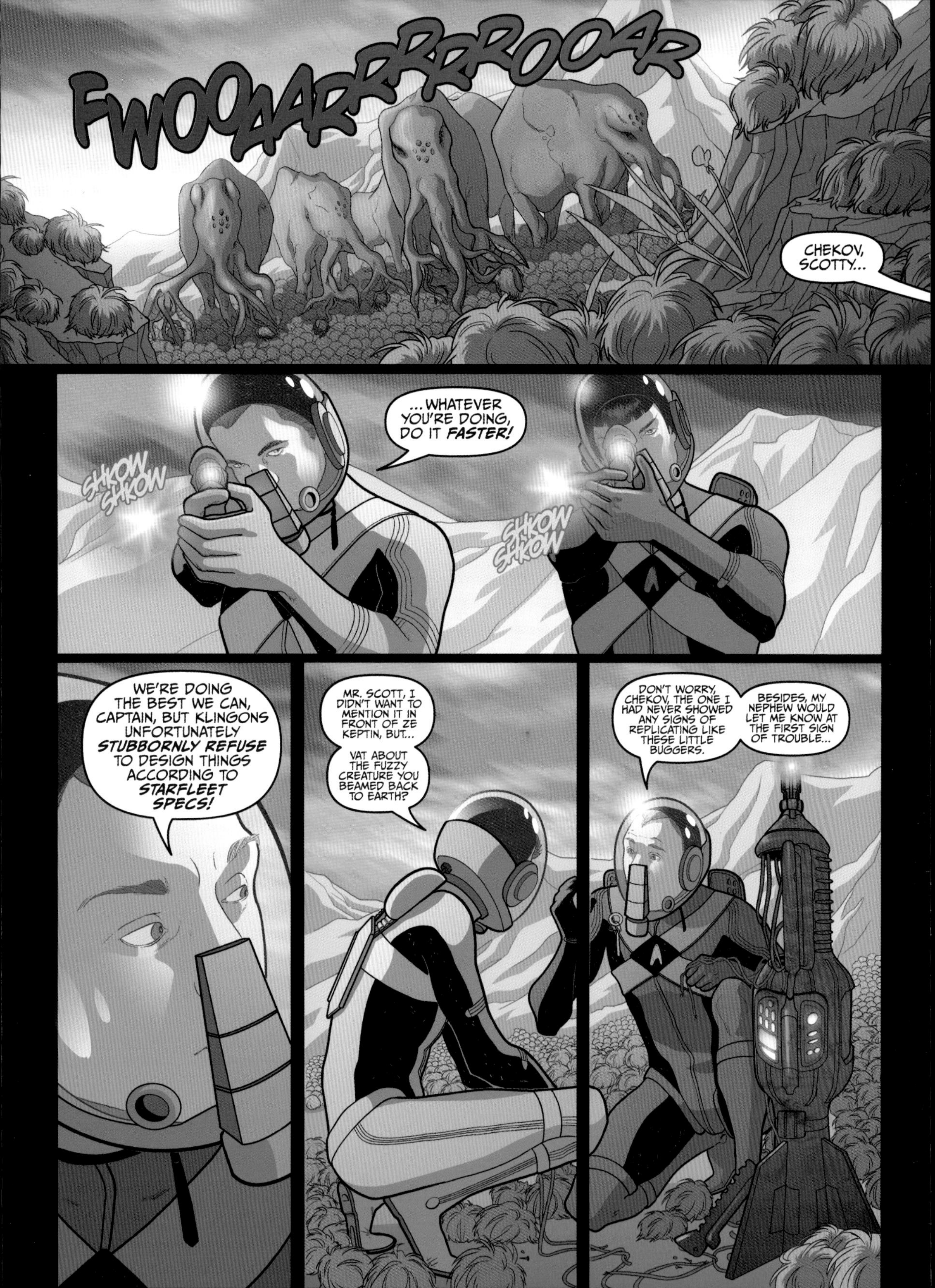
FWOOAARRRRROOAR
CHEKOV, SCOTTY...
...WHATEVER YOU'RE DOING, DO IT FASTER!
SHKOW SHKOW
SHKOW SHKOW
WE'RE DOING THE BEST WE CAN, CAPTAIN, BUT KLINGONS UNFORTUNATELY STUBBORNLY REFUSE TO DESIGN THINGS ACCORDING TO STARFLEET SPECS!
MR. SCOTT, I DIDN'T WANT TO MENTION IT IN FRONT OF ZE KEPTIN, BUT...
VAT ABOUT THE FUZZY CREATURE YOU BEAMED BACK TO EARTH?
DON'T WORRY, CHEKOV, THE ONE I HAD NEVER SHOWED ANY SIGNS OF REPLICATING LIKE THESE LITTLE BUGGERS.
BESIDES, MY NEPHEW WOULD LET ME KNOW AT THE FIRST SIGN OF TROUBLE...

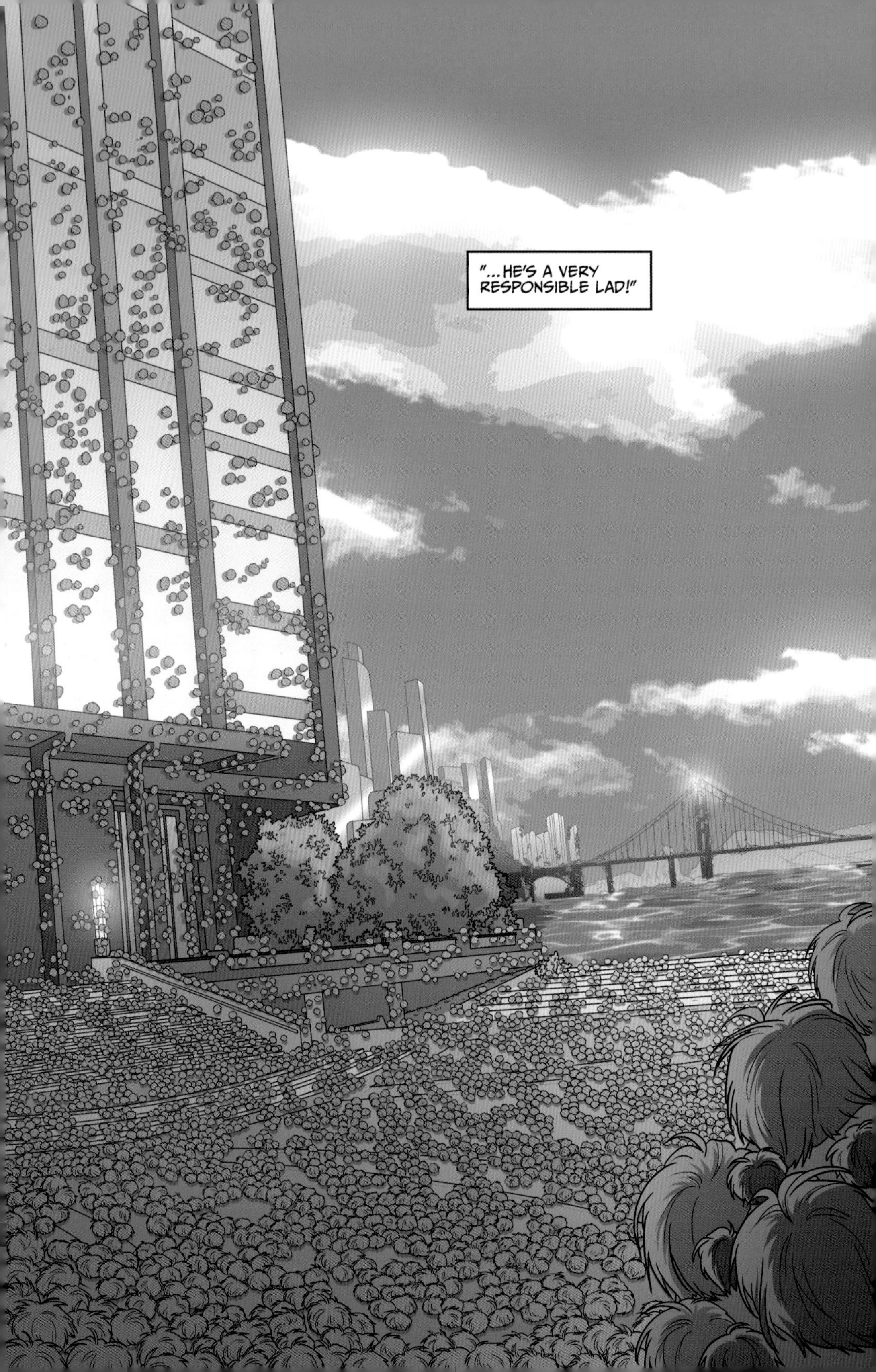
"...HE'S A VERY RESPONSIBLE LAD!"

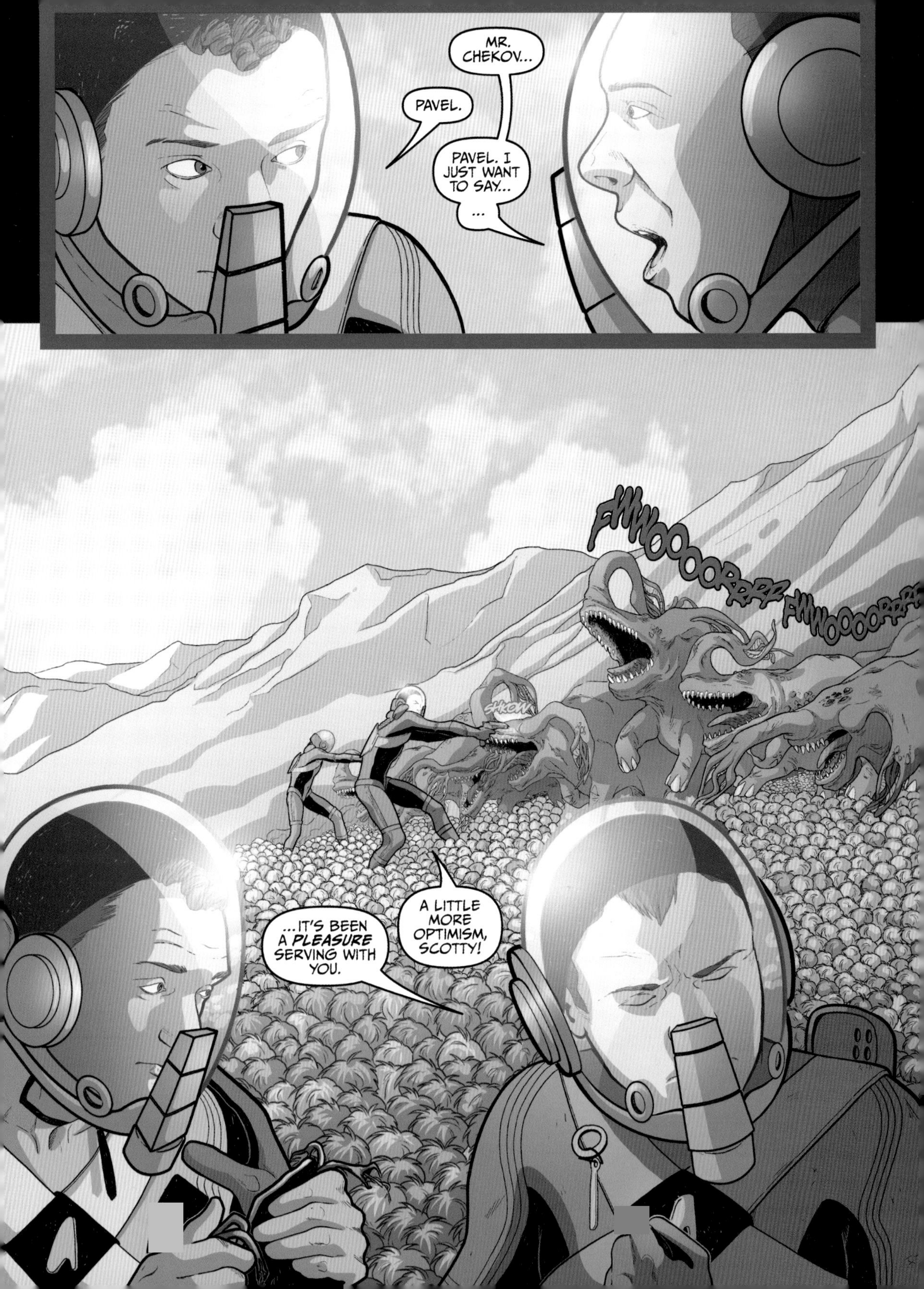
MR. CHEKOV...
PAVEL.
PAVEL. I JUST WANT TO SAY...
...
FWWOOOORRRR
FWWOOOORRRR
SHKOW
A LITTLE MORE OPTIMISM, SCOTTY!
...IT'S BEEN A PLEASURE SERVING WITH YOU.

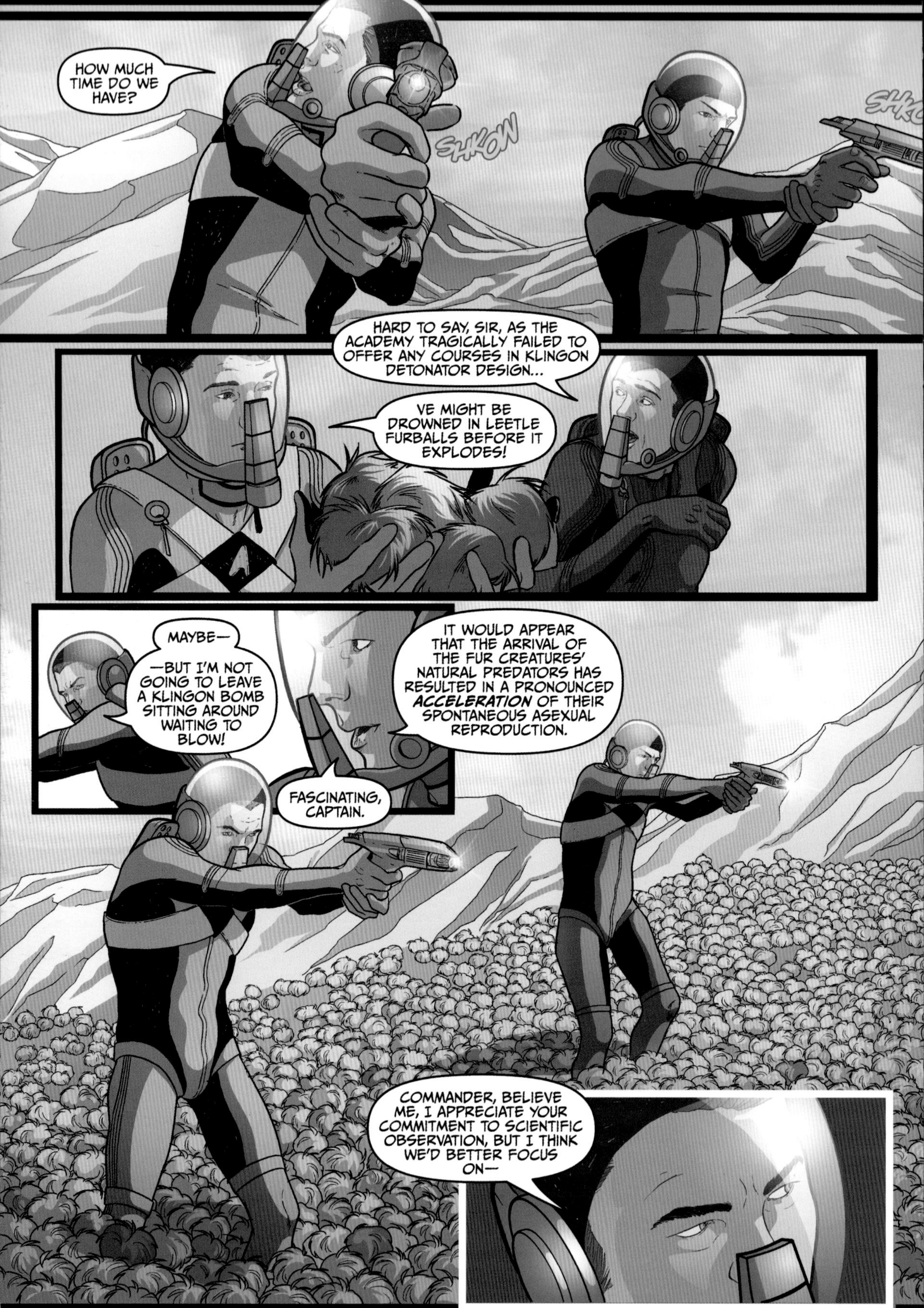
HOW MUCH TIME DO WE HAVE?
SHKOW
SHKO
HARD TO SAY, SIR, AS THE ACADEMY TRAGICALLY FAILED TO OFFER ANY COURSES IN KLINGON DETONATOR DESIGN...
VE MIGHT BE DROWNED IN LEETLE FURBALLS BEFORE IT EXPLODES!
MAYBE—
—BUT I'M NOT GOING TO LEAVE A KLINGON BOMB SITTING AROUND WAITING TO BLOW!
IT WOULD APPEAR THAT THE ARRIVAL OF THE FUR CREATURES' NATURAL PREDATORS HAS RESULTED IN A PRONOUNCED ***ACCELERATION*** OF THEIR SPONTANEOUS ASEXUAL REPRODUCTION.
FASCINATING, CAPTAIN.
COMMANDER, BELIEVE ME, I APPRECIATE YOUR COMMITMENT TO SCIENTIFIC OBSERVATION, BUT I THINK WE'D BETTER FOCUS ON—

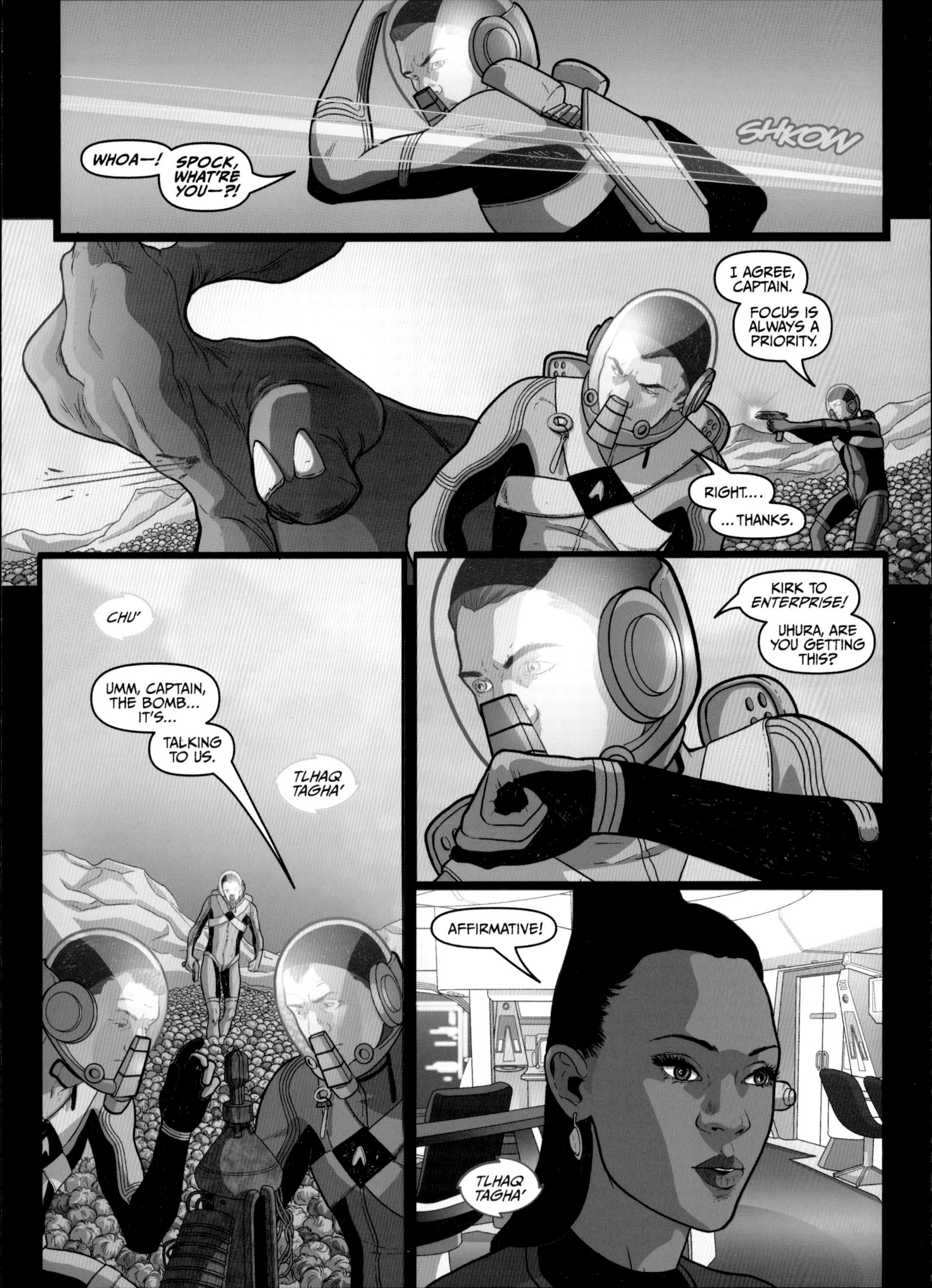
SHKOW
WHOA—!
SPOCK, WHAT'RE YOU—?!
I AGREE, CAPTAIN.
FOCUS IS ALWAYS A PRIORITY.
RIGHT....
...THANKS.
CHU'
UMM, CAPTAIN, THE BOMB... IT'S...
TALKING TO US.
TLHAQ TAGHA'
KIRK TO ENTERPRISE!
UHURA, ARE YOU GETTING THIS?
AFFIRMATIVE!
TLHAQ TAGHA'

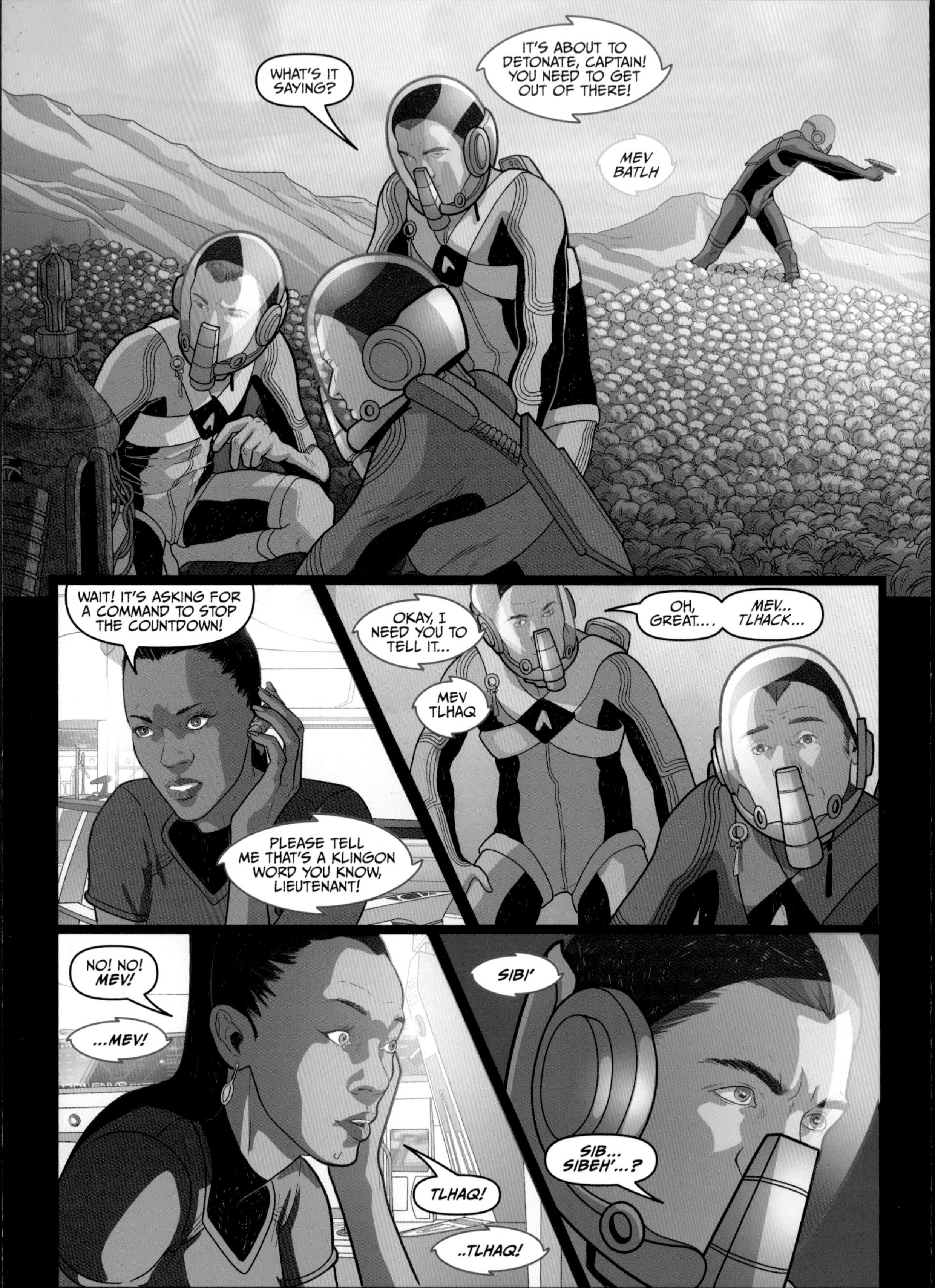
WHAT'S IT SAYING?
IT'S ABOUT TO DETONATE, CAPTAIN! YOU NEED TO GET OUT OF THERE!
MEV BATLH
WAIT! IT'S ASKING FOR A COMMAND TO STOP THE COUNTDOWN!
OKAY, I NEED YOU TO TELL IT...
OH, GREAT....
MEV... TLHACK...
MEV TLHAQ
PLEASE TELL ME THAT'S A KLINGON WORD YOU KNOW, LIEUTENANT!
NO! NO! MEV!
...MEV!
TLHAQ!
..TLHAQ!
SIBI'
SIB... SIBEH'...?

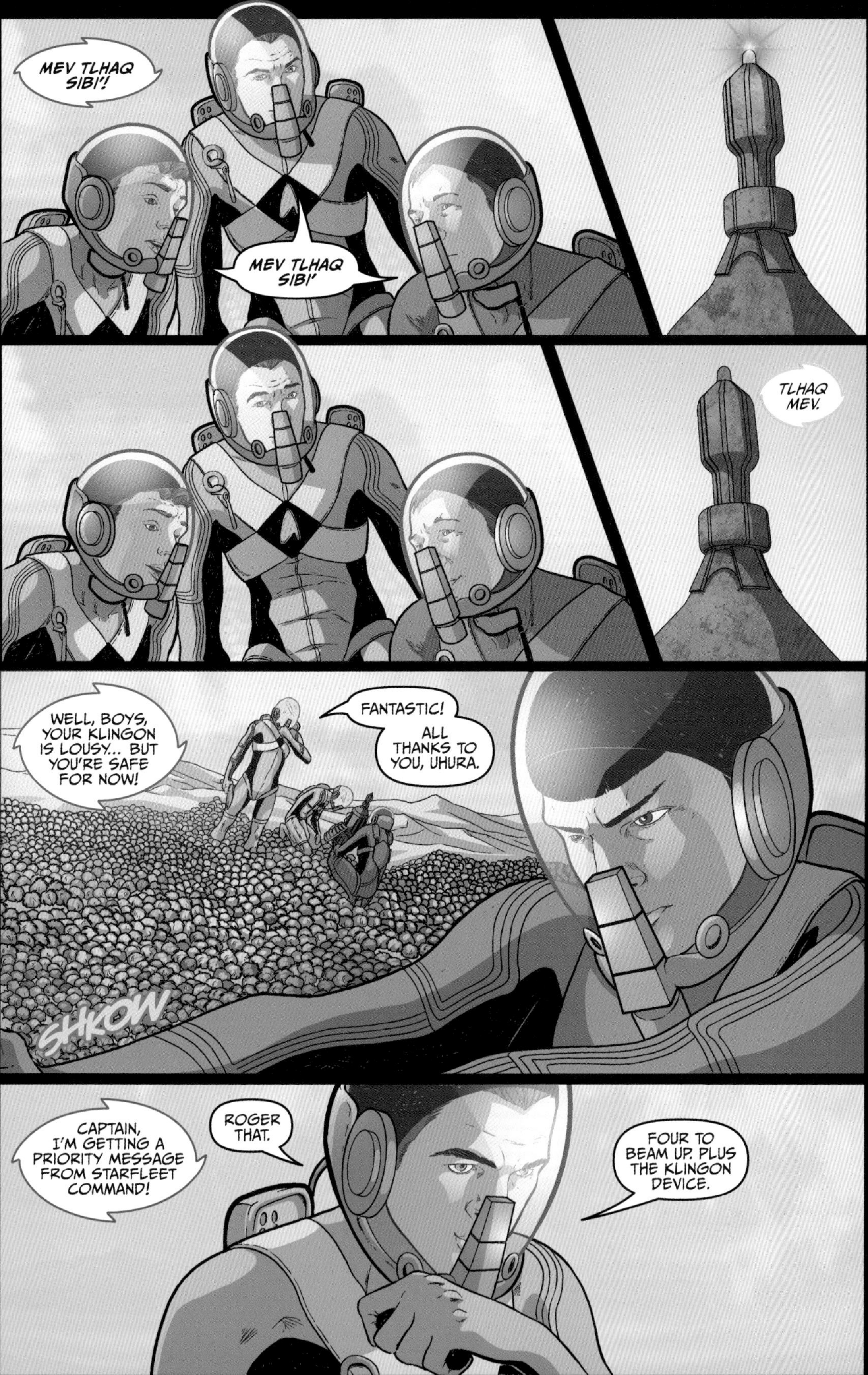
MEV TLHAQ SIBI'!
MEV TLHAQ SIBI'
TLHAQ MEV.
WELL, BOYS, YOUR KLINGON IS LOUSY... BUT YOU'RE SAFE FOR NOW!
FANTASTIC!
ALL THANKS TO YOU, UHURA.
SHKOW
CAPTAIN, I'M GETTING A PRIORITY MESSAGE FROM STARFLEET COMMAND!
ROGER THAT.
FOUR TO BEAM UP. PLUS THE KLINGON DEVICE.

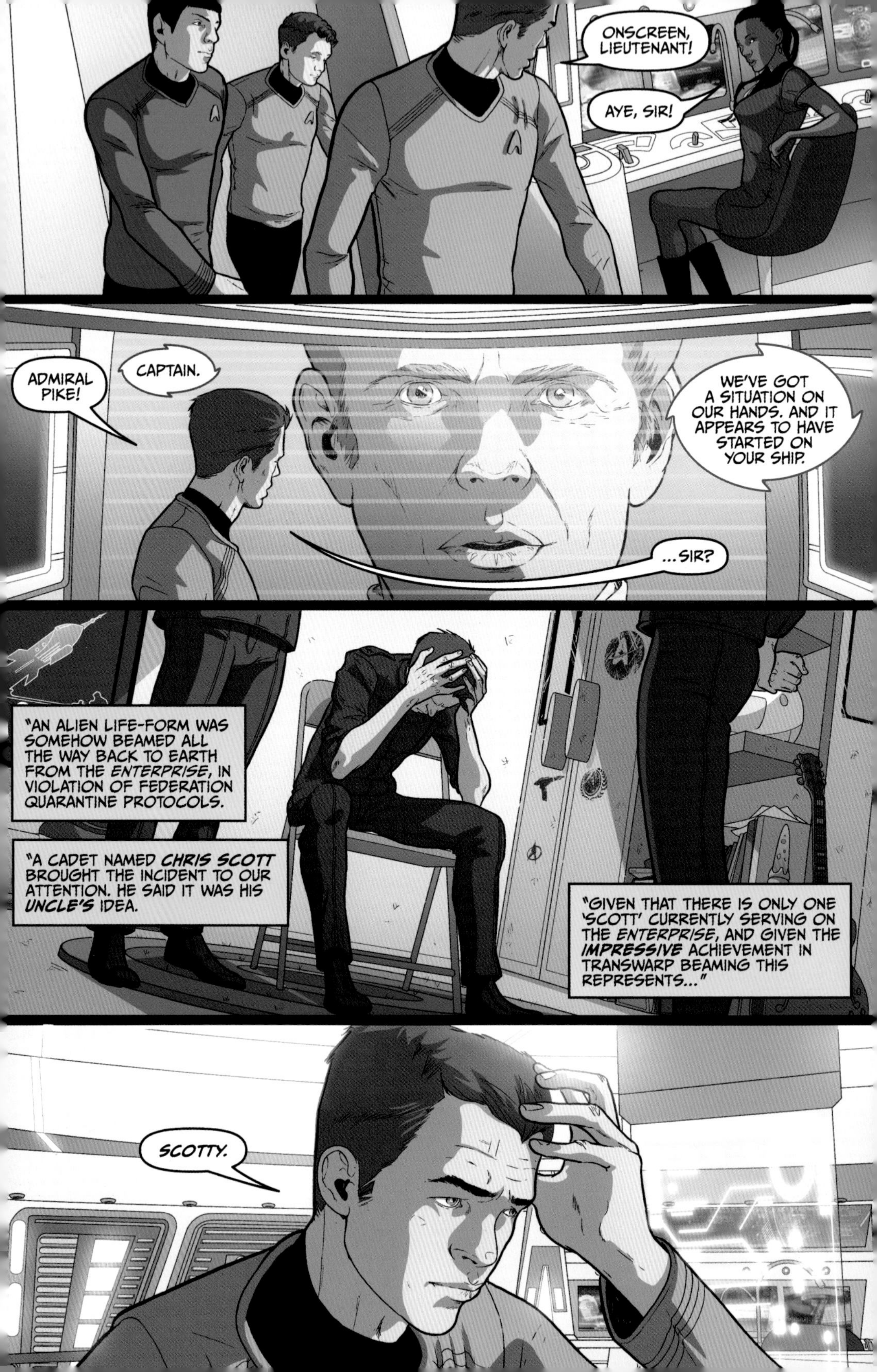
ONSCREEN, LIEUTENANT!
AYE, SIR!
ADMIRAL PIKE!
CAPTAIN.
WE'VE GOT A SITUATION ON OUR HANDS. AND IT APPEARS TO HAVE STARTED ON YOUR SHIP.
...SIR?
"AN ALIEN LIFE-FORM WAS SOMEHOW BEAMED ALL THE WAY BACK TO EARTH FROM THE *ENTERPRISE*, IN VIOLATION OF FEDERATION QUARANTINE PROTOCOLS.
"A CADET NAMED ***CHRIS SCOTT*** BROUGHT THE INCIDENT TO OUR ATTENTION. HE SAID IT WAS HIS ***UNCLE'S*** IDEA.
"GIVEN THAT THERE IS ONLY ONE 'SCOTT' CURRENTLY SERVING ON THE *ENTERPRISE*, AND GIVEN THE ***IMPRESSIVE*** ACHIEVEMENT IN TRANSWARP BEAMING THIS REPRESENTS..."
SCOTTY.

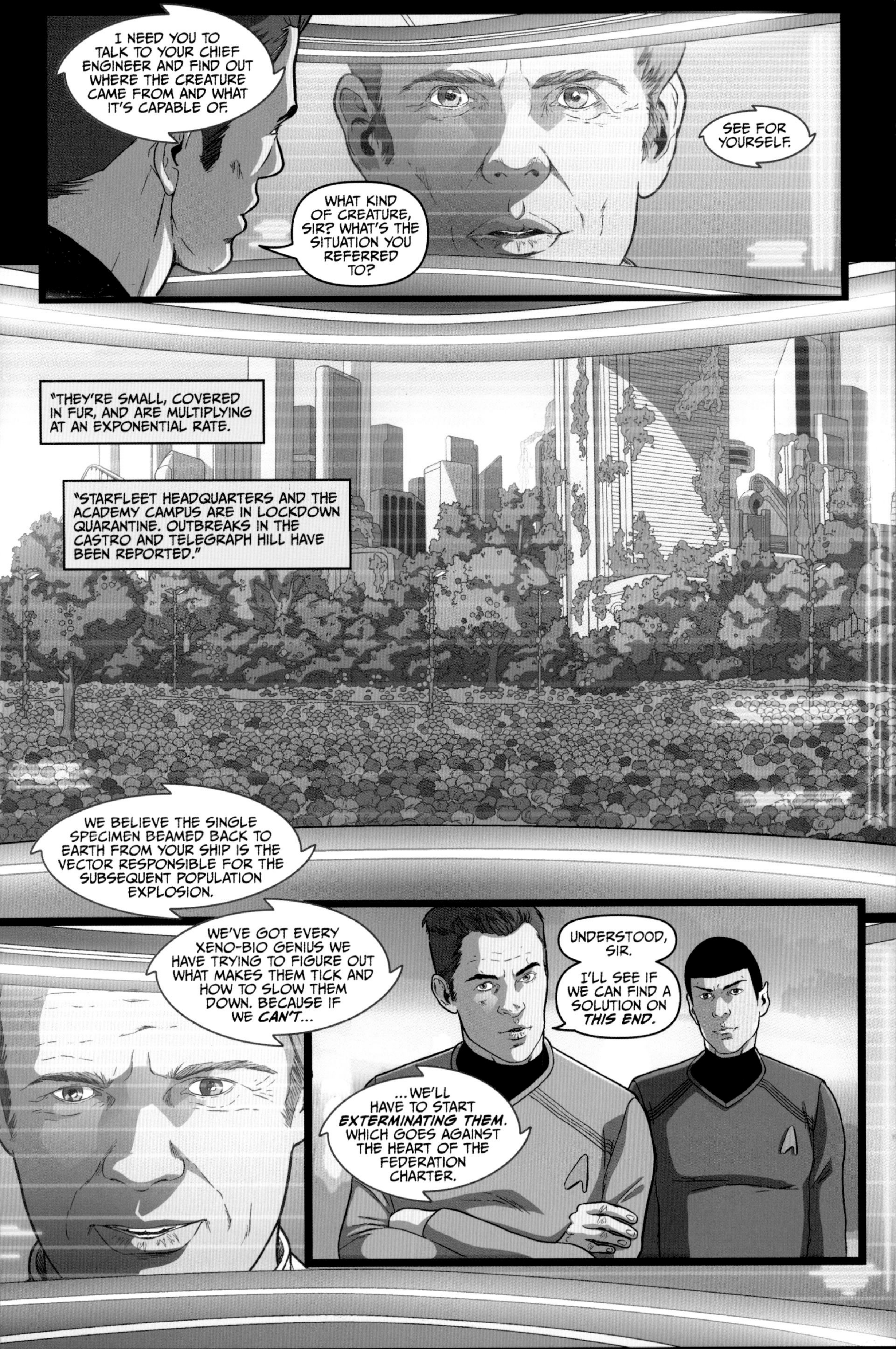
I NEED YOU TO TALK TO YOUR CHIEF ENGINEER AND FIND OUT WHERE THE CREATURE CAME FROM AND WHAT IT'S CAPABLE OF.
WHAT KIND OF CREATURE, SIR? WHAT'S THE SITUATION YOU REFERRED TO?
SEE FOR YOURSELF.
"THEY'RE SMALL, COVERED IN FUR, AND ARE MULTIPLYING AT AN EXPONENTIAL RATE.
"STARFLEET HEADQUARTERS AND THE ACADEMY CAMPUS ARE IN LOCKDOWN QUARANTINE. OUTBREAKS IN THE CASTRO AND TELEGRAPH HILL HAVE BEEN REPORTED."
WE BELIEVE THE SINGLE SPECIMEN BEAMED BACK TO EARTH FROM YOUR SHIP IS THE VECTOR RESPONSIBLE FOR THE SUBSEQUENT POPULATION EXPLOSION.
WE'VE GOT EVERY XENO-BIO GENIUS WE HAVE TRYING TO FIGURE OUT WHAT MAKES THEM TICK AND HOW TO SLOW THEM DOWN. BECAUSE IF WE *CAN'T*...
...WE'LL HAVE TO START ***EXTERMINATING THEM.*** WHICH GOES AGAINST THE HEART OF THE FEDERATION CHARTER.
UNDERSTOOD, SIR.
I'LL SEE IF WE CAN FIND A SOLUTION ON ***THIS END.***

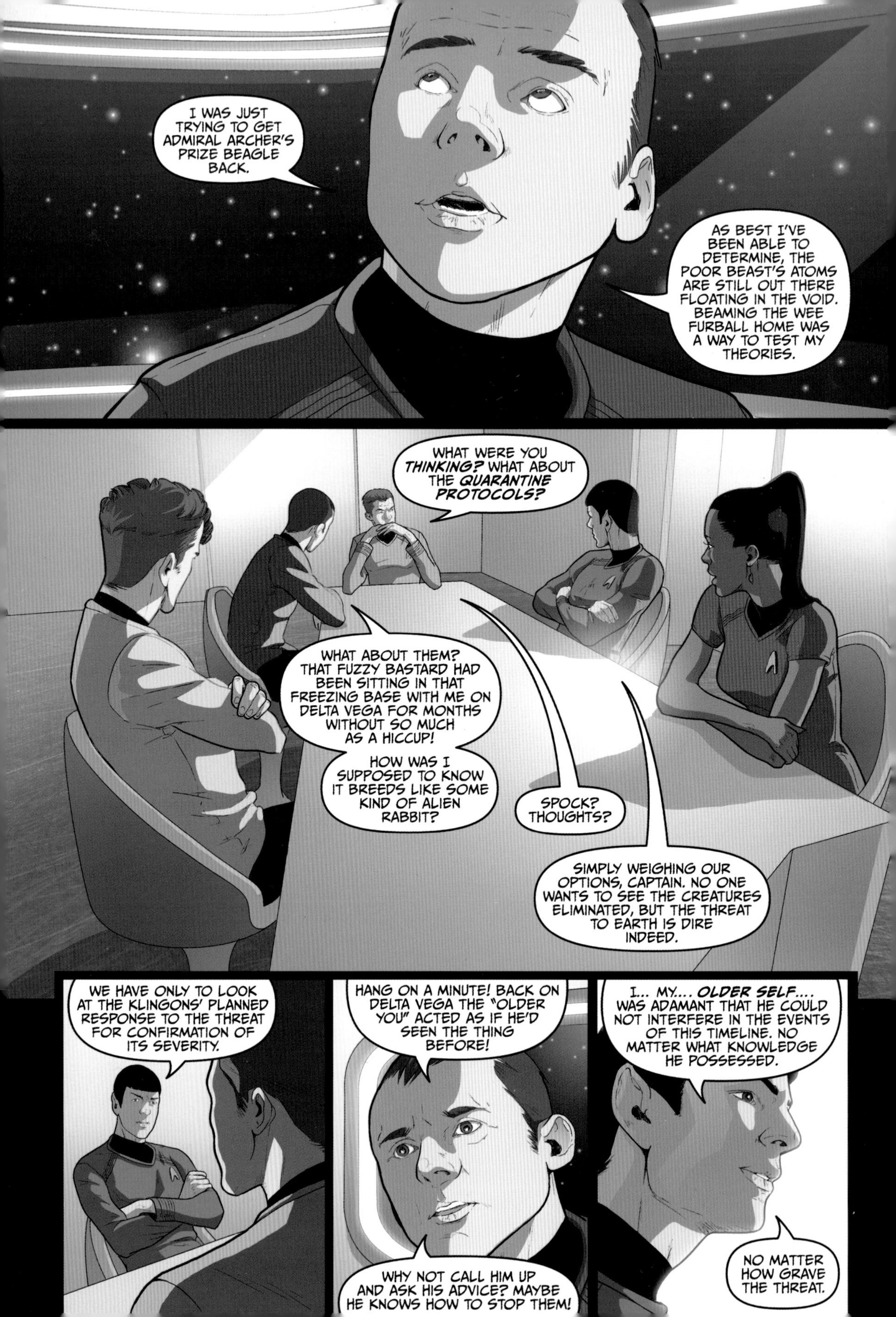
I WAS JUST TRYING TO GET ADMIRAL ARCHER'S PRIZE BEAGLE BACK.
AS BEST I'VE BEEN ABLE TO DETERMINE, THE POOR BEAST'S ATOMS ARE STILL OUT THERE FLOATING IN THE VOID. BEAMING THE WEE FURBALL HOME WAS A WAY TO TEST MY THEORIES.
WHAT WERE YOU *THINKING?* WHAT ABOUT THE *QUARANTINE PROTOCOLS?*
WHAT ABOUT THEM? THAT FUZZY BASTARD HAD BEEN SITTING IN THAT FREEZING BASE WITH ME ON DELTA VEGA FOR MONTHS WITHOUT SO MUCH AS A HICCUP!
HOW WAS I SUPPOSED TO KNOW IT BREEDS LIKE SOME KIND OF ALIEN RABBIT?
SPOCK? THOUGHTS?
SIMPLY WEIGHING OUR OPTIONS, CAPTAIN. NO ONE WANTS TO SEE THE CREATURES ELIMINATED, BUT THE THREAT TO EARTH IS DIRE INDEED.
WE HAVE ONLY TO LOOK AT THE KLINGONS' PLANNED RESPONSE TO THE THREAT FOR CONFIRMATION OF ITS SEVERITY.
HANG ON A MINUTE! BACK ON DELTA VEGA THE "OLDER YOU" ACTED AS IF HE'D SEEN THE THING BEFORE!
WHY NOT CALL HIM UP AND ASK HIS ADVICE? MAYBE HE KNOWS HOW TO STOP THEM!
I... MY.... *OLDER SELF*.... WAS ADAMANT THAT HE COULD NOT INTERFERE IN THE EVENTS OF THIS TIMELINE. NO MATTER WHAT KNOWLEDGE HE POSSESSED.
NO MATTER HOW GRAVE THE THREAT.

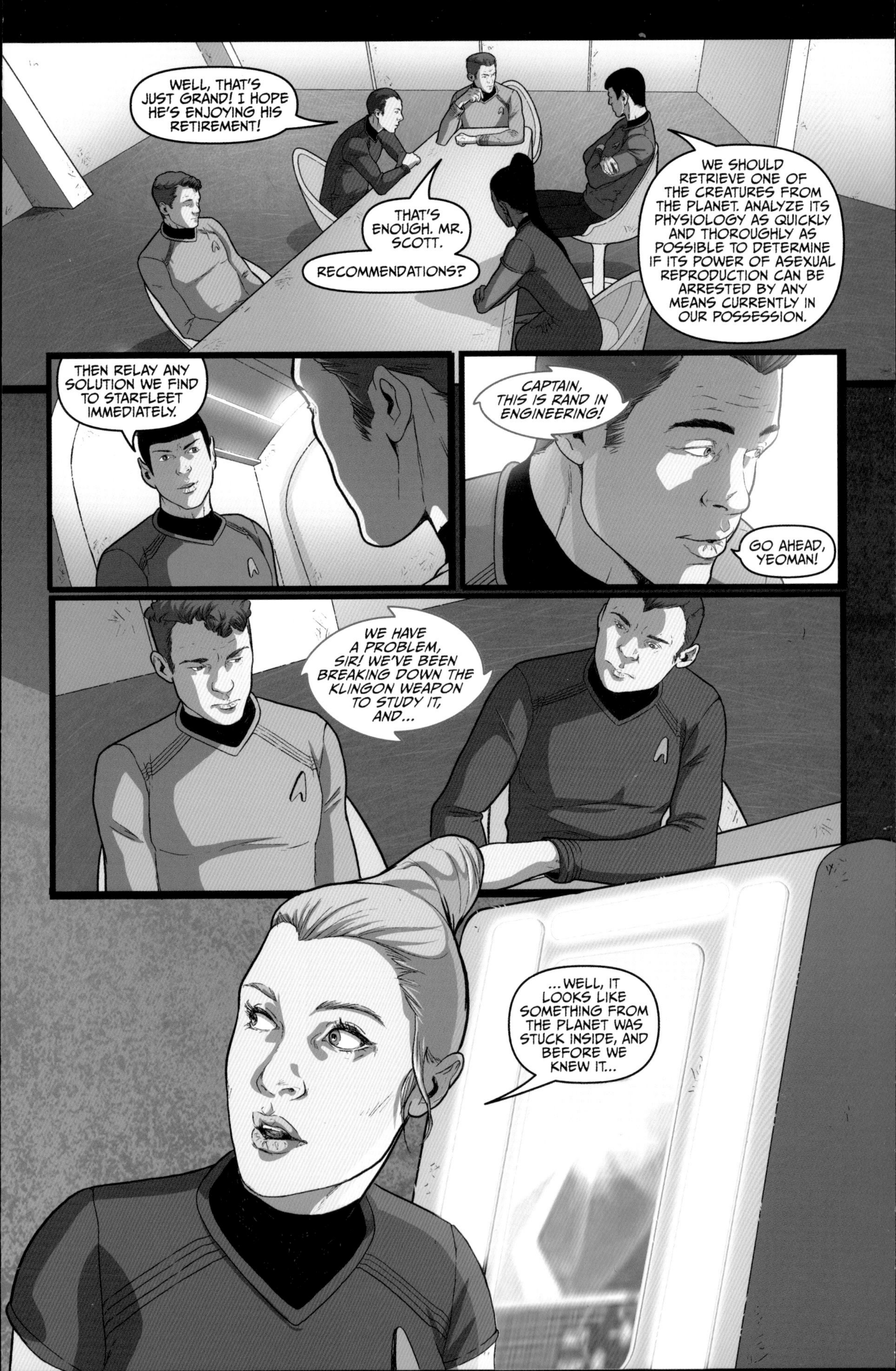
WELL, THAT'S JUST GRAND! I HOPE HE'S ENJOYING HIS RETIREMENT!
THAT'S ENOUGH. MR. SCOTT.
RECOMMENDATIONS?
WE SHOULD RETRIEVE ONE OF THE CREATURES FROM THE PLANET. ANALYZE ITS PHYSIOLOGY AS QUICKLY AND THOROUGHLY AS POSSIBLE TO DETERMINE IF ITS POWER OF ASEXUAL REPRODUCTION CAN BE ARRESTED BY ANY MEANS CURRENTLY IN OUR POSSESSION.
THEN RELAY ANY SOLUTION WE FIND TO STARFLEET IMMEDIATELY.
CAPTAIN, THIS IS RAND IN ENGINEERING!
GO AHEAD, YEOMAN!
WE HAVE A PROBLEM, SIR! WE'VE BEEN BREAKING DOWN THE KLINGON WEAPON TO STUDY IT, AND...
...WELL, IT LOOKS LIKE SOMETHING FROM THE PLANET WAS STUCK INSIDE, AND BEFORE WE KNEW IT...

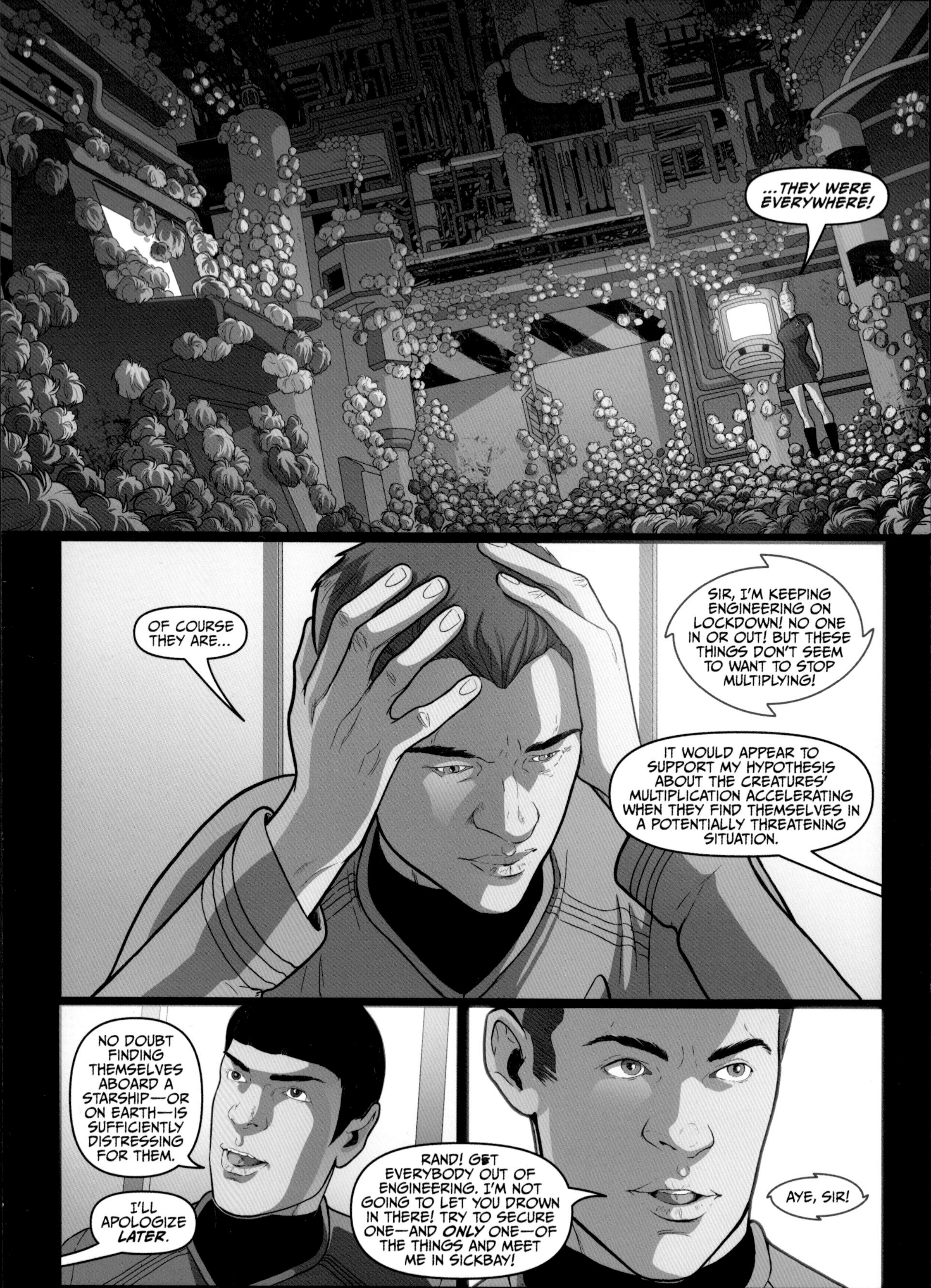
...THEY WERE EVERYWHERE!
OF COURSE THEY ARE...
SIR, I'M KEEPING ENGINEERING ON LOCKDOWN! NO ONE IN OR OUT! BUT THESE THINGS DON'T SEEM TO WANT TO STOP MULTIPLYING!
IT WOULD APPEAR TO SUPPORT MY HYPOTHESIS ABOUT THE CREATURES' MULTIPLICATION ACCELERATING WHEN THEY FIND THEMSELVES IN A POTENTIALLY THREATENING SITUATION.
NO DOUBT FINDING THEMSELVES ABOARD A STARSHIP—OR ON EARTH—IS SUFFICIENTLY DISTRESSING FOR THEM.
I'LL APOLOGIZE LATER.
RAND! GET EVERYBODY OUT OF ENGINEERING. I'M NOT GOING TO LET YOU DROWN IN THERE! TRY TO SECURE ONE—AND ONLY ONE—OF THE THINGS AND MEET ME IN SICKBAY!
AYE, SIR!

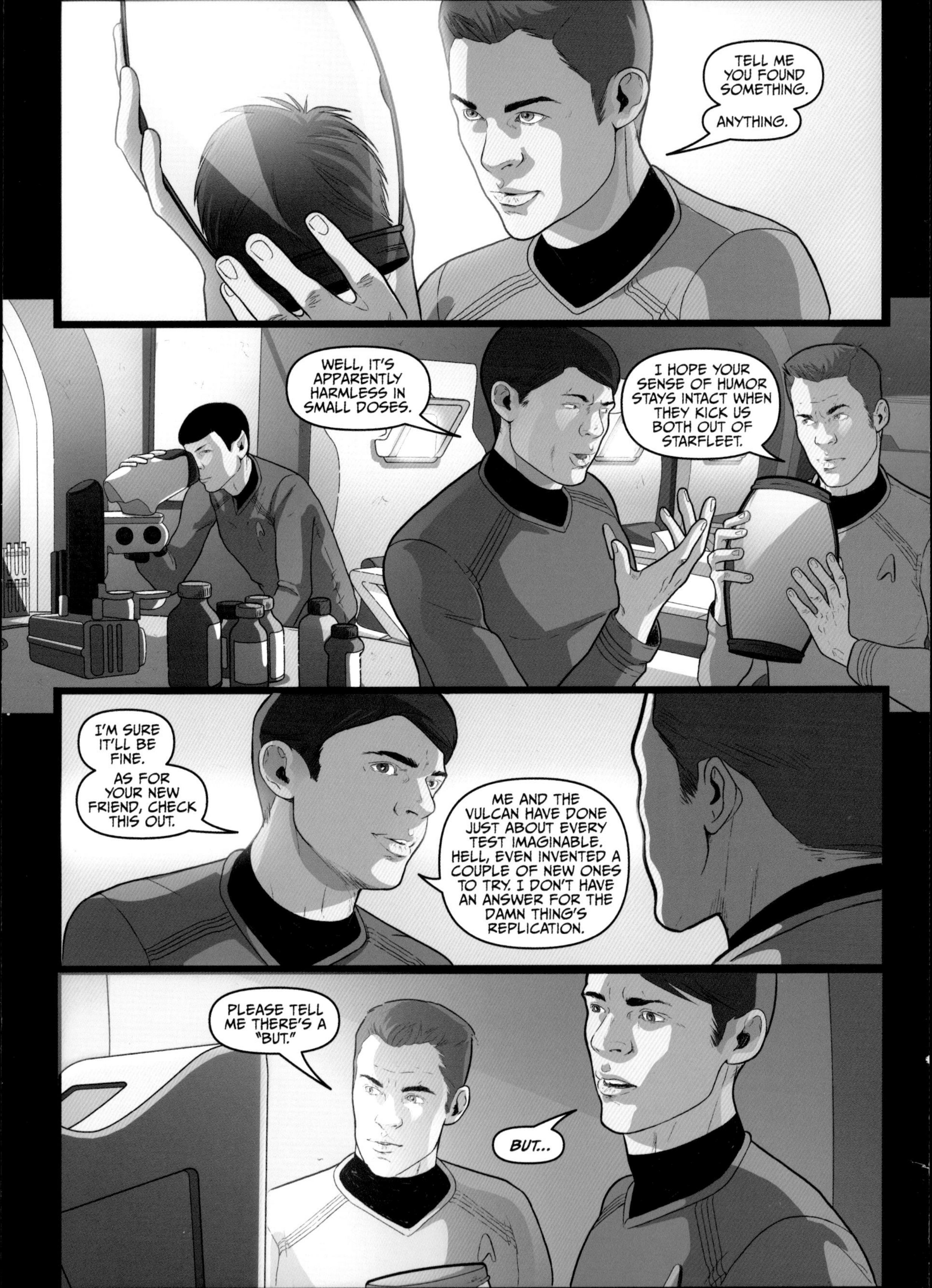
TELL ME YOU FOUND SOMETHING.
ANYTHING.
WELL, IT'S APPARENTLY HARMLESS IN SMALL DOSES.
I HOPE YOUR SENSE OF HUMOR STAYS INTACT WHEN THEY KICK US BOTH OUT OF STARFLEET.
I'M SURE IT'LL BE FINE.
AS FOR YOUR NEW FRIEND, CHECK THIS OUT.
ME AND THE VULCAN HAVE DONE JUST ABOUT EVERY TEST IMAGINABLE. HELL, EVEN INVENTED A COUPLE OF NEW ONES TO TRY. I DON'T HAVE AN ANSWER FOR THE DAMN THING'S REPLICATION.
PLEASE TELL ME THERE'S A "BUT."
BUT...

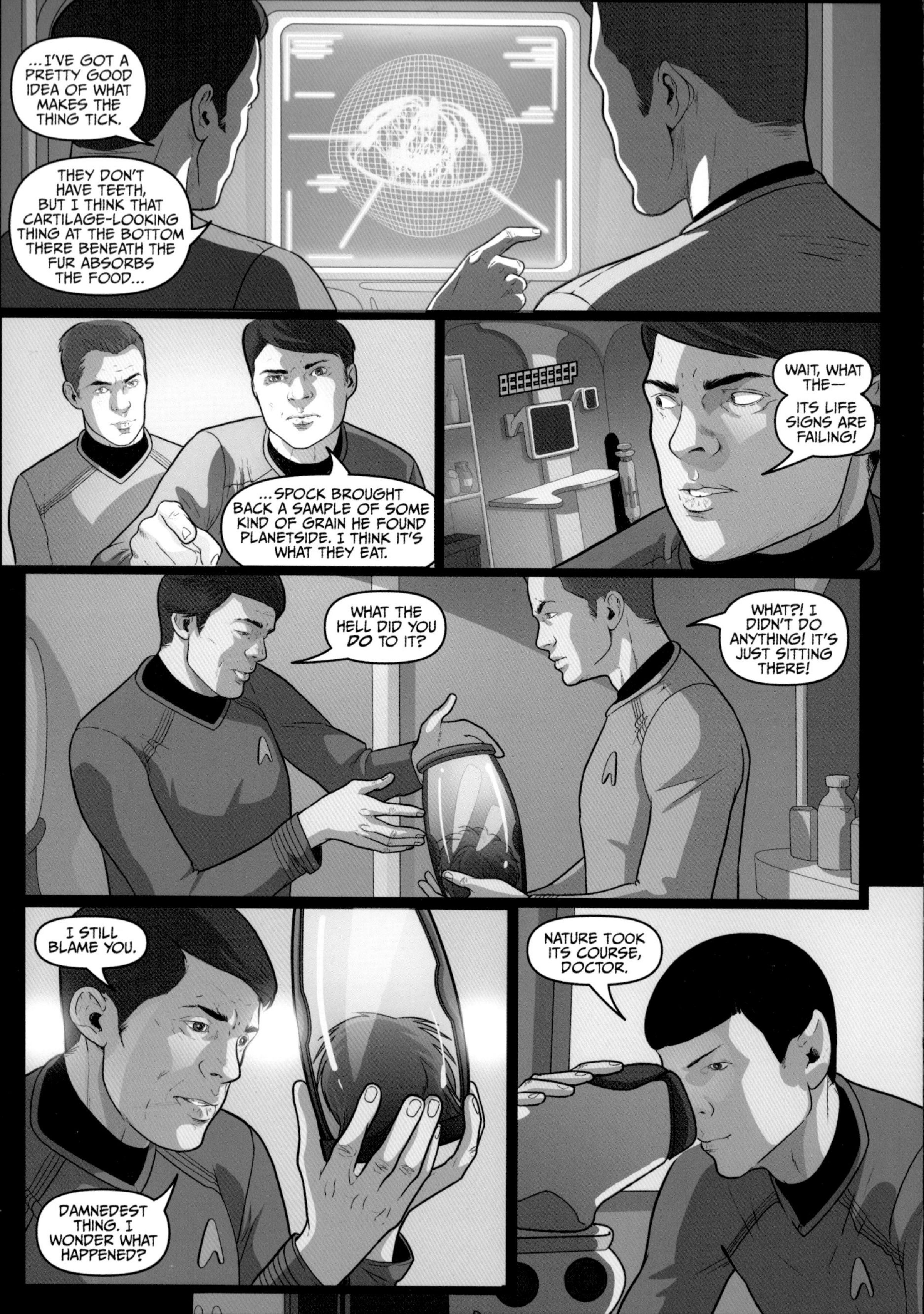
...I'VE GOT A PRETTY GOOD IDEA OF WHAT MAKES THE THING TICK.
THEY DON'T HAVE TEETH, BUT I THINK THAT CARTILAGE-LOOKING THING AT THE BOTTOM THERE BENEATH THE FUR ABSORBS THE FOOD...
...SPOCK BROUGHT BACK A SAMPLE OF SOME KIND OF GRAIN HE FOUND PLANETSIDE. I THINK IT'S WHAT THEY EAT.
BEEEEEEEEP
WAIT, WHAT THE—
ITS LIFE SIGNS ARE FAILING!
WHAT THE HELL DID YOU *DO* TO IT?
WHAT?! I DIDN'T DO ANYTHING! IT'S JUST SITTING THERE!
I STILL BLAME YOU.
DAMNEDEST THING. I WONDER WHAT HAPPENED?
NATURE TOOK ITS COURSE, DOCTOR.

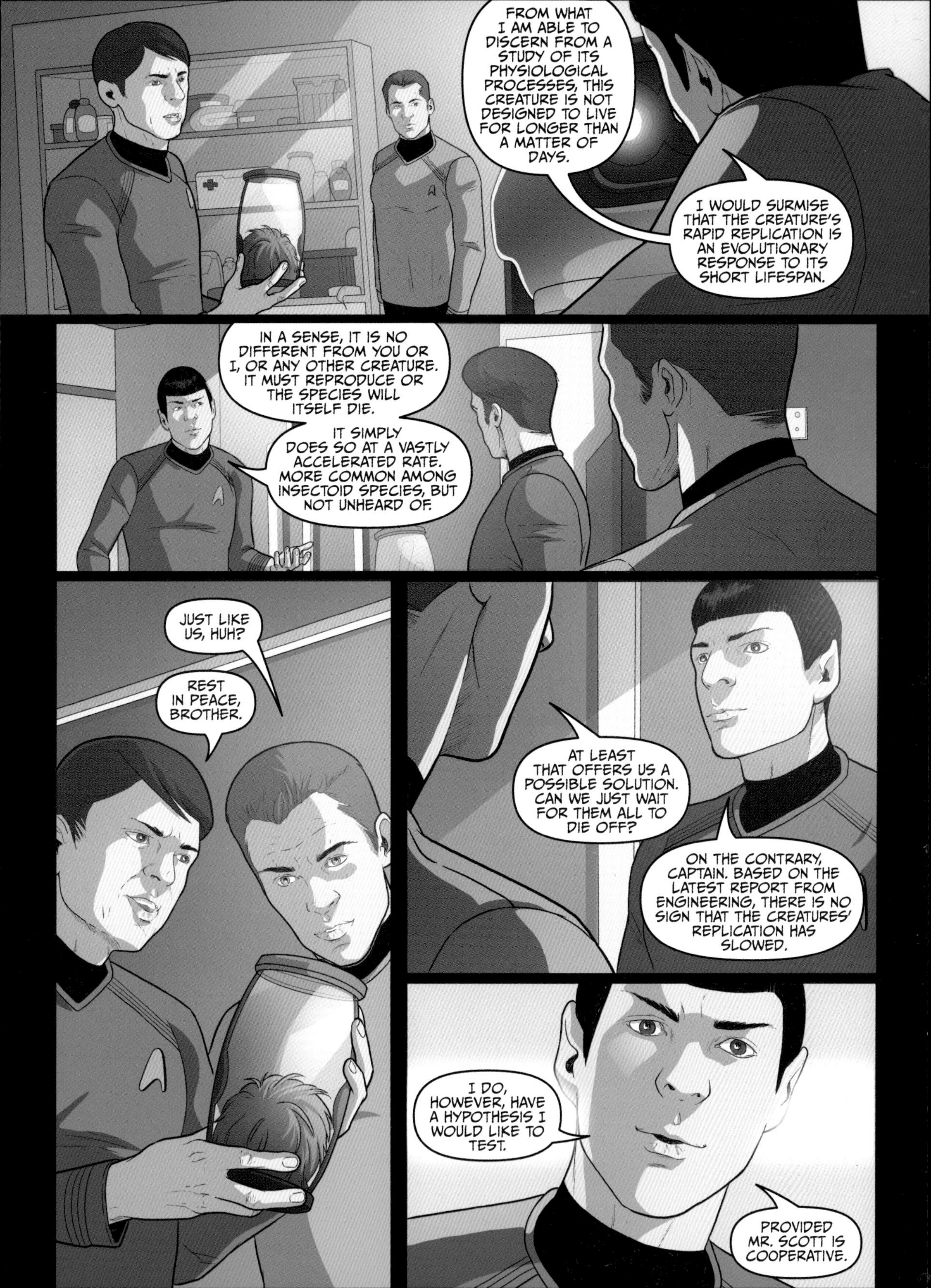
FROM WHAT I AM ABLE TO DISCERN FROM A STUDY OF ITS PHYSIOLOGICAL PROCESSES, THIS CREATURE IS NOT DESIGNED TO LIVE FOR LONGER THAN A MATTER OF DAYS.
I WOULD SURMISE THAT THE CREATURE'S RAPID REPLICATION IS AN EVOLUTIONARY RESPONSE TO ITS SHORT LIFESPAN.
IN A SENSE, IT IS NO DIFFERENT FROM YOU OR I, OR ANY OTHER CREATURE. IT MUST REPRODUCE OR THE SPECIES WILL ITSELF DIE.
IT SIMPLY DOES SO AT A VASTLY ACCELERATED RATE. MORE COMMON AMONG INSECTOID SPECIES, BUT NOT UNHEARD OF.
JUST LIKE US, HUH?
REST IN PEACE, BROTHER.
AT LEAST THAT OFFERS US A POSSIBLE SOLUTION. CAN WE JUST WAIT FOR THEM ALL TO DIE OFF?
ON THE CONTRARY, CAPTAIN. BASED ON THE LATEST REPORT FROM ENGINEERING, THERE IS NO SIGN THAT THE CREATURES' REPLICATION HAS SLOWED.
I DO, HOWEVER, HAVE A HYPOTHESIS I WOULD LIKE TO TEST.
PROVIDED MR. SCOTT IS COOPERATIVE.

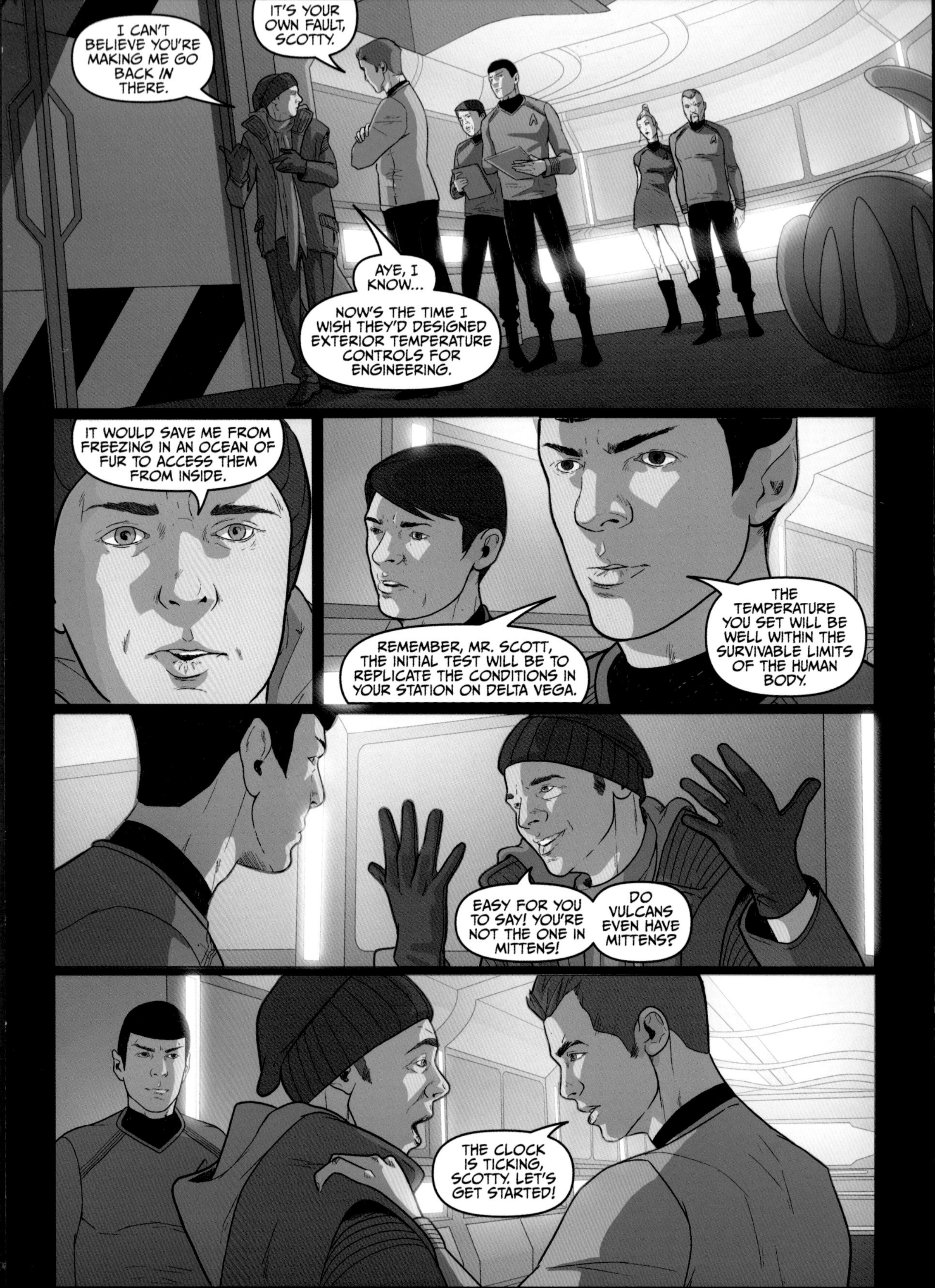
I CAN'T BELIEVE YOU'RE MAKING ME GO BACK *IN* THERE.
IT'S YOUR OWN FAULT, SCOTTY.
AYE, I KNOW...
NOW'S THE TIME I WISH THEY'D DESIGNED EXTERIOR TEMPERATURE CONTROLS FOR ENGINEERING.
IT WOULD SAVE ME FROM FREEZING IN AN OCEAN OF FUR TO ACCESS THEM FROM INSIDE.
REMEMBER, MR. SCOTT, THE INITIAL TEST WILL BE TO REPLICATE THE CONDITIONS IN YOUR STATION ON DELTA VEGA.
THE TEMPERATURE YOU SET WILL BE WELL WITHIN THE SURVIVABLE LIMITS OF THE HUMAN BODY.
EASY FOR YOU TO SAY! YOU'RE NOT THE ONE IN MITTENS!
DO VULCANS EVEN HAVE MITTENS?
THE CLOCK IS TICKING, SCOTTY. LET'S GET STARTED!

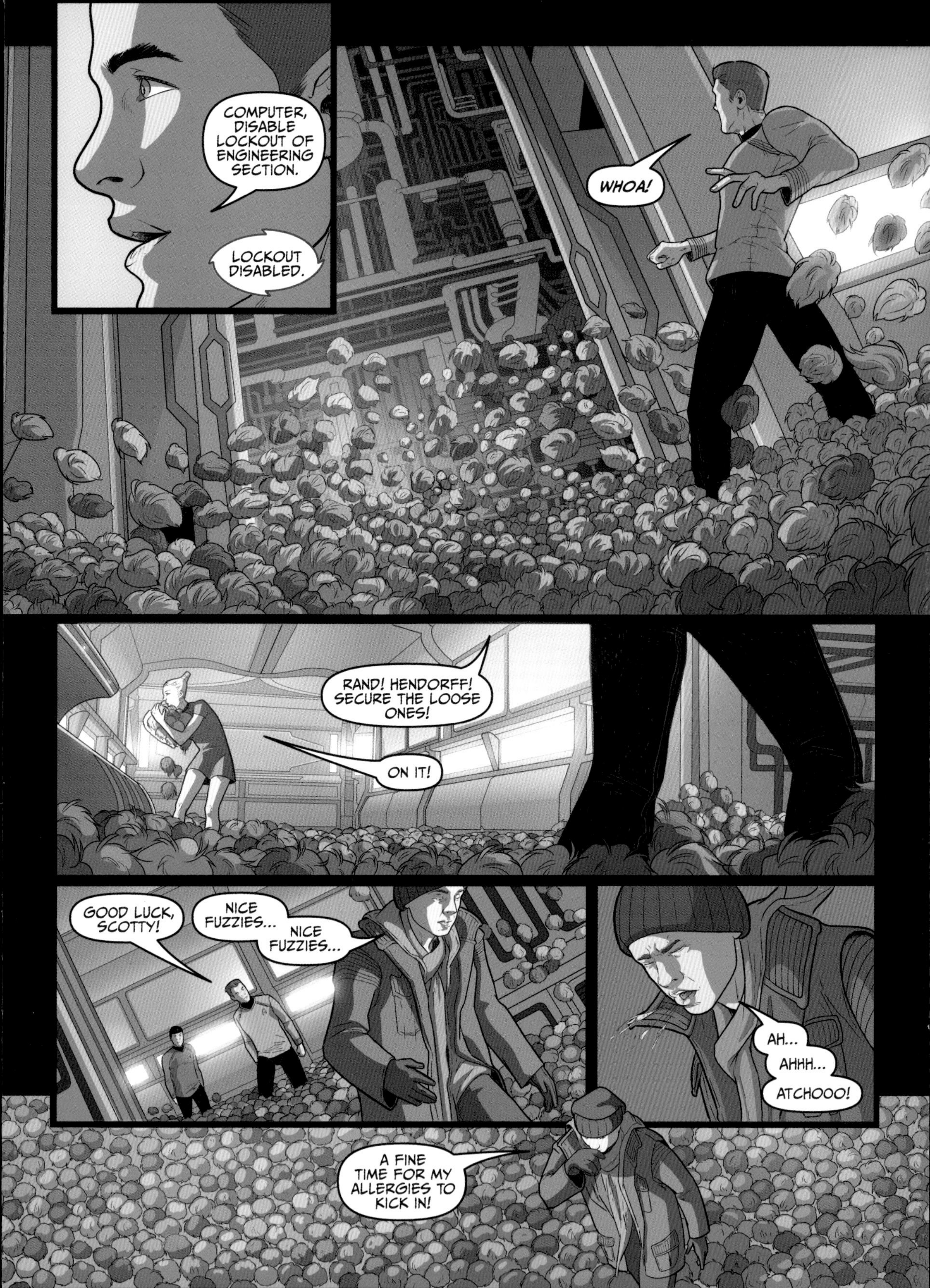

COMPUTER, DISABLE LOCKOUT OF ENGINEERING SECTION.
LOCKOUT DISABLED.
WHOA!
RAND! HENDORFF! SECURE THE LOOSE ONES!
ON IT!
GOOD LUCK, SCOTTY!
NICE FUZZIES...
NICE FUZZIES...
AH...
AHHH...
ATCHOOO!
A FINE TIME FOR MY ALLERGIES TO KICK IN!

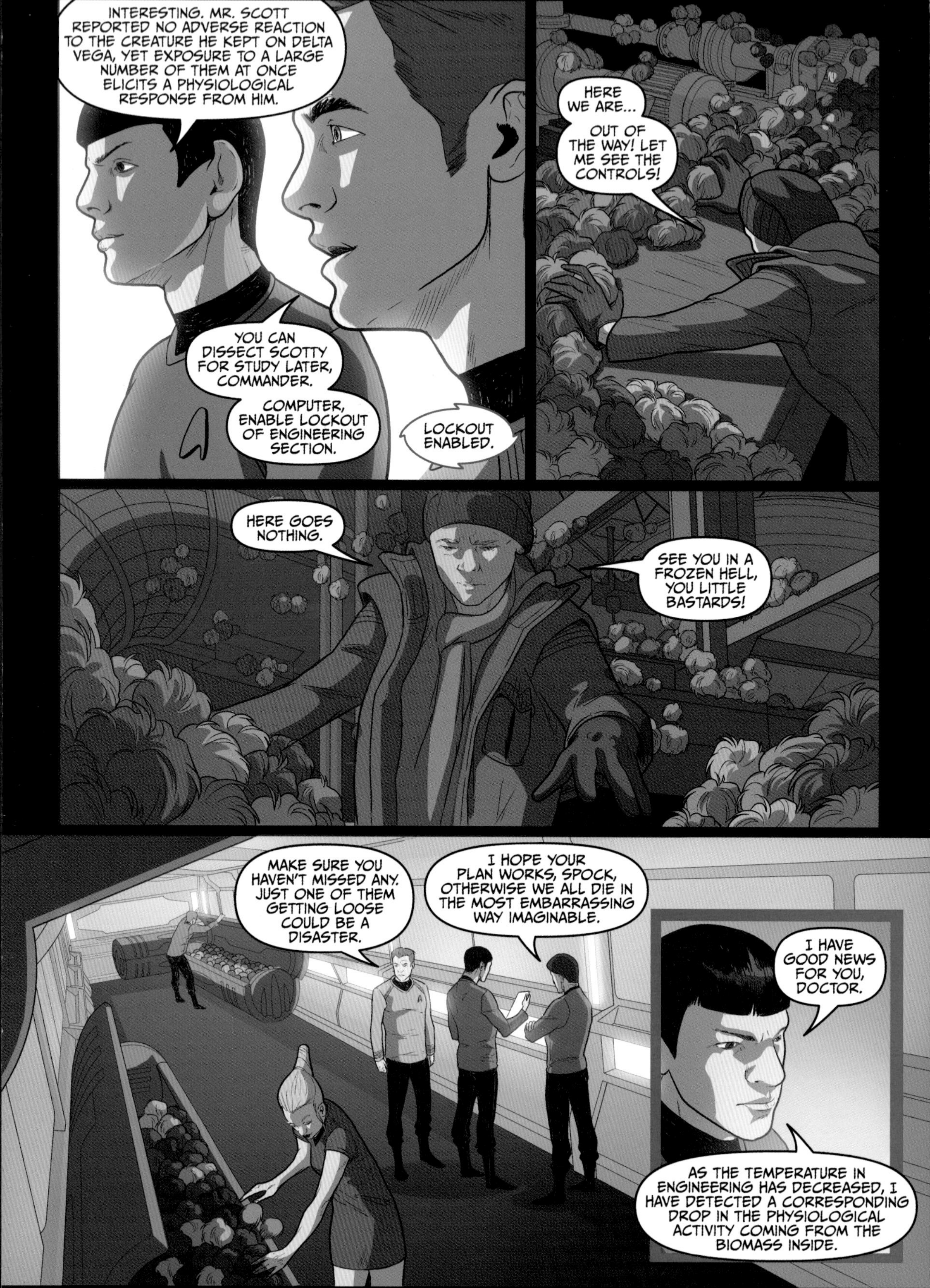
INTERESTING. MR. SCOTT REPORTED NO ADVERSE REACTION TO THE CREATURE HE KEPT ON DELTA VEGA, YET EXPOSURE TO A LARGE NUMBER OF THEM AT ONCE ELICITS A PHYSIOLOGICAL RESPONSE FROM HIM.
YOU CAN DISSECT SCOTTY FOR STUDY LATER, COMMANDER.
COMPUTER, ENABLE LOCKOUT OF ENGINEERING SECTION.
LOCKOUT ENABLED.
HERE WE ARE...
OUT OF THE WAY! LET ME SEE THE CONTROLS!
HERE GOES NOTHING.
SEE YOU IN A FROZEN HELL, YOU LITTLE BASTARDS!
MAKE SURE YOU HAVEN'T MISSED ANY. JUST ONE OF THEM GETTING LOOSE COULD BE A DISASTER.
I HOPE YOUR PLAN WORKS, SPOCK, OTHERWISE WE ALL DIE IN THE MOST EMBARRASSING WAY IMAGINABLE.
I HAVE GOOD NEWS FOR YOU, DOCTOR.
AS THE TEMPERATURE IN ENGINEERING HAS DECREASED, I HAVE DETECTED A CORRESPONDING DROP IN THE PHYSIOLOGICAL ACTIVITY COMING FROM THE BIOMASS INSIDE.

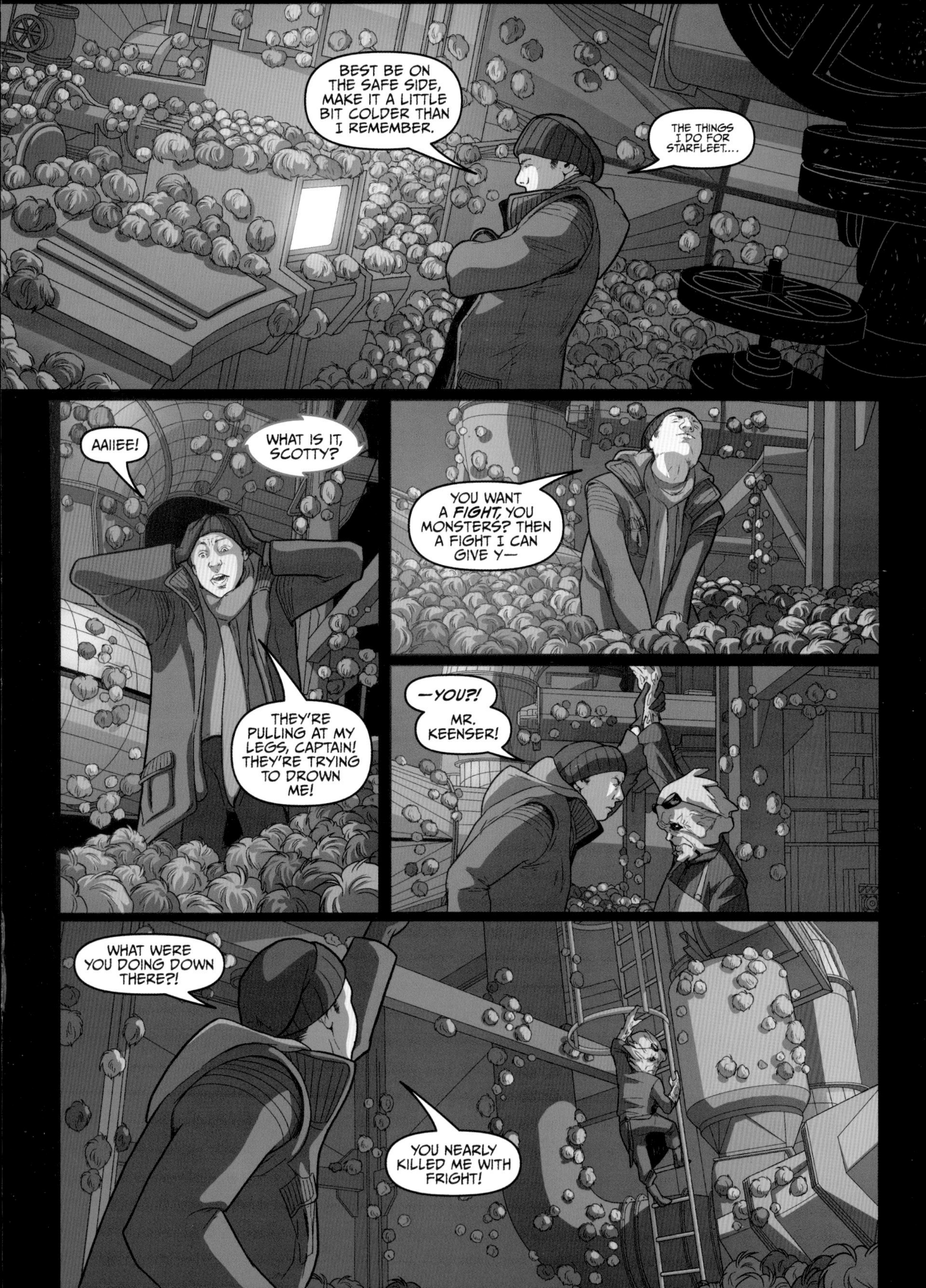
BEST BE ON THE SAFE SIDE, MAKE IT A LITTLE BIT COLDER THAN I REMEMBER.
THE THINGS I DO FOR STARFLEET....
AAIIEE!
WHAT IS IT, SCOTTY?
THEY'RE PULLING AT MY LEGS, CAPTAIN! THEY'RE TRYING TO DROWN ME!
YOU WANT A FIGHT, YOU MONSTERS? THEN A FIGHT I CAN GIVE Y—
—YOU?!
MR. KEENSER!
WHAT WERE YOU DOING DOWN THERE?!
YOU NEARLY KILLED ME WITH FRIGHT!

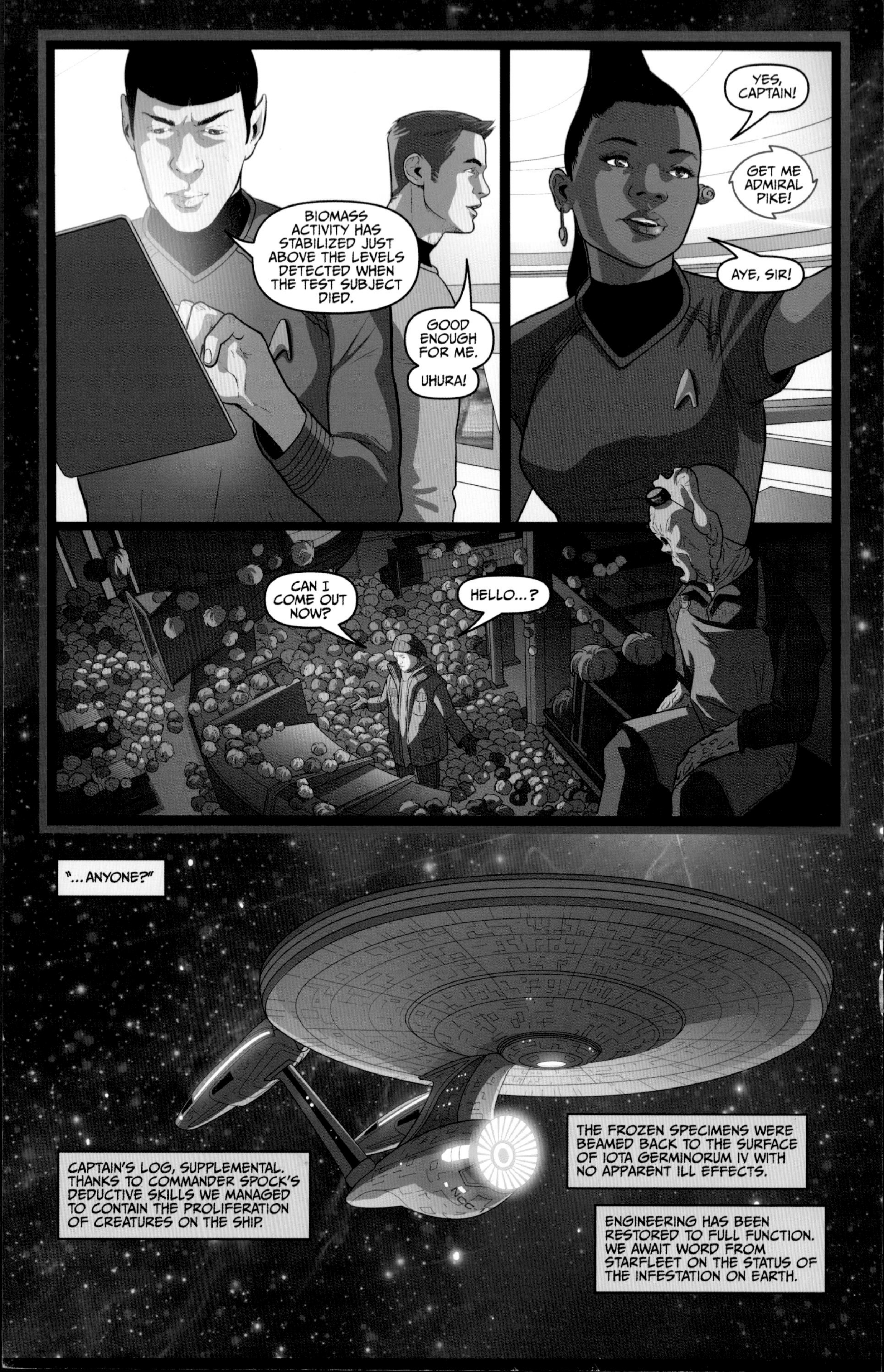
BIOMASS ACTIVITY HAS STABILIZED JUST ABOVE THE LEVELS DETECTED WHEN THE TEST SUBJECT DIED.
GOOD ENOUGH FOR ME.
UHURA!
YES, CAPTAIN!
GET ME ADMIRAL PIKE!
AYE, SIR!
CAN I COME OUT NOW?
HELLO...?
"... ANYONE?"
CAPTAIN'S LOG, SUPPLEMENTAL. THANKS TO COMMANDER SPOCK'S DEDUCTIVE SKILLS WE MANAGED TO CONTAIN THE PROLIFERATION OF CREATURES ON THE SHIP.
THE FROZEN SPECIMENS WERE BEAMED BACK TO THE SURFACE OF IOTA GERMINORUM IV WITH NO APPARENT ILL EFFECTS.
ENGINEERING HAS BEEN RESTORED TO FULL FUNCTION. WE AWAIT WORD FROM STARFLEET ON THE STATUS OF THE INFESTATION ON EARTH.

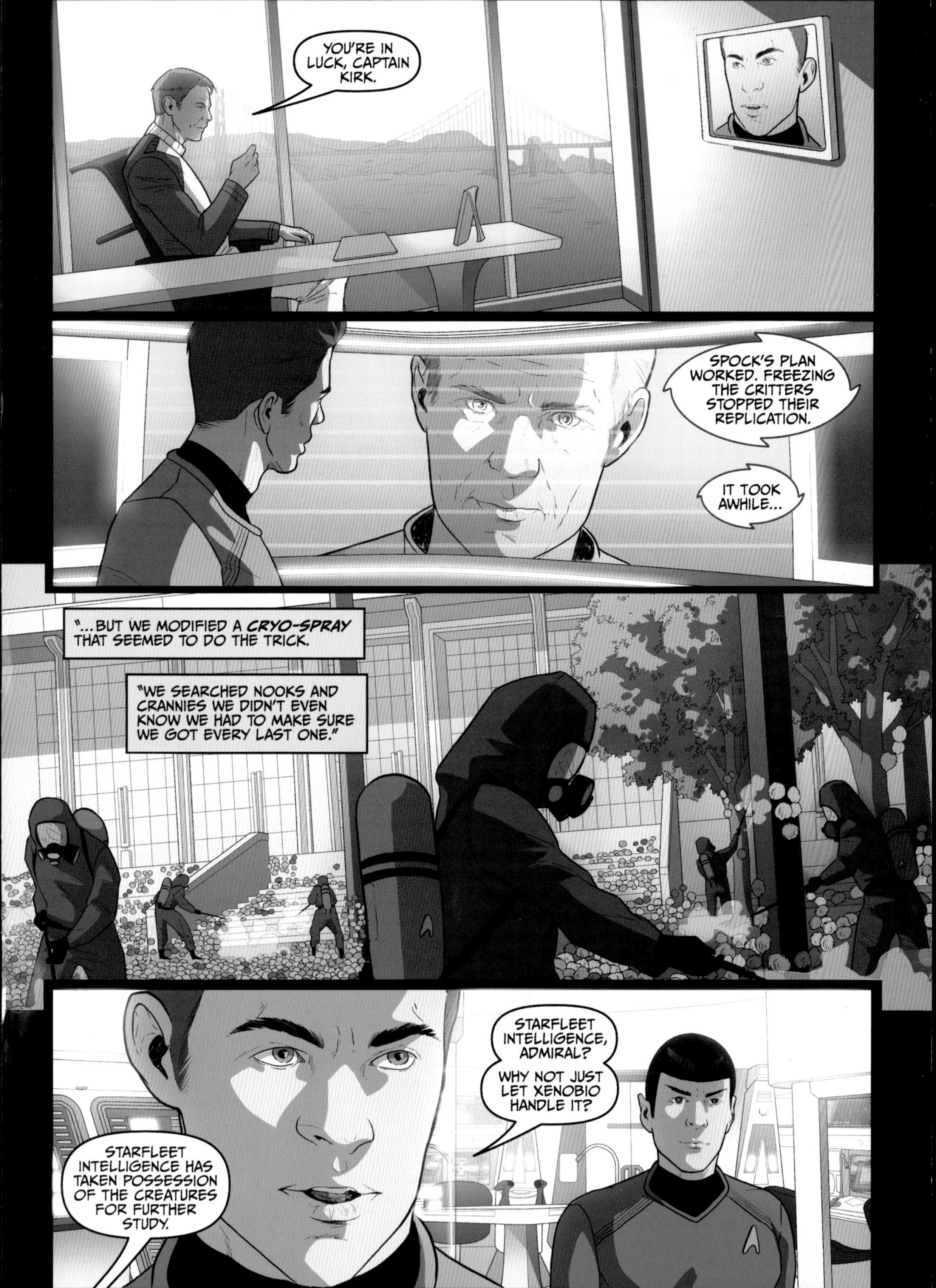

YOU'RE IN LUCK, CAPTAIN KIRK.
SPOCK'S PLAN WORKED. FREEZING THE CRITTERS STOPPED THEIR REPLICATION.
IT TOOK AWHILE...
"...BUT WE MODIFIED A CRYO-SPRAY THAT SEEMED TO DO THE TRICK.
"WE SEARCHED NOOKS AND CRANNIES WE DIDN'T EVEN KNOW WE HAD TO MAKE SURE WE GOT EVERY LAST ONE."
STARFLEET INTELLIGENCE HAS TAKEN POSSESSION OF THE CREATURES FOR FURTHER STUDY.
STARFLEET INTELLIGENCE, ADMIRAL?
WHY NOT JUST LET XENOBIO HANDLE IT?

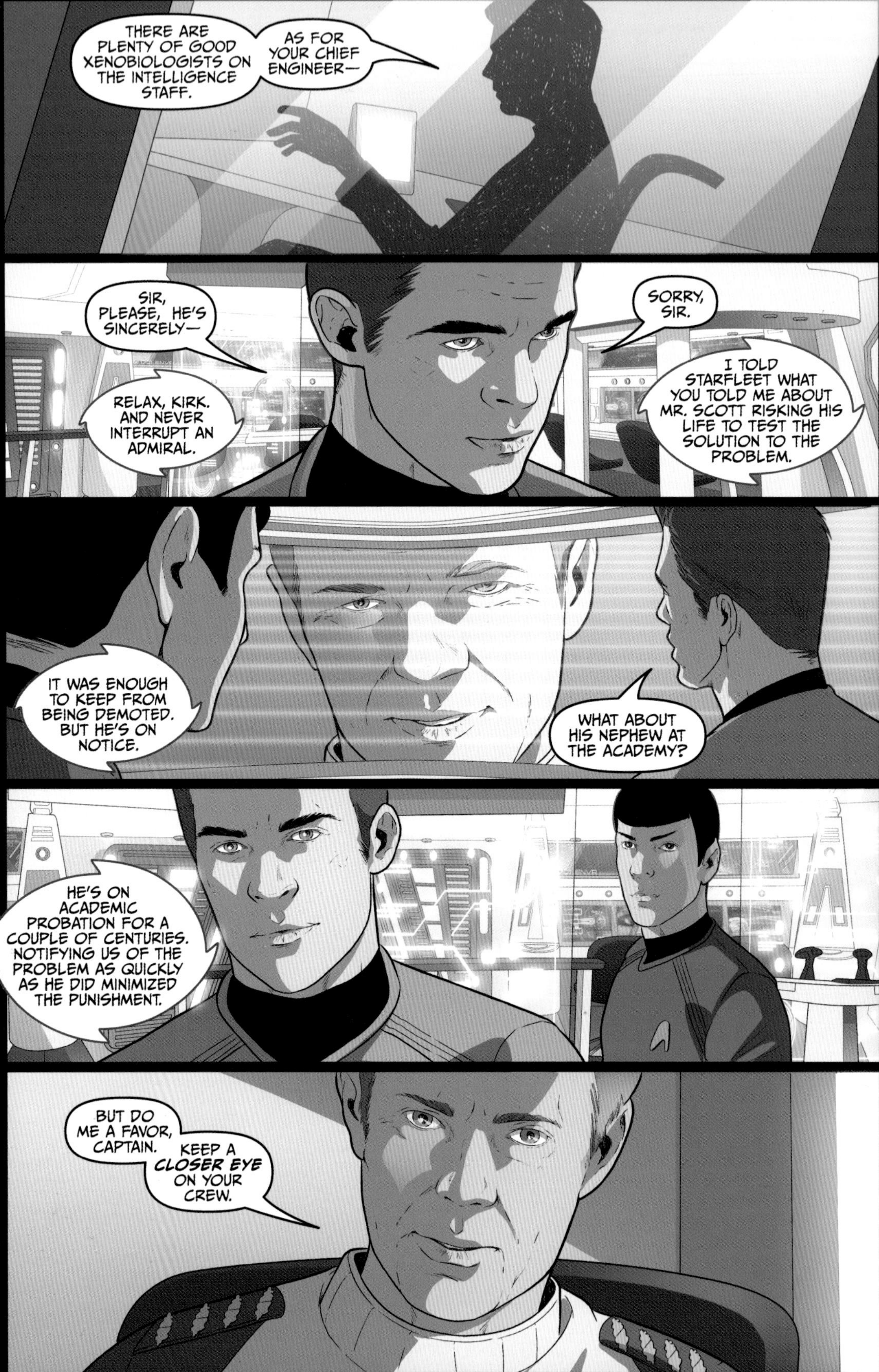
THERE ARE PLENTY OF GOOD XENOBIOLOGISTS ON THE INTELLIGENCE STAFF.
AS FOR YOUR CHIEF ENGINEER—
SIR, PLEASE, HE'S SINCERELY—
RELAX, KIRK. AND NEVER INTERRUPT AN ADMIRAL.
SORRY, SIR.
I TOLD STARFLEET WHAT YOU TOLD ME ABOUT MR. SCOTT RISKING HIS LIFE TO TEST THE SOLUTION TO THE PROBLEM.
IT WAS ENOUGH TO KEEP FROM BEING DEMOTED. BUT HE'S ON NOTICE.
WHAT ABOUT HIS NEPHEW AT THE ACADEMY?
HE'S ON ACADEMIC PROBATION FOR A COUPLE OF CENTURIES. NOTIFYING US OF THE PROBLEM AS QUICKLY AS HE DID MINIMIZED THE PUNISHMENT.
BUT DO ME A FAVOR, CAPTAIN.
KEEP A *CLOSER EYE* ON YOUR CREW.

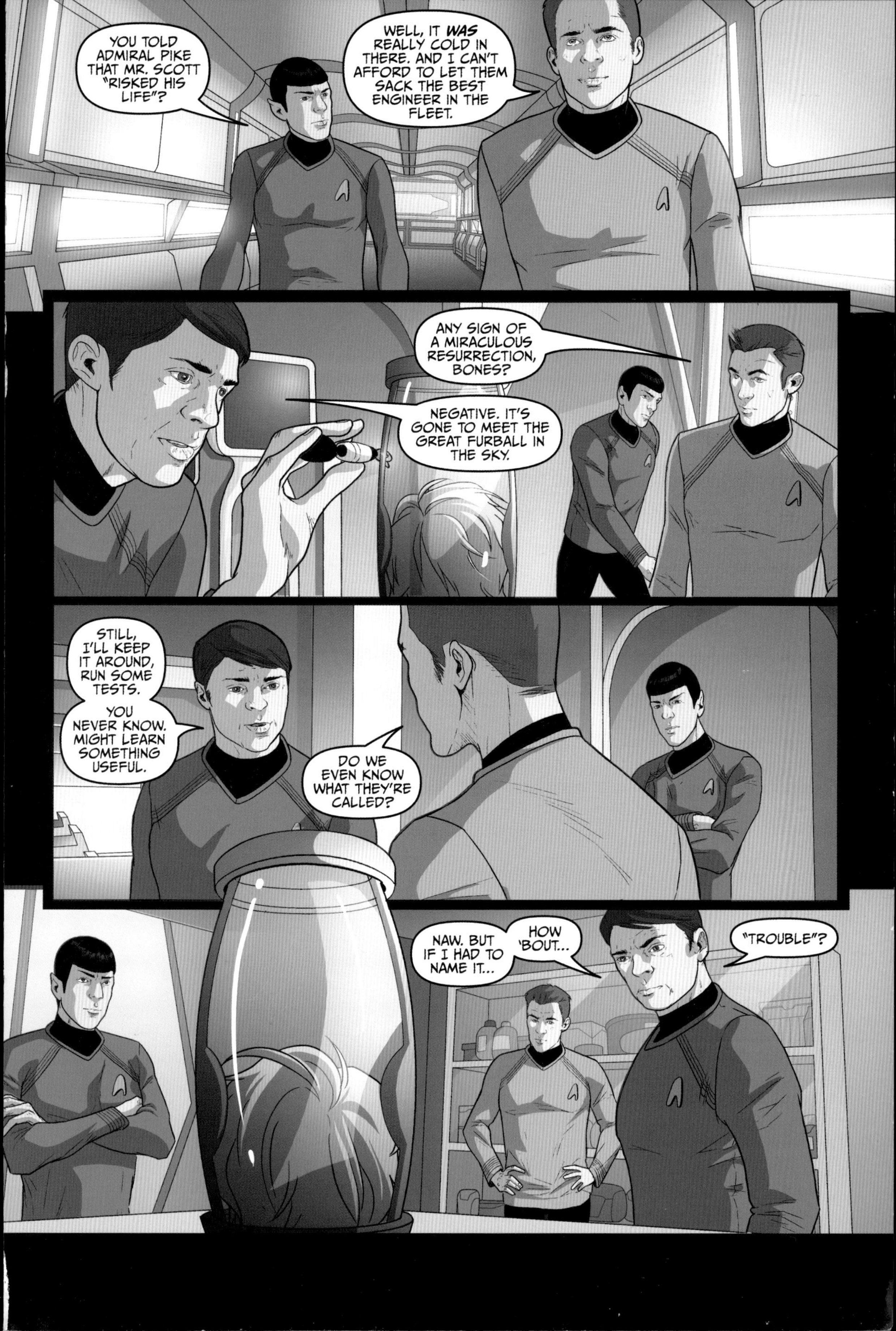
YOU TOLD ADMIRAL PIKE THAT MR. SCOTT "RISKED HIS LIFE"?
WELL, IT WAS REALLY COLD IN THERE. AND I CAN'T AFFORD TO LET THEM SACK THE BEST ENGINEER IN THE FLEET.
ANY SIGN OF A MIRACULOUS RESURRECTION, BONES?
NEGATIVE. IT'S GONE TO MEET THE GREAT FURBALL IN THE SKY.
STILL, I'LL KEEP IT AROUND, RUN SOME TESTS.
YOU NEVER KNOW. MIGHT LEARN SOMETHING USEFUL.
DO WE EVEN KNOW WHAT THEY'RE CALLED?
NAW. BUT IF I HAD TO NAME IT...
HOW 'BOUT...
"TROUBLE"?

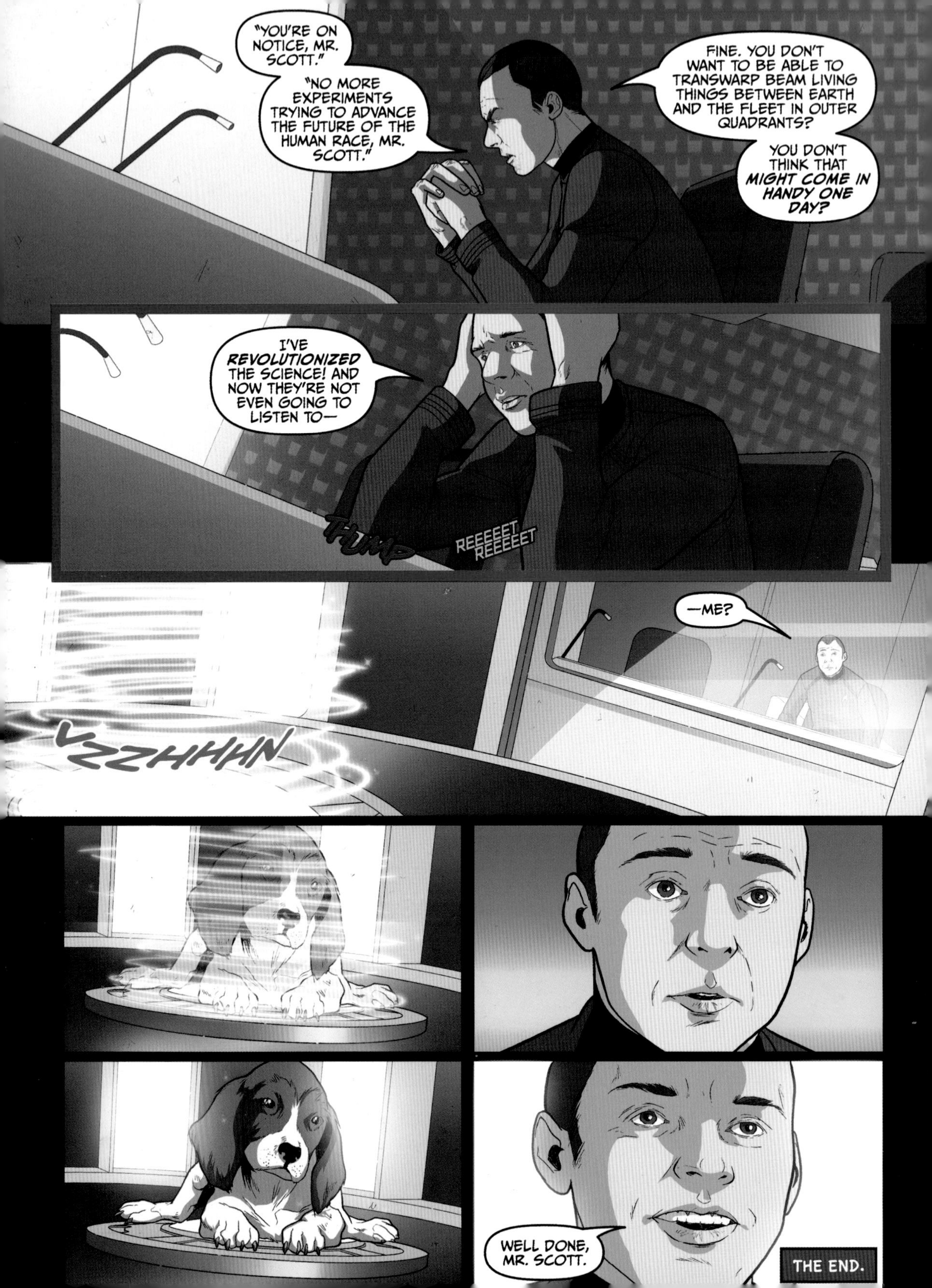
"YOU'RE ON NOTICE, MR. SCOTT."
"NO MORE EXPERIMENTS TRYING TO ADVANCE THE FUTURE OF THE HUMAN RACE, MR. SCOTT."
FINE. YOU DON'T WANT TO BE ABLE TO TRANSWARP BEAM LIVING THINGS BETWEEN EARTH AND THE FLEET IN OUTER QUADRANTS?
YOU DON'T THINK THAT MIGHT COME IN HANDY ONE DAY?
I'VE REVOLUTIONIZED THE SCIENCE! AND NOW THEY'RE NOT EVEN GOING TO LISTEN TO—
THUMP
REEEEET REEEEET
VZZHHHN
—ME?
WELL DONE, MR. SCOTT.
THE END.